Catching Jordan

MIRANDA KENNEALLY

Cover design by Angela Goddard
Cover images © rubberball/Getty Images; Radius Images/Photolibrary

Published by Sourcebooks Fire, an imprint of Sourcebooks, Inc.
P.O. Box 4410, Naperville, Illinois 60567-4410
(630) 961-3900
Fax: (630) 961-2168
teenfire.sourcebooks.com

Library of Congress Cataloging-in-Publication data is on file with the publisher.

Printed and bound in the United States of America.
VP 10 9 8 7 6 5

for sara megibow
and all the other badass chicks out there

Who ever knew throwing a perfect spiral would be simple compared to dealing with guys?

a hail mary and a harem

the count? 21 days until my trip to alabama

I once read that football was invented so people wouldn't notice summer ending. But I couldn't wait for summer vacation to end. I couldn't wait for football. Football, dominator of fall—football, love of my life.

"Blue forty-two! Blue forty-two! Red seventeen!" I yell.

The cue is red seventeen. JJ hikes me the ball. The defense is blitzing. JJ slams into a freshman safety, knocking him to the ground. The rest of my offensive line destroys the defense. Nice. The field's wide open, but my wide receiver isn't where he's supposed to be.

"What the hell, Higgins?" I mutter to myself.

Dancing on my tiptoes, I scan the end zone and find Sam Henry instead and hurl the ball. It flies through the air, a perfect spiral, heading right where I wanted it to go. He catches the ball, spikes it, and does this really stupid dance. Henry looks like a freaking ballerina. With his thin frame and girly blond hair, he actually could be the star of the New York Ballet.

I'm gonna give him hell for his dance.

This is my senior year at Hundred Oaks High, and I'm captain, so I'm allowed to keep my players in line. Even though he's my best friend, Henry has always been a showoff. His antics get us penalties.

Through the speaker in my helmet, I hear Coach Miller say, "Nice throw. This is your year, Woods. You're going to lead us to the state championship. I can feel it...Hit the showers." What the coach actually means? *I know you're not going to blow it in the final seconds of the championship game like you did last year.*

And he's right. I can't.

The University of Alabama called last week—on the first day of school—to tell me a recruiter is coming to watch me play on Friday night. And then a very fancy-looking letter arrived, inviting me to visit campus in September. An official visit. If they like what they see, they'll sign me in February.

I can't screw this season up.

I pull my helmet off and grab a bottle of Gatorade and my playbook. Most of the guys are already goofing off and heading over to watch cheerleading practice across the field, but I ignore them and look up into the stands.

I spot Mom sitting with Carter's dad, a former NFL player. My dad isn't here, of course. Asshole.

Lots of parents come to watch our practices because football is the big thing to do around here. Here being Franklin, Tennessee, home of the Hundred Oaks Red Raiders, eight-time state champions.

Mom always comes to practice—she's been supporting me ever since Pop Warner youth football days, but sometimes she worries I'll get hurt, even though the worst thing that's ever happened was a concussion. Sophomore year, when JJ took a breather, the coach brought in this idiot to play center, the idiot didn't cover me, and I got slammed hard.

Otherwise, I'm a rock. No knee problems, no broken limbs.

Dad never comes to my practices and rarely comes to games.

People think it's because he's busy, because he's Donovan Woods, the starting quarterback for the Tennessee Titans. But the truth is he doesn't want me playing football. Why wouldn't a famous quarterback want his kid to follow in the family footsteps? Well, he does. He loves that my brother, Mike, a junior in college, plays for the University of Tennessee and led his team to a win at the Sugar Bowl last year. So what the hell is Dad's problem with my playing ball?

I'm a girl.

After chugging a bunch of Gatorade, I go find Higgins, who's already attempting to flirt with Kristen Markum, the most idiotic of cheerleaders. I take Higgins aside, avoiding her Darth Vader stare, and say, "Next time try finishing your route instead of staring at Kristen, will you?"

His face goes all red before he nods. "Okay."

"Great."

Then I go pull a sophomore cornerback aside to speak privately. Duckett's a couple inches shorter than me, so I put a hand on his shoulder and walk him down the sideline.

"On that last play, where I threw the long pass to Henry, you left him wide open. And I know how fast he is, but you can't let that happen in the game. You were totally out of position."

Duckett drops his head and nods at me. "Got it, Woods."

I pat his back with my playbook as I take another sip of Gatorade, and wipe the dribble from my mouth. "Good. We're counting on you Friday night. I'm sure Coach is going to start you."

Duckett smiles as he puts his helmet under an arm and heads toward the locker room.

"Awesome job today, guys," I say to a couple of my offensive linemen, then jog over to Henry and look up at him.

He says, "What's good, Woods?"

"Nice move faking out Duckett on that last play."

Henry laughs. "I know, right?"

"Would you quit it with the dancing?"

He grins at me, his green eyes lighting up as he drags a hand through his blond curls. "You know you love it."

Smiling, I shove his chest. "Whatever."

He shoves me back. "Want to come out to eat with us?"

"Who's us?"

"Me and JJ…"

"And?"

"Oh, let's see…Samantha and Marie and Lacey and Kristen."

I stick my tongue out before saying, "Shit, no."

"We're going to Pete's Roadhouse," he says, wiggling his eyebrows.

Damn it. I love going there. It's one of those restaurants where they let you throw peanut shells all over the floor. Still, I reply, "Can't. My brother said he'd watch film with me tonight."

Henry gets this hurt look on his face. "Come on, Woods. You know I want to go to Michigan more than anything, and I'm working hard, but you've been holed up every night since you heard that Alabama is coming to opening game."

I suck in a breath. "Right—I've only got three days left to get perfect."

"You're already, like, one hundred times the quarterback your brother was in high school, you know."

I grin at Henry. "Thanks," I say, even though it's not true.

He wipes sweat off his forehead with his red and black jersey. "How about I come over and watch film with you instead?"

"What about Samantha and Marie and Lacey and Kristen?"

He glances over at the cheerleaders. "They'd wait a year for me."

I shove him again, and he laughs. "Nah, it's okay," I say. "I'm glad you're going out with girls again, even if Kristen is Satan's sister."

"I'd never fool around with Kristen—I have standards, you know."

"Bullshit," I say as JJ and Carter walk up.

With his helmet in hand, JJ drapes an arm around Henry's shoulders. I'm surprised Henry's skinny knees don't buckle under JJ's 275 pounds. "You in trouble again, man?" JJ asks in his deep voice.

"Woods doesn't appreciate my dancing skills."

"No one likes your *dancing skills*," JJ replies. He nods at me. "You in for the Roadhouse, Woods?"

"Can't. Gotta study," I say, holding up the playbook.

"Take a break," JJ says.

"I bet you'd go if they'd picked a place that makes real food, like Michel's Bistro or Julien L'Auberge in Nashville," Carter says in a ridiculous French accent, and JJ, Henry, and I burst out laughing at him.

"Hell no," I say. "All I need is a big slab of meat and a bunch of peanut shells to throw all over the floor."

"Blasphemy," Carter replies.

"You're not going either?" I ask Carter.

He focuses on his cleats before saying, "Can't—it's a practice night, remember?" He's, like, the only person I know whose parents never say anything about school nights—it's always about football practice and games in the Carter household.

"Come on, Woods," Henry whines. "Just for an hour or two."

I hate saying no to him. "If I get through four hours of Alabama film tonight, I'll come out tomorrow."

"Fine," Henry says, smiling.

"As long as you don't bring your harem." I jerk my head at the group of cheerleaders hovering ten yards away near a goal post, making googly eyes at the guys.

"But we're a package deal," he says with a laugh.

"That's 'cause all you ever think about is your package," JJ replies.

"And you don't?" I snap and JJ punches my shoulder, causing me to stumble backward. We all crack up again.

And then two cheerleaders come up and start fawning over Henry and JJ. What took them so long?

JJ and Lacey start kissing as if winning the state championship depends on it, and Samantha intertwines her fingers with Henry's and smiles up at him. Then Kristen and Marie come over, because cheerleaders travel in packs.

"Nice practice today, Jordan," Marie says, giving me a smile. "That quarterback sneak of yours is great."

"Did Henry tell you to say that?" I ask, staring down at her.

"No," she mutters, looking at her pompoms as she ruffles them.

JJ and Lacey break apart, much like unsnapping Velcro, as Kristen says, "Don't get Jordan started, Marie. We'll be here all night listening to stats and pointers on pitching footballs…"

"They're called *passes*, Kristen," I reply. "Don't think too hard. I hear it makes your hair frizzy."

"Ha, ha," Kristen replies, but she subconsciously smooths her brown hair with a hand. It takes everything I've got not to burst out laughing when I see Samantha and Lacey patting their hair too. I sneak a peek at Henry, JJ, and Carter, and they start snickering again. So does Marie.

"Call if you change your mind about getting food," Henry says to me and Carter, and we all knock fists before Henry and JJ trudge off with their fan club toward the locker rooms.

I clutch my playbook to my chest and for a moment, I feel a pang of loneliness and wish that I had asked Henry to come over. He's been sad since his girlfriend dumped him a couple months ago, so he'd probably appreciate the company. Especially since he's been spending time with girls who think a Hail Mary is a prayer to Jesus's mom.

But he'd just distract me—and I need to concentrate on performing well for Alabama.

"Carter, let's go home," I hear his dad call out from the first row of the metal bleachers. "Your mom's keeping dinner warm until we're done working out."

"Have fun watching film," Carter says. "I'll be wishing I'm you as I do sit-ups with Dad tonight."

Carter jogs over to his dad, who immediately starts talking and gesturing with his hands, probably giving a play-by-play critique of how practice went.

I wish Dad would talk with me like that.

• • •

Back at home, I take a seat at the kitchen table and open my playbook. I peel a banana as I study the formation for Red Rabbit, this crazy cool flea-flicker play Coach wants us to try tomorrow. It'll be hard, but Henry and I can pull it off.

Mom comes in, lays her pruning shears and gardening gloves on the counter, and then pours a glass of water. "Why didn't you go out with your friends tonight?"

"I'm not ready for opening game," I reply, training my eyes on the *X*s and *O*s scrawled across the paper.

"From what I've seen at practice, you're definitely ready. I don't want you to burn out."

"Never."

"Maybe you need a massage. A spa day...so you'll be all fresh and relaxed for Friday. We could go on Thursday after I'm done volunteering at the hospital."

I slowly lift my head to stare at Mom. *Yeah, I'm sure the guys would take me seriously if I show up with pink fingernails on Friday night.* "No, but thanks." I give her a smile so I won't hurt her feelings.

She smiles back. "What are you planning to wear on your trip to Alabama?"

I shrug. "I dunno. Cleats? And my Hundred Oaks sweats?"

Mom sips her water. "I was thinking maybe we could go shopping for a dress."

"Nah, but thanks."

God, if I wore a dress, the Alabama guys would laugh me right out of Tuscaloosa, right back to some pitiful Division II school. "The Alabama head coach is a big Baltimore fan. Maybe I'll wear a Ravens jersey."

Mom laughs. "Dad would kick you out of the house."

"Why am I kicking my daughter out of the house?" the *great* Donovan Woods asks as he comes into the kitchen and gives Mom a kiss and a hug.

"No reason," I mutter and flip a page in my playbook.

Dad grabs a bottle of Gatorade, the strawberry-plum shit he does advertising for, and takes a gulp. He's still buff as ever, but his black hair has started to turn salt-and-peppery. At forty-three years old, Dad has tried to retire after each of the five previous seasons, but he always comes back for some reason or another. Over the years, this has become a joke to sportscasters, so unless we want to get yelled at, we never ask when he's actually going to retire.

He stares down at my playbook and shakes his head.

"You coming to my game on Friday?" I ask Dad.

He looks at Mom when he replies, "Maybe. I'll think about it."

"Okay…"

"How about I take you and Henry fishing on Saturday morning before we go to your brother's game?" Dad smiles at me expectantly.

What total bullshit. He'll go to Mike's game, but won't come to mine? And he tries to suck up by asking me to go fishing?

"No thanks," I say.

The grin dissolves from Dad's face. "Maybe next weekend then," he says softly.

"And maybe you could come to my game on Friday," I mumble to myself. "Mom, where's Mike?" I'm anxious to start watching more Alabama film. Even though I've watched hundreds of college and pro games, I love getting an expert opinion and, well, Dad's never willing to give it.

"Oh," Mom replies. "His coach called a team meeting. Mike said to tell you he's sorry."

"That's cool," I say quietly.

Mom starts telling Dad all about her roses and sunflowers, gesturing out the kitchen window toward the garden. "The sunflowers have almost reached a state of Zen, don't you think?"

Dad wraps his arms around Mom, and I swear I hear him murmur, "I'm in a state of Zen right now too."

Before I reach a state of upchuck, I grab my playbook and a package of chocolate-chip cookies and head downstairs to our basement, where I turn on the TV and put in a DVD of last year's national championship game—Alabama vs. Texas.

I flip off the lights, settle down on one of the leather sofas, and dig into the cookies as I push the play button on the remote.

So. My friends are off hooking up with cheerleaders.

My dad cares more about sunflowers reaching a state of Zen than my feelings.

At least I've got football.

It's been my life since I was seven, but sometimes Henry says I need to spend less time focusing and start "living life like I'm going to hell tomorrow."

But I feel like a normal teenager. Well, as normal as I can be. I mean, obviously I think Justin Timberlake is a mega-hunk, but I'm also over six feet tall and can launch a football fifty yards.

Other ways I'm not normal?

A girl who hangs with an entire football team must hook up all the time, right?

Nope.

I've never had a boyfriend. Hell, I've never even kissed a guy. The closest I've ever come to a kiss happened just this past summer, but it was a joke. At a party, one of those cheerleaders suggested we all play a game of seven minutes in heaven, you know, the game where you go into a closet and kiss? Somehow Henry and I got sent into the closet together, and of course we didn't kiss, but we ended up in a mad thumb-wrestling match. Which turned into a shoving match. Which turned into everyone thinking we'd hooked up in the closet. Yeah, right. He's like my brother.

It's not that guys aren't interested in me, because they are, it's that most of the guys I know are either:

1. Shorter than me;
2. Pansies;
3. On my team;
4. All of the above.

I would never let myself date guys on my team. And I'm not interested in any of them anyway. Riding buses to and from games for years has turned me off to all of them 'cause one bus ride with my team produces more gas than a landfill.

Besides, I don't have time for guys, and if I suddenly were to start acting like a girl, the team might not take me seriously. And I can't afford to lose my confidence—because I'm the star of the Hundred Oaks Red Raiders.

The star Alabama will love on Friday night.

knee problems

the count? 20 days until alabama

"Take five," Coach calls out.

Wednesday afternoon. Two days until our opening game.

I rip my helmet off, jog over to the bench, take a seat, and open my playbook.

"Woods," Henry says, sliding up next to me on the bench. "Take a break."

"I couldn't get the timing for the screen pass right."

He leans over onto his knees and spits between his cleats. "You saved the play by handing off to Bates. Don't be so hard on yourself."

"How can you be so calm?"

Looking over at me, his blond curls fall into his eyes. "I'm not scared for you. You're the best player in Tennessee." He laughs. "But me, I should be learning how to drive a semi like my dad or practicing how to say, 'Attention Wal-Mart shoppers, do not, I repeat, do not go in the men's restroom until further notice. We've had an atomic disaster.'"

I laugh. "Stop. You're the fastest person I know—if you can't get a scholarship to play ball in college, no one can. You're a kickass wide receiver, and you're smart."

Smiling, he leans back and folds his hands on top of his stomach. "Are we still on to do something after practice?"

"I should watch more film..."

"Woods, you promised!" He scrunches up his face at me.

"I doubt Liz Heaston and Ashley Martin partied much in high school."

"I'm not talking about partying. I'm talking about you and me hanging out—same ole, same ole. Besides, they were kickers. It doesn't take a lot to kick an extra point."

"And look at them! Liz Heaston? Two extra points in her whole college career! And that was just Division III. And Ashley? Well, sure. She kicked three in a game. And that was Division I—Jacksonville State, but still." I shake my head. "I wanna play for real."

"But we've barely seen each other in a week," he says quietly, and I think about how much it would suck to achieve my dream of playing for Alabama but have no one to share it with, 'cause my best friend has found better stuff to do.

"Forget the film—we'll go out. Just us, right?"

"Of course." He leans over onto his knees and says, "So what do you think of Marie Baird?"

"She's better than Kristen, I guess."

"I'm thinking of asking Marie out."

"What happened to Samantha?"

Henry focuses on the ground and kicks a rock. "I dunno...the sex is okay...but I don't really like her."

"Why do you keep sleeping with girls you aren't dating? Isn't this, like, three girls since Carrie Myer dumped you? Why don't you just get back together with her?"

Henry's face grows pink, pinker than those ridiculous bras

Mom recently left on my bed when she decided I needed something more feminine than a sports bra. "Marie seems really cool..."

"You mean for actual dating, not just fooling around?"

"Maybe."

"I like Carrie." Of all the girls I know, she's the only one I consider a friend. When we started ninth grade, the first day in the locker room after practice was a true nightmare. I made the mistake of changing out of my uniform in front of the cheerleading captain, who proceeded to make fun of my flat chest in front of twenty other girls. And Carrie, a brand-new freshman cheerleader, walked up to the captain and told her to knock it off, which took mucho guts.

"I bet you'd like Marie too if you'd give her a chance."

I shrug, thinking I'm not hanging out with anyone who's friends with Kristen Markum. "Why did Carrie dump you anyway?"

"I've told you, Woods. It's private."

"But we've never kept secrets from each other."

"Then why won't you tell me why you hate Kristen so much?" He smiles, and I punch him in the arm. "Truce!" he says, rubbing his bicep. "So do you wanna go to the Fun Tunnel and play skee-ball?"

"Perfect. Then dinner at my house?"

"Hell, yeah. It's fried chicken night, right?"

"You'd better believe it."

Henry usually eats at our house a few nights a week, and sometimes he sleeps over. Technically, he's supposed to stay in the guest room, but he's been sneaking into my room since we were eight. When Mom found out, she started forcing him to sleep head-to-toe with me. To make me laugh, he always has excuses as to why we should be allowed to sleep head-to-head, like it'll be easier for him to protect me if an attacker were to come in, or because my feet reek.

"Break's over!" Coach shouts. "Woods!"

Jumping to my feet, I sweep my long blond hair back up into my helmet and jog over to the fifty-yard line. "'Sup, Coach?"

"Try out the hook and lateral play we talked about."

"'Kay." This is not an easy play, but Henry and I can handle it. I'm supposed to throw a short pass to Henry and as the defense moves in to tackle him, he pitches it to a running back who plows up the middle.

I jog to the center of the field and huddle with the guys.

"What's the play?" JJ asks.

"Red Rabbit," I reply.

"Oh hell, yeah," Henry says, clapping his hands together once.

We all get into position and as JJ hikes the ball to me, I only hear silence. Coach Miller always talks to me through the speaker in my helmet, so when he doesn't, I'm surprised. What the hell is he doing? Glancing out of the corner of my eye, I spot the principal walking toward Coach with this incredible-looking guy in tow. Suddenly I have the first knee problems of my life:

They turn to rubber.

I keep staring, and I'm knocked off my feet by a linebacker—Carter and his 250 pounds. I fly backward, slamming to the ground, my head rattling around inside my helmet. Ow.

• • •

Where the hell is JJ? Why didn't he protect me? This is the first time I've been tackled in forever. With my footwork and JJ's muscular, continent-sized body, it should never happen.

"Jordan!" I hear Mom shout from the stands.

Henry comes running up, ripping off his helmet and kneeling down next to me. Biting his lip, he puts a hand on my arm. Then

Carter falls down next to me too. "I'm so sorry, Woods. I tried to stop. Why the hell were you just standing there?"

"Woods!" Coach yells, running over. "You okay? What the hell happened, JJ? Carter—how could you be dumb enough to hit our quarterback two days before the opening of the season?" Coach throws his clipboard onto the ground. How cheesy.

"I'm fine, Coach," I say. I'm not hurt, but I don't want to stand, because I'm just as embarrassed now as the time my bathing suit top fell off on that waterslide in Florida.

I can't believe I just got sacked. Dad will be furious when he finds out I got blindsided during a practice…great. Just what I need two days before opening game. More damned stress.

"My fault, Coach," JJ says. He holds out a hand and quickly pulls me to a standing position.

"Don't let that happen on Friday night!" Coach shouts, pointing a finger in JJ's face.

Under my helmet, I breathe deeply. JJ didn't have to take the blame—it wasn't his fault. But he did owe me. Last Saturday, I covered for him when he was late for practice—he'd been making out with Lacey and had lost track of time.

Speaking of making out, I see Chace Crawford's twin standing with the principal, looking concerned. Crap. So he saw my spill too. I'm glad I'm wearing my helmet, because my face feels hotter than a potato on a grill.

He has this sandy blond hair that stands up in places and sweeps across his forehead. His blue eyes remind me of a Crayola crayon, the truest blue there is, and his worn-out polo shirt and faded jeans just hang off him.

You can't buy jeans that look like that—you have to wear them out for years to make them so perfect. I wonder if I could buy them off him. Wait—why would I do that? Nothing else he'd wear could compare with those jeans. I'm also glad to see he's taller than me by a few inches and has a great tan. And, oh the heavens, his body. What does he do? Work out for a living?

Wait. *What the hell is this guy doing on my field?*

I feel like I could simultaneously fly and barf. I need to get my head back into practice.

Luckily, the principal starts speaking, distracting me. "Coach Miller, I'd like you to meet Tyler Green. His high school football team won the Texas state championship last year. I know it's a bit late for a tryout, but his family just moved here and I hope you'll consider him for the team. I can explain more later."

Coach nods. "Thanks."

The principal disappears back into the school, to the comfort of air conditioning.

Wait. Did the principal just say something about Tyler and football? And trying out for *my* team? I need to stop staring and figure out what's going on here.

Tyler, with his hands stuffed deep in his pockets, toes the yard line, then glances around at the team. Why's he so nervous? For someone who won a state championship, you'd think he'd be this pompous asshole strutting around like he's fucking Tom Brady.

"So, Tyler," Coach says.

"Call me Ty, Coach."

"Okay. So Ty, what position do you play?"

"Quarterback, sir."

I take a step back, and everyone else on the team laughs.

The position is mine.

It's been mine for two years and this new kid isn't going to take it away.

"Quiet!" Coach yells. He gives the team a scary look and we all stop talking and laughing. One of those looks means: if you don't behave, you're gonna run five miles *while* wearing pads. "Ty—we already have a starting quarterback. An all-state quarterback."

Ty's eyes seem to fill with pain, and he looks down at the ground. I've never seen a QB act like this before. Most are cocky, full of attitude. Leaders. I can't imagine following a guy whose eyes give so much away. But he's buff, and obviously good if he played for a Texas championship team. Texans take their football seriously. It's practically a religion down there.

So what's wrong?

Wait. What's all this sympathy? Jordan Woods isn't sympathetic. I'm a rock.

"But we could always use another good backup," Coach says. "Our captain will run you through some drills. Woods!"

Though my knees are still wobbling, somehow I run over to Coach. Ty stretches out his hand to shake mine. When I grasp his hand, I squeeze as hard as possible. Gotta show him that I'm captain, that I'm in charge.

Ty eyes my hand in his, then quickly releases it. "Ow," he says, smiling. The sight of his smile makes my body melt like the Wicked Witch of the West.

"Woods—run some drills with him," Coach says. "Do a few quick passes, some intermediate. Hit Henry on a five-yard slant. Do a post route with Higgins."

"Yeah, Coach," I say, glancing at the cheerleaders. They've stopped doing their pyramids and jumps. They're all mesmerized by Ty, just like me.

"Woods?" Coach says. "You paying attention? Take off your helmet—I want to check your eyes. You took a pretty hard hit there."

I slowly take off my helmet. I pass the helmet to Henry and start running my hands through my hair, pushing it away from my face so Coach can look in my eyes. Henry watches me, his mouth falling open.

Ty gasps. Then smirks and laughs. He obviously had no idea I'm a girl.

"Dude, you'd better watch it," Henry says, taking a step toward Ty.

When JJ slaps a hand on Ty's shoulder, my mind flashes back to last year when JJ punched a guy from Northgate High for grabbing my butt after a game. "Show Woods some respect! Or I'll kick your ass."

"No disrespect intended," Ty says, holding a hand up to JJ's chest. "I'm surprised…and impressed. That's all."

After taking a look in my eyes and confirming all's okay with me—I mean, besides the fact Ty is completely throwing me off my game—Coach says, "Let's go. We've wasted enough practice time."

I take my helmet from Henry and stuff it on my head, then pick up the ball and yell, "Henry! Go long!"

He takes off running down the field and changes directions a few times. I launch a thirty-five-yard deep pass that drops right into his hands. Thank God. I'm back. I'm myself again.

"Nice," Ty says, nodding. He has this deep, sexy Texas accent.

"Your turn," I say, grabbing another ball and tossing it to Ty. "Higgins—post route!"

Higgins jets down the field, then takes a quick left. Ty bombs the ball right into Higgins's arms. I'm impressed—I couldn't have done it any better, and Ty doesn't even know how Higgins moves. We run a few more drills and Ty makes them all look effortless. We're equals.

And I'm scared.

Ty's bigger, obviously stronger, and, unlike me, he probably didn't screw up in the final two minutes of a state championship game. Johnson City beat us 13–10 because I threw an interception and they returned it for a touchdown.

What if Coach gives my position to him? I try to shake this thought from my mind—I've worked years for this. I've earned it. For the coach to give away my position, I'd have to mess up in a spectacular way. Like five interceptions followed by a fumble.

Finally, Coach Miller comes back over. "Woods, Ty—let's talk," he says, gesturing for us to walk away from the rest of the players. Henry glances at me as we move toward Coach.

"Ty—that's quite an arm you've got there. And you've got highly developed instincts as well," Coach says.

"Thanks, sir."

"You're a senior?"

"Yeah."

"And you started for your team in Texas when you won the championship last year?"

"Yeah."

Now it's my turn to stare at the grass.

Thanks to our boosters, mostly wives of former Titans players who still call Franklin home, Hundred Oaks has the best high school football program in Tennessee. We have shitloads of money to put toward buying state-of-the-art equipment and paying first-rate staff. Coach Miller used to coach college ball, but gave it up for a slower pace of life when his wife got sick. His expertise has led several players to get full rides to college.

I bet that's why Ty wants to play for Hundred Oaks. It's like we're in the same league, but he's one step higher. Tears sting my eyes. I need to focus. I can't cry in front of my team.

Damned estrogen.

Coach narrows his eyes. "Why would you give all that up? Your parents couldn't stay in Texas one more year to ensure you got your choice of colleges? And why Franklin? If you had to move to Tennessee, I'm surprised your parents didn't search for a school district lacking a star quarterback."

The pain returns to Ty's eyes. "I did what I had to do, sir. I just moved here with my mother and sister." Mussing his sandy hair, Ty peeks at me. "Some things are more important than football."

What? A Texas football player who doesn't kneel down and pray to the Cowboys every Sunday?

Epic.

Coach nods. "I see. Well, you're on the team, but I don't know how much playing time I can guarantee you."

"Thank you, sir. Being on the team is good enough for me," Ty says with a hint of a smile. He stuffs his hands into the pockets of his jeans.

"Great. We'll get you a uniform—wear your jersey on Friday for the pep rally," Coach says. "That's enough for today, Woods. No practice tomorrow—the team needs to rest before the game."

"Got it, Coach." I walk back to my team and yell, "No practice tomorrow. Don't do anything stupid on your day off."

I pull my helmet off and head to the girls' locker room as quickly as I can—I need to get in and out before cheerleading practice ends or they'll quiz me for information about their crushes, aka my teammates.

They don't seem to understand that the guys don't spend all their time talking about girls. Only about, I'd say, ninety percent of their time is devoted to that. And even then, it's only about who's hooking up with who, and who wants to hook up with who. The day I hear JJ talking about his feelings is the day I'll run to a nuclear fallout shelter and pray for my life.

About halfway across the field, JJ, Carter, and Henry jog up behind me. Henry throws an arm around my shoulders as he pulls off his helmet, shaking his curly blond hair loose. He wipes a few curls off his forehead and whispers, "So Coach is letting that Ty dude on the team?"

"Yup," I reply, straightening my jersey.

"That's bullshit," JJ replies, cracking his knuckles.

"What's his story?" Carter asks.

"No idea," I say, but I'm dying to know. I start wiping the dust from my hands and off my football pants.

Henry looks at me and whispers, "You sure you're okay?"

"Totally." I hear my voice wobble.

"That guy's got nothing on you," JJ adds, looking over his shoulder at Ty, who's talking to Coach.

"We both know that's not true. Did you see his footwork? Ty's incredible."

"Yeah…incredible," Henry says, closing his eyes, pulling me in closer to him as we approach the girls' locker room.

Yanking the door open, I say, "'Kay, Henry—see you in a few," leaving him outside. He swings his helmet back and forth like a pendulum, staring at me as I let the door slam.

I walk through the white concrete locker room, which is covered with old red and black checkered carpet. I take a seat on a bench, then yank off my practice jersey and pads and walk into the showers. The cold water feels great, and finally, I cool down.

When I'm finished, I pull on a pair of mesh shorts and a T-shirt before walking back into the locker room. Parading around in my plain white underwear in front of cheerleaders isn't my idea of fun.

I hear the giggling when I'm still ten yards away from the other girls. Shuddering, I head to my locker, open it, and yank my bag out.

"I think JJ will tell me he loves me soon," Lacey says to Kristen.

"He definitely will," Kristen says. "I can tell by the way he looks at you."

I force myself to cough so I won't laugh. JJ stares at Lacey the way he stares at every single one of the Titans' cheerleaders. It's the same way he stares at cheese fries, for that matter.

"Hey, Jordan," Lacey says, brushing her brown hair. Must she stand around in skimpy black underwear? She'd get more coverage wearing a spool of thread than those things.

"Hi," I say, focusing on packing my bag and getting the hell out of here. I ignore my wet hair; brushing it will take too much time.

"When's the last time you shaved your legs?" Lacey asks.

I bite the inside of my cheek. Sometimes Lacey makes me feel so shitty. I mean, what if Ty notices I haven't shaved in, like, a week?

"So, um, has JJ mentioned me lately?" Lacey says.

You mean, besides to tell me you guys slept together in the back of your mom's car last night? I'm still trying to figure out how JJ could fit horizontally inside the back of a Ford Taurus, but I'll take his word that it actually happened.

"Nope," I say. "Hasn't said a word."

Lacey slams her hairbrush into her bag.

I try to cobble together a sympathetic look, but it's harder than I thought it would be.

I've never told anyone this, not even Henry, but one time I overheard Lacey and Kristen talking bad about me in the bathroom…

I remember hearing Lacey whine, "I don't understand why JJ hangs out with her so much. It's not like she's cute—she's huge!"

"I dunno," Kristen had replied. "Sam Henry fawns over her too, even though she's a dyke."

"JJ promises me that he's not sleeping with her…"

"Maybe she's sleeping with both him and Henry." And that wasn't a one-time diss. Kristen's a repeat offender.

Right then, Marie and Carrie, Henry's ex, come in through the locker room door.

"Sam Henry asked me out," Marie is saying to Carrie, who purses her lips, biting them. "Do you mind if I say yes?"

"No…I'm glad," Carrie says, focusing on me, and then she motions for Marie to follow her.

They head straight over to my locker. "Who's the new guy?" Carrie asks me.

"His name's Ty Green," I reply. "He just moved here from Texas."

"He looked pretty good out there," Lacey says. "I mean, in terms of football obviously."

I snort. Like Lacey knows *anything* about football.

"Jealous?" Kristen asks. "He seems just as good as you."

"No. I'm glad to have a great backup," I respond, grabbing my bag. "He plays quarterback like me—you know, it's a position in this game called football."

Kristen rolls her eyes and goes back to staring at herself in the mirror. "Why's your face all red?"

I jet for the door.

the great donovan woods

I walk back across the field toward my truck, and on the way, I spot Coach Miller talking to Ty. Coach is frowning and scratching his chin, his glance alternating between Ty and the ground. They stop talking and, like me, Ty heads toward the parking lot.

"Hey," he calls out, jogging toward me. My hands fly to my wet hair, and I try to smooth it and get some of the tangles out, but I'm sure it looks like knotted yarn. God, I'm as bad as the cheerleaders.

"Hi," I reply. Suddenly we're walking right next to one another.

"You're amazing," he says.

"Excuse me?"

He clears his throat. "I mean, you're a great quarterback. I haven't seen any guys our age as good as you."

I nod as I approach my truck, my Dodge Ram, a sixteenth birthday gift from my dad. I throw my bag into the truck's bed.

"Hot ride," Ty says, smiling and patting the side of my truck.

"Thanks." I turn away from him. His smile is a virus. A virus sweeping through my body, rendering it useless. "What do you drive?" I ask.

"Nothing. No car," he says. But he doesn't seem embarrassed.

Crossing his arms, he leans up against my truck. "So what's your first name?" he asks. "I hope it's not Woods."

"Jordan."

He nods. "You related to Donovan Woods?"

"Yeah," I mutter. "He's my dad." I start peeling the label off my Gatorade bottle.

"That explains your style and mechanics."

Damn, he must've been watching me pretty closely. "You a Tennessee fan?" I ask. Maybe he was into the Oilers before they moved from Houston to Nashville.

He laughs. "Of course not. Cowboys all the way, man. I remember watching your dad play for my team back when I was a little kid."

My dad is the last thing I want to talk about right now. When people meet me, that's all they think of—the great Donovan Woods, two-time MVP of the NFL Two-time Heisman Trophy winner. The great Donovan Woods, surely a first-round Hall of Fame selection.

The *great* Donovan Woods who doesn't believe in me or my dreams of playing ball at the collegiate level.

"I'd better get going, Ty. Nice work today. I'm glad you made the team." I'm keeping it smooth and professional. "If you don't have a car, how're you getting home?"

He shrugs. "Walking, I guess."

I gasp. "No one in Tennessee walks—sidewalks barely exist here. You're not walking."

He's a teammate now, and teammates take care of each other.

I scan the parking lot. Henry is the only guy out of the locker room so far—he's talking to Kristen and Marie. What the hell do the guys do in there anyway? How could it possibly take me less time to get ready than them? "Henry," I call out.

Henry abandons the cheerleaders and jogs over, then steals the Gatorade bottle from my hand, takes a swig, and hands it back to me while staring Ty down.

"Make sure Ty gets home okay," I say.

"What about our plans?" Henry asks. He cradles the back of his neck with a hand and smirks at Ty.

"I don't feel well," I reply, touching my stomach. I just need to be alone right now, so I can think about what's happened today—how this guy swooped in to steal both my position and my cool.

"That's all right," Henry says, but he looks hurt. "Kristen and Marie just invited me to study anyway."

"Can you take Ty home first?"

"Why can't you take him home?"

Um, because he's driving me nuts? "Take him on your *study* date. It'll be good for him to meet some of the local bimbos."

Ty smiles.

"Fine, but I get Marie. Give me just a sec, Ty." Henry puts his arm around me and leads me away from Ty. "What do you mean you aren't feeling well? Was it the hit you took?" he whispers.

"Yeah, I think so."

"Guess I'm not coming over for dinner then?"

"Just go have a nice time with Marie, okay? I want you to date someone who makes you happy again." Henry nods and rubs his chin, looking up at me, staring right in my eyes. Ever since Carrie dumped him, he's seemed so sad.

"Thanks, Woods. Maybe we'll catch up sometime soon," he says, giving my shoulder a squeeze before he walks off. "Ready to go, Ty? I think you'll like Kristen."

Ugh. Kristen has the same IQ as a tree stump. I've gotta get out of here before I punch her or something. I climb into my truck, lean my head out the window, and smile. "See you tomorrow, guys." Through my rearview mirror, I see Ty staring at me as I drive away. Why didn't I just offer him a ride?

I know why.

I have to focus. I can't risk my season. I can't blow it again this year. I *need* to get a football scholarship.

And to do that, I have to win the state championship.

• • •

Walking in the back door of my house, I drop my bag on the floor. I have a date with my bed: hiding beneath my pillow and listening to some Guns N' Roses. That'll make me feel better.

I go through the kitchen, grabbing a banana and Gatorade on the way to my room, and run into my brother, Mike, and his friend Jake, who's an awesome wide receiver. Like my bro, Jake also plays for the University of Tennessee at Knoxville. Jake is originally from California, so he's spent most of his summer living here so he can be closer to school for football practice.

"Hey, sis," Mike says, giving me a side hug. "Mom said you took a bad spill at practice. You okay?"

"I'm fine."

"How's it goin', Jordan?" Jake says, eyeing me up and down. Remember how I said that guys are interested in me? Yeah, he's one of them. I think Mike would kill him if he tried something, though, and I wouldn't want Jake to go after me anyway. He's hot, but he seems like one of those guys who's been with about a hundred girls.

"Good," I say.

Jake slips an arm around my waist. "Mike says you're having problems with algebra? Want some help?"

"What the hell do you know about math, Reynolds?"

"Not only can I teach you math, I can teach you math in bed, Jordan. You know, I'll add the bed, you subtract the clothes, you divide the legs, and I'll multiply."

This is standard Jake Reynolds behavior, so Mike does the typical rolling of his eyes as I say, "Charming," and shove Jake against the dishwasher.

Then I run upstairs to my room and flop down on my bed, which is covered in a new fluffy white duvet. I used to have this blue checkered bedspread that looked like graph paper. One day this past summer when Henry was over, he said that graph paper bedding turns guys off and that if I ever want to get laid, I can't bring a guy home to a room that reminds them of algebra and the nerdy girls on the math team. Not that I care what guys think of my bedding, but the math team is the last thing I want to be associated with, so I got rid of the old spread for something neutral.

Grabbing my stereo remote, I flip on the classic eighties station and stare out my window into our backyard, which ends at the banks of a lake. *My* lake actually—Lake Jordan. Having a dad who plays pro means we aren't lacking in amenities. Our house is huge, with hardwood floors everywhere and giant windows overlooking the woods and trails. The best thing about our house? My parents' room is on the other side of it, so it's like Mike and I have our own private wing. Dad never comes up here.

Sometimes I'm embarrassed about how lavishly we live, because a lot of families around here don't have much. Tennessee's a weird place—it's like you're really rich, like me, or you're really poor, like Henry. There's not much in between. If Dad wanted to, he could be making fifteen or twenty million bucks a year. But with the NFL salary cap rules being what they are, he chose to take a pay cut so the Titans could pay other players more money. He'd rather have a killer offensive line protecting him than a bit more cash.

Lying on my bed, I try to drown myself in the ancient rock music, and try to forget that I got sacked today. Try to forget about Ty's body.

I bury my face in a pillow and hit it with a fist. Rolling over, I jump out of bed and pace back and forth across the hardwood floors, biting my knuckle. Then I flop back down and grab my Gatorade from the bedside table and start slapping the bottle against my palm.

I squeeze the bottle to see if I'm strong enough to bust it. I dig my fingertips into it, but it doesn't budge, so I hurl the damned thing across the room at my dresser, knocking a bunch of the lotions and perfumes and other shit Mom buys me to the floor.

I go pick the girly stuff up and put it back on my dresser, and the birthday gift from Mom peeks out from behind my sophomore MVP trophy, taunting me. For my seventeenth, she bought me this lame journal.

"Jordan," she said, "writing allows me to blah, blah, blah, think deeply about karma, blah, blah, blah, and helps me figure out my problems."

Mom should get a job creating lame-ass mantras for the bottoms of juice-bottle lids.

But was she right?

I pick up the Moleskine and thumb through the blank, crisp pages.

Sitting back down on my bed, I open the journal. It's not like the paper will judge me, or question my sanity, or doubt my ability to lead a football team. No one could know about it—the guys would make fun of me for eons if they found out.

At least by writing stuff down, it's out of my head, out of my body.

I reach over to my bedside table and push a stack of *Sports Illustrated* magazines aside to find a pen, then I write:

> I've never seen anyone so freaking gorgeous. No one's ever distracted me like this...But I'm so far behind everyone else—I've never even seen a guy naked...Well, I guess I've seen Henry in his boxers bunches of times, and his body is hot—scalding hot wings hot, so Ty must be gorgeous. And I want to touch—

God, what the hell am I writing!?

I scribble through the shitty words.

As I chew on my pen, thinking what to write about Ty, something that isn't complete crap, I hear a knock at the door. "Who is it?" I say, stuffing the journal under my pillow.

"Mike."

"Enter."

My brother comes in and sits down next to me on the bed.

"Where's your other half?" I ask.

Mike laughs. "Jake? In my room, calling up some girls we met the other night. So what happened at practice today?"

I bury my face in my pillow. "You have to promise not to make fun of me."

He rubs my shoulder. "I promise."

"Carter accidentally sacked me."

"Carter sacked you? Where the hell was JJ?"

"It was my fault. I wasn't paying attention," I say, groaning into my pillow.

"That's hard to believe. When you're in the zone, you're in the zone. I mean, I've never seen you lose concentration."

I turn over and stare up at Mike. "Um…a new quarterback tried out for the team today. He just transferred here from Texas. And he's good. Damned good. Better than me."

Mike whistles and runs his fingers through his hair. "The coach would be pretty stupid to make a QB change two days before the opening game. You're going to start, sis."

I slap Mike's arm. "Of course I'm starting."

"I don't get it then. Are you threatened by him?"

I take a deep breath, sit up, and lean back against my pillows. I can tell my bro about Ty—Mike won't mention him to anyone else. I just can't tell him about wanting to tackle Ty in the guys' locker room.

"I think I like him."

Mike starts coughing, then smiles. "You? Jordan Woods? Has a crush? Yeah, right."

"I told you not to make fun of me." I shove him off my bed.

Grinning, Mike stretches out on the hardwood floor and puts his hands behind his head. "I'm not making fun. I think it's great. It's about time you started noticing guys."

"Oh, shut up. I notice guys. It's just…this was so weird, when he walked onto the field, I just lost it…"

"So whatcha gonna do about it?"

"I dunno. Try to keep my head on straight for practices and games. I can't date a guy who's on my team. Especially not a rival for my position."

Mike nods. "Good luck. Just keep your head in the game and you'll be fine. And don't look at the sidelines too much. You might get hungry for this hunk of man meat."

"Dude! Shut up!" I yell, throwing my pillows at him. "You're awful." I cover my face with my hands. God. Why couldn't Ty have moved here after the season was over?

"What's his name?"

"Tyler Green. Ty."

"Well, Ty's a lucky guy if my sister is interested in him. I can't wait to meet him at the game Friday night."

"You aren't heading back to school before then? Don't you have a game Saturday?"

"Coach says it'll be okay if I drive back on Saturday morning. Besides, this'll probably be the only game of yours I'll get to see this year. I wanna see which schools have recruiters checking you out besides Alabama. I'll chat them up a bit."

I smile at Mike. "Thank you!"

"You're going to have your pick of scholarships. Imagine it. You'll be the first girl to ever play QB at the collegiate level."

I sigh. "I wanna go to Alabama so bad. I just wish Dad would support me. Doesn't he think I'm good?"

"He knows you're good," Mike says, ruffling his hair, avoiding my eyes. "Dad's just...scared. He knows you can take all these fools at the high school level, but college is a different beast."

I nod slowly, then smile at him. "I can't wait for your game on Saturday. You're gonna kill the Gators."

Mike waves a hand, but he looks pleased. "Thanks. We've got it. As long as we play good."

"Mike, Jordan, Jake! Dinnertime," Mom yells from downstairs.

"Don't tell Mom and Dad about Ty," I warn Mike.

"But they'll be so glad to hear you aren't gay!"

• • •

You know those scenes on the news where people from "Food

for Peace" take big bags of wheat to starving children in Somalia? Hundreds of people crowd around the trucks and knock each other down to get one bag of corn.

That's what dinnertime is like at my house. When I sit down at the table, I'm like a stealth bomber as I secure four pieces of bread, because if I don't do it now, I won't get any later. Mike and Jake spoon big globs of mashed potatoes onto their plates, and I take three chicken legs. We won't start eating until Dad gets his ass in here, but we're all poised to dig in.

Mom brings in a pitcher of lemonade and pours me a glass. She looks at all of us and sees Henry's empty chair. "Where's Sam?" Mom asks.

"He had a study date," I reply.

"A *date* date?" Mike asks, narrowing his eyes.

"I guess."

"With who?"

"I dunno…some cheerleader. Marie Baird."

"I figured he'd get back together with Carrie," Mom says. "The other day, he told me he was going to ask her out again."

"I dunno. He didn't mention it to me when I suggested that," I say, focusing on my chicken leg. I can't wait to eat this thing. Mike glances at Mom, who shrugs. Why are they so interested in Henry's love life? Or should I say sex life?

In more important news, I'm dying to dig into dinner. All this thinking about Ty has made me ravenous. I didn't know crushing on a guy would require me to up my caloric intake.

The *great* Donovan Woods finally comes in and sits down at the head of the table. He plops a bottle of Gatorade next to his plate and grabs his napkin.

I can tell from the scowl on his face that Dad's in a horrible mood, so I wonder if Titans practice sucked or something. When he finally picks up a fork and starts eating his salad, the rest of us start shoveling food into our mouths as if we actually are those poor starving Somali children. A minute later, Dad drops his fork onto his plate. Everyone looks over at him.

"Don?" Mom says.

Dad ignores Mom and focuses on me. "Jordan, I seriously think it's time for you to consider quitting football."

"Dad, come on," Mike says. Jake picks up his silverware and napkin and sits on the edge of his chair and stares at Dad, almost as if he doesn't want to witness this, but can't help but stay and watch.

"Mike, keep out of this," Dad says, focusing on me again. "Joe Carter called to tell me his son hit you hard today."

"It was no big deal," I say, pushing my salad around on my plate with a fork.

"But it could've been a big deal, Jordan. I don't think you understand how dangerous this sport is," Dad says with a shaky voice. I hope he doesn't use that tone in front of his teammates, because it makes him sound like a complete pansy.

"Dad, I've been playing for ten years!"

"Joe Carter weighs 250 pounds. You weigh 170. You're lucky you didn't get knocked out." Dad starts cramming salad into his mouth. Mike bites into a chicken breast like he's a vulture or something and shakes his head at Dad.

"Well, nothing happened," I say, "and I'm not quitting."

Dad rubs his eyes. "What exactly do you want to do with football anyway? No women have ever been in the NFL, 'cause they'd get killed."

"I don't know, Dad. Right now, all I want is to play in college, and see what happens there."

"You could seriously get hurt. The guys in college play at a totally different level than high school."

"Don't you know how good I am?"

"You shouldn't be playing a sport with guys who are twice your size." Dad stabs at his chicken with a knife and fork, ripping the meat off the bone and forcing it into his mouth.

"Maybe you'd know how good she is if you ever showed up to one of her games, Dad," Mike blurts. Jake lets out a low whistle, and I think he's about to take off, when Dad suddenly stands up and throws his napkin down on the table. He shoots Mike a look—the look of death, which I haven't seen since Henry and I accidentally drove Dad's ATV into the lake.

"Thanks for dinner, Julie," Dad says, bending over and kissing Mom's cheek. He picks up his plate, puts the bottle of Gatorade under his arm, and leaves the room. A few seconds later, I hear the door to his study slam shut.

My appetite gone, I pick up my plate and hold it out for Mike and Jake. My brother grabs the bread and chicken and Jake scoops the mashed potatoes onto his plate.

Mike rips into his second chicken breast, then wipes the grease from his lips with a napkin. "Dad's such a jerk."

Grinning at my brother, I stand up and take my plate to the sink. Before heading upstairs, I pause outside the dining room because I hear Mom speaking quietly. "Mike, I know you're mad, but you will show your father more respect."

"Yes, ma'am," Mike replies softly.

I wish Henry was here to make me laugh right now, because I

feel like shit. To get my mind off Dad's assholishness, I run upstairs to my room and grab the stupid journal. Then I go outside into the backyard, through the gardens to Mom's potting shed, this rickety oak shack that's covered in ivy and moss. It's totally *Scotland*.

Looking over my shoulder to make sure no one's watching me, I slip inside and shut the door and take a seat next to the shovels in the corner, where streams of light from our deck shoot through the window and the cracks in the siding, illuminating the dirt floor.

I love hiding in the shed when I need alone time. When we were little, Henry and I used to play house in here. We'd make long-winded announcements about how we would never get married to anyone, and I liked to pretend we had a bowling alley, and Henry would talk about having a helipad, and I'd trump that by pretending to have a transporter like on *Star Trek*.

I find my flashlight. And holding it using my chin, I open the Moleskine to a blank page and try to think of something to write, besides fantasies of seeing Ty's…

"Jesus, Woods," I mutter. "Get a hold of yourself."

I doodle. A few pictures of footballs, some pinwheels, the Alabama Roll Tide logo about thirty times. I draw a bunch of *X*s and *O*s, which aren't hugs and kisses, but offensive plays from the team playbook, and—okay, okay—I write J.W. + T.G., which I scribble over immediately.

I rip out the page of doodles and wad it up.

> Ode to Ty…I love your three-step drop and that quick release.

I laugh as I rip that page out too.

evolution

(aka second attempt at tackling a poem)

I'll admit it
When I first saw Jake Reynolds
    I thought I'd died and gone to the Super Bowl
        (as starting QB)
That blond surfer-boy hair
That tan body that won't stop
That bottom lip: upturned, a sexy invite
And then he spoke
"Damn, Jordan. You should play tight end
    because your ass is wound tighter than a baseball."
Now every time I see a hot guy
    my first reaction is to brace myself
Wait for the sewage to seep out of his mouth
I thought Henry was the last of his kind
I thought hot nice guys had gone extinct
Be still, my hormones
Ty is here to repopulate the species

mudding

the count? 19 days until alabama

The next morning, I wake up a little earlier than usual. Mike, Jake, and I run five miles together and then we lift weights before I hop in the shower. When I shave my legs for the first time in a week, I actually try to hit all the tricky spots—around the ankles, behind the knees. It's like when Mom spends hours making sure each weed has been plucked from her vegetable garden.

I also mess around with the assorted lotions, body washes, and conditioners that Mom puts in my bathroom. I hope Ty likes shea butter.

Ugh. All I've done since yesterday is think about him. I only got two hours of sleep last night. Imagine that—me losing tomorrow's game against Lynchburg High School, the worst team in our district—because I'm worn out from thinking about a guy all night long.

Yeah, I know. I make myself sick too.

Yet here I am at 7:00 a.m., actually trying to decide what I'm going to wear to school today. I spend two minutes brushing my hair, which is about two minutes longer than usual, then I pick out a nice pair of jeans, and since I don't have practice today, I try on a pushup bra and matching underwear that have infiltrated my underwear drawer. The lacy blue underwear barely covers anything and offers virtually no support.

Mom must really want me to get a boyfriend.

As uncomfortable as I feel, I keep the girly underwear on anyway. Who knows? Provided they stay the hell out of my butt crack, they might make me feel sexier later on today.

And instead of my usual ratty "Titans" and "Bell Buckle Moon Pie Ten-Mile Race" T-shirts, I pick out a plain black fitted tee. I know, I know—I'm wild. But seriously? For me, this fitted tee is totally dressing up, and it shows off my boobs. I don't think too many people even realize I have boobs. Not even Jake, the total horndog, knows I have a chest.

I top off the outfit with flip-flops and chapstick. Ty better appreciate how hard I've worked to make myself attractive for him this morning, because I am fucking spent.

• • •

At lunchtime I head to the cafeteria, which always smells like a mixture of meatloaf and salad dressing, like those odors have seeped into the concrete walls and tile floor. I grab a slice of pizza, a salad, and a couple cartons of chocolate milk. I know I'm seventeen and that those little milk cartons are for kids, but I love them.

Today, I'm the first person to sit down at the football team's table, and when I look up at the lunch line to see where the rest of the guys are, there he is. Ty. He stares at me, smiling. From across the cafeteria, he mouths the words, "Can I sit with you?"

I take a bite of pizza and point at the table. He grins again. Suddenly I seem to lose the ability to chew.

He drops his tray down and slides in beside me. Our elbows touch. "Hey, Woods."

I nod once. "Ty."

I scan the cafeteria for the rest of the guys, hoping they'll be here soon. JJ and Carter are talking to a tableful of freshman girls. From a few tables away, Lacey is glaring at JJ, but he doesn't even notice because some redhead is feeding him French fries. Carter is listening to a girl with long brown hair, gazing at her as if she's saying very important things, like giving a play-by-play account of Super Bowl XXXVIII. In all actuality, she's probably giving him a play-by-play account of some romance novel where some chick is in love with a boy who's really a werewolf, and a vampire who's really a dragon with enormous wings, and a handsome king who's really a vampire.

Henry is standing over by the windows talking to Carrie Myer. He's leaning against the glass and frowning at her. Is Mom right? Are they going to get back together? Carrie says something, and they both turn and look at me. She stares at me for a sec, then turns back to Henry and says something.

What's that about? I wish I could read lips. Then he drags a hand through his curls and focuses on the ceiling tiles. Carrie wipes a tear off her face, turns, and walks toward the doors. Her eyes are all puffy and red. Henry follows her out into the hallway, frowning.

Even though she said she's glad, maybe Carrie is actually pissed that Marie went out with Henry yesterday, thus breaking the cardinal rule of cheerleading. JJ once told me that if a guy dates one cheerleader, the rest of the cheerleaders will never, ever date him because of squad loyalty. Yeah, JJ didn't understand it either. It's not like anyone is getting married. But when it comes to Henry, the rule doesn't apply: the girls disregard it and mess around with him anyway.

Too much drama for me.

Speaking of fooling around, Ty's sitting so close I can smell him. The scent of soap and detergent wafts up to my nose.

Ty leans over and whispers in my ear, "I don't know whether to thank you or hate you for sending me home with Henry yesterday."

"Oh hell," I say. "What did he do?"

He stuffs a few French fries in his mouth, but keeps talking. "First he takes us to this diner. Those friends of his, Kristen and Marie, are all over us. Which isn't necessarily a bad thing, but Kristen doesn't seem to have anything between her ears."

I snort and chocolate milk comes out my nose. Yeah, I know, I'm the sexiest creature on the planet. Ty grins at me.

"Go on," I say, wiping up my chocolate snot.

"So we stay at the diner for a couple hours, talking about absolutely nothing. And I mean *nothing*. Oh yeah—there was no studying going on either. Henry and Marie made out for, like, an hour."

I start cracking my knuckles as Ty goes on. "Then we go out to his truck, and I'm thinking, great—finally, I get to go home. My grandfather's probably worried sick about me. But no, Henry doesn't take me home. He drives us way out into the country into this field. It's basically a giant mud puddle."

I grin. "Henry took you mudding?"

"Yup. So we're in the field, and Henry drives his truck around in circles at about eighty miles an hour. I think I'm gonna die. Everybody's screaming. He rolls down the windows and mud's flying all over the place, all inside the cab of the truck. I'm covered in muck. Finally he stops the truck and we all fall out into the giant mud puddle." He looks down at his cheeseburger, picks it up, and takes a bite. With food in his mouth, he says, "Pretty soon I'm the only person still wearing clothes. And then Kristen—" Ty suddenly grabs some fries and eats them, his face growing pink.

I'm jealous out of my mind, but I'm still laughing hysterically. Only Henry would do this to the new guy on his first day at a new school.

"You think it's funny, do you?" Ty says, grinning. "I didn't get home until after midnight. I showed up covered in mud and now I'm in trouble."

"Hell yeah, it's funny."

"And that Kristen chick has been stalking me all day."

I glance over at the cheerleader table, where Lacey continues to glare at JJ and the redheaded French fry slave. I locate Kristen, who is gazing over at us. She waves at Ty and blows him a kiss. I'm tempted to catch the kiss and pretend to crumple it up with my hand, throw it on the ground, and stomp on it.

Instead, I sip my chocolate milk and say, "Sucks to be you, man."

He elbows me. "I think you planned the whole thing."

"Did not."

"Did too."

"Did not." What is this? Third grade?

"Make it up to me." He stares straight into my eyes.

Breathe, Jordan, breathe. "I didn't do anything wrong, so I'm not making anything up to you."

"What are you doing after school today?"

JJ and I are going out to eat after school. I could invite Ty to get grub with us. I want to, but I just can't—if he comes, I won't be able to relax at all, and I need to freaking relax before tomorrow night's game.

JJ and Carter finally come sit down at our table. The minute JJ's back is turned and he's facing me, I see Lacey stand up and go over to the redheaded freshman. I don't need to read lips to know what Lacey's saying. I'm pretty sure she just called the girl a whore. The redheaded freshman gets up and rushes her tray to the dishwashing window, then bolts out of the cafeteria as tears fill her eyes.

Ty leans over to me. "Did you see that?"

"Yup."

"I take it she's a bitch?"

"Yup. I'll go make sure that freshman's okay once I'm done eating." Gotta keep my energy up for the game tomorrow.

He stuffs more fries in his mouth. "You know, there's no more dangerous creature on Earth than the teenage girl."

"Hey! I'm a girl." I punch him in the arm.

"Ow..." he says, rubbing his bicep, but then he smiles. "So about this afternoon?"

"I'm sorry—I have plans."

"Oh, okay..."

"So who's the redhead?" I ask JJ.

"No idea," he says, shrugging. "Cute though, don't you think?"

I don't know what comes over me when I grab some of Ty's French fries and say, "Hey, Ty, guess who I am?" and lean across the table toward Carter and start trying to feed him.

JJ and Ty laugh.

"Nasty," Carter says, batting my hand away. "You know I hate school food, Woods."

"What are you talking about?" I ask, sitting back down in my chair. "These are the best steak fries in town."

"Agreed," Ty says. Smiling, he opens his mouth, like he wants me to give him a fry. So I pop one in his mouth.

Oh my God.

Did I just feed Ty a fry?

I should probably take my temperature.

stupid fitted tee

"What the hell's wrong with you, Henry?" I say, shoving him up against a locker.

"What?" he says, shoving me back.

"I told you to take Ty home, not let him get molested by Kristen."

"He wasn't complaining last night! I think he had a great time."

I shake my head.

"What do you care what he does, Woods?" Smiling, he raises his eyebrows at me and looks down at my black tee.

"I don't care."

Henry keeps grinning. "Yeah, that's bullshit. Since when do you wear shirts like that? We never get to see your boobs." I shove him again. "Fuck, Woods, do you like this guy or something?" he whispers, shoving me back.

I move to shove him yet again, but he jumps out of the way. Damned ballerina reflexes. "I care about my team. Ty told me you didn't drop him off until late. You shouldn't be out past midnight two days before our first game."

"So he made it home then?"

"What do you mean?"

"He wouldn't let me take him all the way home. He had me let him out on the highway. It was weird, but I could tell he was serious. He didn't want me anywhere near his house."

How bad could his house be? Half the guys on my team live in trailers—it can't be worse than that.

I stare into Henry's eyes and tan face, which has broken out recently. He never used to have acne, but now he's got a smattering of it.

"Sam?" I say, grabbing his hand.

"Yeah?" he says, burying his other hand in his crazy hair.

"Um, I'm wondering if everything's okay with you. Are you stressed out or anything?"

He sighs and leans against the lockers. "Yeah—maybe a little."

"Is it Carrie?"

He shakes his head.

"Then what's up?"

He brushes the curls off his forehead and stares at his flip-flops. "I dunno…a lot's up…Dad's never home and Mom's sadder than ever…I'm worried about college. I want to go so bad and I think a football scholarship is the only way my family will be able to afford it."

Judging by his eyes darting around and that familiar twitch of his mouth, I can tell he's hiding something. But I rub his arm anyway and play along. "I know. But you're great—just keep playing hard and you'll be fine. And I'm sure you can get some money since you have great grades."

He stares at flyers tacked all over the bulletin board on the other side of the hallway. "I hope so. My future's riding on football."

"I get it," I say, and looking away from Henry, I notice Ty coming down the hall. He stops for a sec when he sees me with Henry, but just passes right by us and doesn't say anything as he goes into the art room.

Henry smiles, shaking his head. "Listen, I won't say anything to anyone about your liking Ty. Promise."

I wince.

He bumps his fist into mine, then puts an arm around me and walks me down the hall toward music appreciation class. Now that we're seniors and only concentrate on football, I swear, we are taking some of the stupidest classes ever. Today we're learning how to play the xylophone.

"Just keep wearing those shirts," he says with a wink. "He'll notice those boobs for sure."

• • •

Before music appreciation/xylophone class starts, Henry and I are huddled over a piece of scrap paper, playing Hangman. I jot down _ _ _ / _ _ _ _ _ _ _. "Category is famous football players."

Henry says *E*, and I draw a head hanging from a noose. "*A*," he says, and I fill in the second letter of both words. Then Marie walks up behind us, looks over Henry's shoulder at Hangman, and says, "I know it."

I snort, and Henry elbows my side and gives me a look. He pulls her onto his lap and wraps an arm around her waist. I sit up straight when he gives her a peck on the lips.

"I wish you could've come out with us yesterday, Jordan," Marie says, and I shrug. "Ty was asking about you."

"What? Sizing up his competition?" I ask Henry, who starts staring at the idiots trying to smash each other with cymbals on the other side of the room.

"No," Marie says, smiling. "He wanted to know what you're interested in. He wished you had come out too."

I sit up even straighter. "I had stuff to do."

"How's getting ready for Alabama going?" Marie asks me as she drapes an arm around Henry's shoulders.

"Why do you want to know?" I ask.

"I know it's important to you," she mutters. Then she climbs off Henry's lap and walks back toward her desk. "Dan Marino," she calls out over her shoulder.

How the hell did she know the answer?

I start filling in the other letters, and Henry whispers in my ear, "Not every girl is bad."

"You wouldn't know, 'cause they fawn over you all the time. You don't see how Kristen and Lacey treat other girls, how they treat me in the locker room and bathroom, and back in—"

I shut up, not wanting to talk about what happened in seventh grade, and start drawing Alabama Roll Tide logos.

Henry whispers, "I really doubt Marie's ever said anything bad to you."

I shrug again.

"Give her a chance," Henry says, "I bet you'll like her." He takes the pen from my fingers, pulls the scrap paper closer to him, and writes _ _ _ _ _ _/_ _ _ _ _. "Dan Marino," he says with a smile. "I knew it the second you wrote out the blanks."

"Bullshit," I say, and he punches my thigh and we laugh.

"*A*," I say, and Henry draws a head. He looks over at Marie.

Staring at him, I call, "Yo, Marie. Come help me figure out Henry's puzzle."

• • •

After school, JJ and I jump out of my truck and head into Joe's All-You-Can-Eat Pasta Shack. I don't know why Joe decided to call his place a shack, considering shacks don't make anyone think of Italy, but the food is amazing. Before every game, JJ and I come here and load up on carbs for hours. We've been doing this for just about forever. Not only does this give us the opportunity to de-stress, but we get to eat tons of food while talking strategy.

I grab our usual spot, and JJ squeezes into the other side of the booth. I have to pull the table back toward me so he'll fit comfortably. Joe comes over and we order water and our first plates of spaghetti.

"So," I say to JJ, "ready for tomorrow?"

"Yeah—nothing to worry about. It's just Lynchburg," JJ replies, taking a sip of water. He pulls a pen and a book of crossword puzzles out of his bag. He clicks the pen and shuffles through the book. This is how he de-stresses. "You worried at all?" he asks.

"Hells no, I'm not worried about Lynchburg."

"Worried about anything else?" He glances up from his book and looks at my face, then down at my shirt. Why in the hell did I wear this fitted tee?

I shake my head and drink some water. Then I start playing with the salt and pepper shakers. I do that game where you put one shaker on top of the other, then pull the bottom shaker out quickly so the top one falls straight down onto the table. But you can't let it fall over. Or you lose.

"You sure, Woods? I hope you're not upset about Ty Green. I can't believe Coach let him on the team." JJ clenches his fists and starts clicking the pen repeatedly.

"It's not a big deal. I'm not sure what the story is, but apparently Ty just had to move here with his family and didn't have a choice. I think he just wants to play ball." I cough, then take another sip of water, which I proceed to choke on. I hit myself in the chest with my fist.

JJ focuses on his crossword puzzle. "Let me know if he's a problem."

Hiding behind my glass of water, I smile. How does he keep his "love" life with Lacey separate from ball? Maybe it's different for him since he's a guy.

But I'm practically a guy. I mean, except for these fucking hormones that make me want to jump Ty and Justin Timberlake. I don't obsess over things that other girls care about, like clothes, movie stars, hair, painting nails, knitting, or whatever shit they're into.

I just want to eat a bunch of hot wings, sleep, play ball, and maybe, someday, make out with Ty.

"JJ? Um, how do you feel about Lacey? Like, do you love her… or anything like that?"

JJ drops the pen on the table and looks up at me. He narrows his eyes. "Why? Has she been asking about me or something?"

"Yeah, once…but I don't really care what she feels about you, I'm more wondering what you think of her?"

"She's a good lay," he says, picking his pen back up. He chews on the end of it and focuses on his book. "What's a four-letter word for a past Russian leader?"

"How the hell should I know, man? Anyhow…how do you manage to keep your, uh, thoughts of Lacey separate from football?"

"Look, Woods, I hate talking about this shit, but if you must know, I don't really think about it. I enjoy sleeping with her and that's all. It helps me relax, which helps me play football better."

I chew on my lip. A "stress reliever" is the last thing I want to be. Is Ty the kind of guy who would only care if I'm a good lay?

Are these the kinds of things cheerleaders discuss at slumber parties?

JJ continues, "Now shut up about Lacey and feelings and shit and tell me the capital of Yemen. Five letters."

• • •

Last year, in biology, we dissected frogs, and when I cut the frog's stomach open, it was just full of flies. The teacher said he'd never seen a frog with such a full stomach. If some higher being were to dissect me right now, I can't imagine how grossed out he'd be by the inside of my stomach. I'm stuffed with spaghetti. Now I'm super-glad I didn't invite Ty to Joe's All-You-Can-Eat Pasta Shack, because he'd probably never want to look at me again. I'm a blimp.

Opening the back door, I walk into my kitchen and hear Mike and Dad yelling. The noise is coming from the dining room so I jog in there to find Henry arm-wrestling with Jake Reynolds. Both of their faces are red and Jake is clenching his teeth.

"How long has this been going on?" I whisper to Mike.

"Forty seconds!"

I gasp. It's not every day a high school senior holds his own against a sure-to-be-first-round draft pick. Henry glances up at me, so I yell, "Go, Henry! Kick this pretty boy's ass!" Smiling, Henry bites into his bottom lip and starts to force Jake's arm down. Jake seems to grip Henry's hand harder. With one swift movement, Henry slams Jake's hand down to the table.

"Good God!" Dad says.

"Holy shit!" Mike exclaims, whacking Henry on the back.

Jake's face is all puffy. "Damn it," he mutters.

Dad squeezes Henry's shoulder. "I can tell how hard you've been working out, Sam. Keep it up, and you'll get into a great college program. I'm really proud of you."

Henry's eyes find mine, and he doesn't look away.

My dad is such an asshole. The *great* Donovan Woods would never stoop so low as to compliment his own daughter—a daughter who has just as much of a chance at getting into a great program as Henry.

• • •

A few minutes later, Dad takes Henry, Mike, and Jake out into the backyard to throw a ball around for awhile. When I start to head outside with them, Dad tells me to help Mom with dinner. What a sexist pig. I carry the lasagna to the table, I carry the bread to the table, I carry the water pitcher to the table. I'm tempted to spit on my dad's plate, but decide to act mature, unlike the *great* Donovan Woods. I'm slamming plates and glasses on the table when Henry comes up and shakes my shoulders.

"You'd suck as a waitress, Woods."

"Maybe you should tell Dad that." I drop a fork onto a plate, causing a clanking sound.

"Tell me what?" Dad says as he walks into the dining room. He sees Henry standing there with his hands on my shoulders, and instead of acting all pissy, Dad actually smiles at us.

"Nothing," I say quickly. I wiggle away from Henry, shrugging him off me. I finish setting the table, taking care to put all the forks and knives in the wrong places. And even though I just ate about a hundred pounds of spaghetti, I start shoveling lasagna onto my plate. Henry sits down next to me, and Jake takes a spot across the table. There's a mad scramble for garlic bread, but I manage to come out victorious with five pieces. I'm not hungry; I just don't want my family to think I'm getting soft.

Mike frowns at me because he's only managed to wrangle three pieces. Since I'm still stuffed from Joe's All-You-Can-Eat Pasta Shack, I donate two pieces of garlic bread to Mike's stomach.

"So," Dad says, looking from Henry to me as he pulls a piece of bread apart. "How's school?"

"Good," Henry replies. "Jordan and I are rebuilding a school bus engine in auto mechanics this semester."

Dad smiles at me. "How's that going?"

"Okay so far," I say, sipping lemonade. "Once we've rebuilt it, our class is gonna put it in an old broken-down bus we're refurbishing."

"What are you gonna do with the bus?" Dad asks.

Henry sets his fork down and wipes his mouth. "Jordan suggested we donate it to the Haskell Youth Center. You know, the orphanage? The kids like coming to watch our games, but they don't have an easy way to get to them."

Dad says, "I think it's a great idea. When do you think it'll be ready?"

"Definitely by the end of the semester, so we'll give it to them for next year," Henry replies.

I add, "We're missing a few parts, but we'll take a look through Murphy's Junkyard next week."

"Let me know if I can help," Dad says before drinking more Gatorade. "Some guys on my team might want to donate money for parts. Hell, I bet they'd buy them a bus."

"Thanks, Mr. Woods," Henry says. "If we screw it up, we'll definitely take you up on the offer."

"But we won't screw up," I say. Henry and I grin at one another.

For a few seconds, I only hear forks and knives clinking against plates, but then, as usual, Dad speaks up—silence makes him uncomfortable or something.

"You look nice today, Jordan."

How lame. He wants to fill the lull by discussing my fashion choices? We'd have a lot more to talk about if he'd just discuss ball with me. *Like that'll ever happen.*

So I ignore Dad and crunch on my salad. Sipping my lemonade, I look up and see that Jake's staring at my chest.

"Yeah—you look nice," Jake says. Beneath the table, I kick him in the knee. Hard. His eyes clench shut and he coughs. I grin.

"I think we all agree that you look nice," Dad says, taking another bite of lasagna. "I'm glad you're starting to act like a lady."

I drop my fork onto my plate. "Just out of clean T-shirts, Dad," I say. "Mom? May I be excused? I ate too much at Joe's today."

Mom nods and reaches out for me, so I walk over and bend down so she can kiss my cheek.

After taking my plate to the kitchen sink, I run up to my room. I've gotta get rid of this stress, or I'll be a wreck at tomorrow night's game, so I pull on workout clothes and trainers.

Outside, I run up and down the little country roads near my house. The streets haven't been paved in forever, so it takes a lot of concentration to make sure I don't trip on bumps or fall in holes and hurt myself. As I run, I let daydreams of playing for Alabama totally absorb the part of my brain that isn't focused on running.

I pretend I'm carrying the ball for a touchdown. I dart left, then right, dodging an imaginary cornerback, and run even faster.

Then I hear footsteps behind me, so I peek over my shoulder and see Henry trying to catch up to me. His curls are bouncing all over the place. "Woods," he calls out. "Your dad was all trying to talk about college with me, and I told him to shove it!"

Laughing, I speed up. Soon I'm sprinting as fast as I can go, but Henry catches up anyway. He's so damned fast. He might as well be Forrest Gump. Passing by me, Henry runs to the end of the block, where he turns around and does this stupid victory dance. It looks like he's roping a bull at a rodeo.

I'm still running at full speed, so I crash into him, catapulting him into a ditch. "Show off!"

"Shit!" he shouts, laughing as he picks himself up. He wipes grass and dirt off his shirt and dusts his hands.

"How did Dad react when you told him to shove it?"

"He laughed in my face."

"That sucks."

"I don't care," he says, looking into my eyes.

"Why'd you say that anyway?"

"If he's not going to support you, then there's no way in hell I'd ever let him support me."

I smile at Henry. My best friend believes in me. What else does a girl need?

Still, I should be happy for him, because Dad's comments about football must mean a whole hell of a lot to Henry, whose own dad is never home and never talks to him about his future. Henry's father probably expects him to become some kind of a bum, working in a factory, or hell, driving a truck too.

"I can't believe you destroyed Jake at arm-wrestling," I say.

Henry grins. "Yeah, I'll never forget that."

I take a deep breath. "I was thinking. Maybe you should talk to Dad about Michigan. Maybe you could ask him to come watch you at one of our games. He might be able to help."

Henry's eyes find mine, but he stays quiet.

"Want to race back?" he asks finally.

"Does the winner get the necklace?" I put my hand on the plastic football charm hanging from a cheap silver chain that Henry always wears.

"Hell, no," he says, fingering the Cracker Jack prize we've been fighting over since we were nine. I'll never forget how we were sitting out in Henry's front yard playing rock, paper, scissors while eating a big box of Cracker Jacks. I pulled the prize out, and we both desperately wanted it. Since we were at Henry's house and they were his Cracker Jacks, he thought he deserved the plastic football. But since I'm the one who pulled the football out of the box, I thought it should be mine.

So we rock, paper, scissors-ed for it. I made scissors with my hand. He made rock.

He's worn the charm around his neck ever since.

"How about we race for an ice cream?" Henry says. "First person back has to make the other a hot fudge sundae."

I sprint off, passing a tractor chugging down the road. I yell, "You're on!"

The sun starts to set, and we race into the pink-lemonade sky.

pep

I understand the importance of pep rallies.
The cheerleaders can show off, doing tricks
  and the guys can strut around acting all big and badass.
For me, the important thing is that I get out of class for an hour this afternoon.
Coach introduces all the players, starting with me.
The school goes wild when I wave.
But the applause I get
  is totally lame compared to what Henry gets.
He does some of his stupid dances
  and all the girls swoon and say, "Aww" and "He's so cute."
But the applause Henry gets
  is totally lame compared to what Ty gets.
He does his signature smirk
  and all the girls swoon and say, "He's so hot."
So I'm even happier when Ty jogs over to me
  knocks his fist into mine and pats my shoulder.
I'm never washing my jersey again.

game #1

the count? 18 days until alabama

Five minutes before the game is to start, the sky has opened up and rain is drenching me. But I barely feel it—I can only concentrate on the game and the Alabama recruiter. I ignore the dozens of reporters taking pictures of me from behind the fence.

I'm desperate for air. I try to suck in as much oxygen as possible through my face mask, but it's not working. I pick up a football and twirl and flip it over and over again.

A hand comes down on my shoulder, and I turn and find Mike. His blond hair is plastered to his face, and his polo shirt and jeans are soaked. My bro is about the only person Coach allows on the sidelines during a game.

"Hey, sis." He leans in close and whispers, "So where's Ty?"

"Shut up," I say. "I'm trying to concentrate. And you need an umbrella—you'll get sick before your game tomorrow."

He shrugs, then rubs my arm. "You need to loosen up, or you're gonna be stiff as Grandpa Woods."

I flash him a withering look. Doesn't he know how important this game is?

"Yes, I know how important this game is," Mike says.

"Yo, Woods."

I see JJ walking up. "Yeah?" I say.

"I wasn't talking to you, I was talking to your bro," JJ replies, shaking Mike's hand. "Nice to see you, man."

"You too, JJ. So where's this hot new quarterback, Ty?" Mike asks. JJ glances at me. I'm glad I'm wearing my helmet, 'cause I can feel my face heating up again.

"Number fifteen," JJ mutters.

"Thanks," Mike says, slapping JJ on the back and wandering away.

"What was that all about?" JJ asks.

"I dunno. I told him how good Ty is. He's interested."

"Well, Ty better not try to take the spotlight away from you, or I'll kick his ass. I can't believe he fucking tried to come in here and take your position," JJ growls.

"Take it out on Lynchburg, okay?" I say, laughing.

I watch as Mike goes up to Ty, shakes his hand, and claps him on the back. Ty yanks off his helmet and smiles at Mike, and they begin to talk animatedly. Mike points at the field, probably describing how crappy Lynchburg's field is, pointing out all the divots in the ground.

I feel fingers poke me in my sides, and I whirl around to find Henry carrying an umbrella under his arm. He whips it out and opens it up, holding it above me.

"Stop it," I hiss. "You're making me look like a pansy."

"Fine," Henry replies. I can see him smiling behind his face mask. He takes two giant steps away from me, but keeps the umbrella out and stands under it alone. Henry jerks his head toward Mike and Ty. "So what's going on down there?"

I sigh. All my guy friends are way too protective and nosy. "He wanted to meet Ty. I told him how good he is."

"How good he is, eh?"

"Shut up, Henry. I'm trying to get in the zone."

"Dude, we're playing Lynchburg! We might as well be playing a Pop Warner team." Henry moves closer to me again and hands the umbrella to a freshman. Squeezing my hand, he says, "You're gonna rock tonight."

"You too," I reply as Mike and Ty walk up.

Henry sees Mike leaning in close to me and quickly moves over to listen. Mike whispers, "The Alabama coach is here."

Henry and I twirl around to face the fence where boosters and alumni usually stand and take notes. Sure enough, a man wearing a red Alabama Roll Tide windbreaker is there.

Mike continues, "Recruiters from Ohio State are here too."

"They must be here for Carter." I feel awful that recruiters from Michigan aren't here. Henry's wanted to go to school there for as long as I can remember.

"Knock 'em dead, Woods," Henry says. He slaps my back as the referee motions for captains to take the field for the coin toss. I jog toward the fifty-yard line with JJ and Carter and soon I'm standing in the center of the field with Carter on my right and JJ on my left. The ref tells me to call it.

"Heads," I say. The ref flips the quarter up into the air, and it hits the ground and lands on tails. The Lynchburg captain says they'll kick off. Looking at the field, I say we want to defend the less muddy side. I don't want our defense slipping and falling all over the place. I'd rather run through the mud on the other side. JJ, Carter, and I jog back over to the sidelines, where I knock fists with Henry before he heads out to return the punt.

"That's cool that Ohio State's here," I say to Carter. He shrugs, which surprises me. I figured he'd be ecstatic. Joe Carter Sr. was a starting linebacker for Ohio State, not to mention the Miami Dolphins and the Titans!

As the other team kicks off, Ty joins me. Together, we watch as Henry catches the ball and takes off down the field. He's at our twenty, then our thirty...he zigs and zags past a couple cornerbacks, who trip and fall into the mud. Then Henry drives straight down, and he's past the other team's twenty, then the ten. And touchdown!

Our cheerleaders cheer like crazy; our marching band plays a fight song. We are awesome.

"Damn," Ty says. "He made that look easy."

Screaming, I jump up and down. I shove a freshman, who stumbles and falls onto the bench. I shove JJ, who doesn't budge of course, but it's the principle of the shove that matters. I knock fists and give high-fives to other guys on the sidelines, including Ty. When our hands high-five each other, I feel this, like, bolt of electricity between us.

Henry spikes the ball and starts to do a dance, but then stops. I guess he realizes a dance isn't worth a penalty in this weather. After our kicker makes the extra point, our defense hustles out and doesn't allow Lynchburg even one first down.

Showtime.

Jogging out onto the field, I take my position behind JJ.

Lynchburg's nose tackle says, "Hey, dyke. Your ass looks better than it did last year."

"Shut your mouth, asshole," JJ says, slapping the tackle's face mask.

"It's okay," I say to JJ, loud enough for the tackle to hear me, "The only girlfriend he'll ever have is his right hand."

Coach talks to me through the speaker in my helmet. "Only carries tonight, Woods. No flashy passes."

"Red fifty!" I yell. "Red fifty! Blue twenty-five!" The cue is blue twenty-five, meaning JJ hikes the ball to me, I hand it off to our starting running back, Drew Bates, and he drives it up the middle. We get the first down easily.

JJ slammed the hell out of the nose tackle, who's now lying on the ground, clutching his stomach. "Nice," I say with a laugh.

The weather is causing Lynchburg to play even worse than usual, which is pretty damned bad, so we keep driving down the field.

After I hand the ball off for the second touchdown, I hear Mom screaming for me from the bleachers. She's sitting with Carter's mom, Henry's mom, and JJ's parents.

I didn't figure Dad would come, but my head droops when I see he's not here.

Sopping wet with rain, Mom grins as she screams my name. I can't wait to tell her how much I love her.

By halftime, the score is 28–0. I'm embarrassed for Lynchburg, but I'm playing an amazing game even if I'm only handing the ball off and not throwing any long passes. I did run for a touchdown, though, just because I need to show off for the Alabama guy. Normally I don't do things like that, but if I can't throw any long bombs in this weather, I've gotta do something to make myself stand out.

Now we're in the guys' locker room, and since we're winning, Coach doesn't have to yell at us about what we're doing wrong, so I drink some Gatorade and dry off. My hands are so soaked they look like raisins. Henry squeezes in on one side of me on the bench, and Ty squeezes in on the other. Because we're slaughtering Lynchburg, I feel like I can relax a bit, so I leave the football zone and start thinking of Ty again. His elbow is touching mine. Breathe, Jordan, breathe. Don't think about his bicep. Don't think about that swatch of tan skin, peeking out from under his uniform, right above his hip. Wouldn't it be great if we were the only two people in here right now? We could rip our uniforms off and—

"Woods!" Coach says.

"What's up?"

"I'm taking you out of the game for the second half."

JJ, Carter, and Henry jump up. They all start yelling, "Are you serious, Coach?" and "She's rocking this game!" and "An Alabama coach is out there!"

Coach holds up a hand. "Woods has shown she's perfectly capable of running a football field. But the weather is getting worse out there, and I don't want her to get hurt."

"You sound like my dad."

Coach yanks off his hat and rubs his head, frowning at me. "I bet your dad would agree with me. I'm putting Ty in for the second half."

"Damn it!" I say, standing and marching out of the locker room. When I'm out in the hallway, I take a long, deep breath and run my hands through my wet hair.

How could Coach do this to me? Alabama's here to see me. Me. Jordan Woods.

Not Ty.

It's like everyone on the freaking planet is out to stop me from playing ball and achieving my dreams. Everyone except the guys on my team.

My team…

No one respects a captain who acts like that, no matter if Coach is just plain idiotic tonight, so I go back into the locker room. "Sorry, Coach," I say. "Won't happen again."

Coach smiles, tossing a ball to me. "Great. Help Ty warm up."

• • •

Thank the Lord that Coach isn't a meteorologist, 'cause his predictions suck.

The weather's getting worse, my ass. By the time Ty is warmed up, bright stars fill the clear sky.

I'm yelling instructions at the defensive players on the field when Mike comes and stands next to me. "You played a hell of a game, sis."

"Thanks," I mutter. "Can't believe Coach pulled me out."

"Doesn't matter. You showed everyone your stuff."

"Did you talk to the Alabama recruiter?"

He grins. "Yup."

"What did he say?"

"Now's not a good time. Focus on the game. Talk to you at home." Mike wanders back over to the fence where the Alabama and Ohio State guys are still standing with Carter's dad. I wish I had my bro's schmoozing skills.

We don't let Lynchburg get a first down, so it's already our ball. Ty runs out onto the field, making even jogging look effortless.

The Lynchburg defense seems to relax when they see I haven't rejoined the game. Big mistake. Big. Even though Ty's only had one practice with our team, a practice that lasted about twenty minutes, he will destroy Lynchburg.

JJ hikes the ball to Ty. He takes a five-step drop and scans the field. JJ lets a defenseman get past him. On purpose, obviously. JJ would never let a Lynchburg linebacker get anywhere near me. It doesn't matter, though, because Ty sidesteps the linebacker and launches a deep pass to Henry, who's vying with a cornerback in the end zone. The ball sails right into Henry's open arms.

Shit.

Ty just threw a forty-yard pass! God, I don't think I could've done that.

I turn to find Mike and the college recruiters. The coaches are speaking quickly to a gaping Mike, who says something to them. The recruiters scribble something in their notebooks.

Ty's name.

Will the Alabama guy even remember me after seeing Ty's pass?

After yanking his helmet off, Ty comes jogging over. He drops a hand onto my shoulder and pulls me close. I quickly shake his hand off.

"I'm sorry, Woods," Ty says in his thick Texas drawl.

"It's okay," I mutter. "Nice pass." After JJ hikes the ball so our kicker can take the extra point, I pull him aside. "JJ, don't ever do that again."

"Do what?"

"Let a linebacker go after a player like that. Ty could've gotten clobbered. Thank God it's only Lynchburg."

"What the hell do you care? The dude stole your position."

"JJ, I don't care if he threatens to kill my unborn children. Ty is still part of the team. We take care of each other. Understand?" I smack JJ's helmet hard enough to make his head hurt, to make a point.

"Yes, ma'am."

Then I see Ty talking to Duckett, who's wearing his "I'm freaked out of my mind" face, so I go see what's happening there. I hear Ty say, "You can't interfere with a receiver like that—you just cost us fifteen yards!"

Ty's advice is right on, but he's not the coach, and he's certainly not captain. "Duckett," I say, "You're playing a fantastic game, but Ty's right. Don't let it happen again."

"Got it, Woods." Duckett glares at Ty and walks away.

"You were too nice to him," Ty tells me.

"I'm the captain here. There's a big difference between being brutally honest and telling people what they need to hear. Understand?"

Ty stares at me like he's never taken directions from anyone before.

I grab him by the jersey and pull him closer. "You got a problem with one of the players, you bring it to me. Understand?"

"Sorry," he mutters. He rubs the back of his neck, furrowing his eyebrows at me.

"I run the field for Hundred Oaks. Not you."

"Understood." Ty shoves his helmet back onto his head and runs out for our next play. Henry and JJ follow Ty, but once they're gone, Carter comes over to me.

"I don't like this one bit, Woods," Carter says. "Something's off about that guy—he assumes way too much."

"It's under control," I reply in a tone that tells Carter to go away, which he does. But I can't help but wonder if Carter's right. This is my team. It's only our first game, and Coach has already taken me out and put in our far-better quarterback, a quarterback who's used to calling the shots and getting his way.

But I won't be controlled by anyone. No matter how cute he is.

• • •

As usual, I'm the first one out of the locker room and seated on the bus. I pull out my iPod and stretch across the last row. JJ and I always sit in the last two bus benches—it's one of those senior perks. Closing my eyes, I listen to some rap music and hope the beats will relax me. I can't wait to get home and hear what the recruiter said to Mike about me. Of course, he might have already forgotten about me—considering I'm only the second-best high school QB in Tennessee now.

We won 42–0. Ty was nice enough to take it easy on Lynchburg, only throwing two long passes, both to Henry. Three touchdowns for Henry in one game is awesome—the college coaches definitely must've noticed that. I find myself smiling at the memory of Henry's dance at the end of the game. In the end zone, after his third touchdown, he did this one move called "The Lawn Mower," where he pretends to start a lawn mower. Then he did "The Sprinkler."

That one got us an unsportsmanlike conduct penalty and then we had to kick off from fifteen yards back. Coach got angry about Henry's showboating, but I didn't care.

Suddenly, the rest of the team gets on the bus, and the bus starts bouncing and shaking, and the other players' yelling distracts me from the music and my thoughts. I close my eyes again. I feel a tap on my foot, and expecting to see JJ, I look up and find Ty standing in front of me. He pushes my legs, causing me to sit up and my feet to fall to the floor, and starts to squeeze in next to me on the bench.

"Woods likes to sit alone," Carter calls out. "Get your ass to your own seat."

Ty turns and glares. "Mind your business, Carter. I need to talk to Woods about the game." He slides in, hip-checking me up against the window.

Crap. I must smell awful, like a mixture of sweat, wet dog, and the odor of diesel gas that has seeped into the vinyl bus seats. But it doesn't matter what I smell like. I can't let my guard down with this guy, or he won't just take over my position. He'll take over the entire team.

"Hey," he says, patting my knee. "Great game tonight. You're really good."

I fold my arms across my stomach. "You're good too."

"I'm just glad I got to play—I love football so much."

"Me too..." I pause for a beat before adding, "I've loved it ever since I was five, when Dad took me to my first pro game—Super Bowl XXXII."

Ty smiles. "Broncos-Packers?"

"Yup."

"Awesome game—my man John Elway destroyed Brett Favre."

I say, "Favre sucks," and Ty says, "I can't stand Brett Favre," at the same time, and then we both say, "Jinx." I pinch his forearm as he pinches my thigh.

We laugh, and he leans into my shoulder, and then we smile at each other. His eyes are so blue...

"So what did you want to talk about?" I ask.

Ty grins that wicked smile of his again. He whispers, "I lied. I just wanted an excuse to sit with you."

Right then, Henry grabs the seat directly in front of us, quickly glances into my eyes, and then sits down and faces forward. Normally, he hangs over the back of his seat and chats with me, but he slouches so far down in his seat that I can't even see him.

I put my headphones back on and recline against the vinyl seat, and Ty nestles his arm up against mine—it feels warm.

When we get back to the school parking lot, I say goodbye to the team, knock fists with everybody, then head to my truck.

"Yo, Woods," Henry says as he jogs up. "Want to come to Higgins's party with me?" He rubs his palms together, then drops his thumbs into the pockets of his jeans.

I hurl my bag into the bed of my truck. "Thanks, but I'm gonna head home."

"You gonna let Ty go home with you too?" he snaps.

"He was just sitting with me," I mumble. What the hell is Henry's problem?

Henry heads toward his rusty maroon truck and turns around to face me as he walks backward. After glancing over at Ty, he locks eyes with me and says, "Well, you know where the real party is if you decide you don't want to be alone." Then he shouts to the masses, "Party at Higgins's! Who's with me?"

The team erupts, and five members of Henry's harem miraculously appear and drape themselves all over him.

Ty comes over to me, shaking his head at Henry. "You going to the party?"

"Nah," I respond. "I've got to hit the sack. I'm going to my brother's game tomorrow in Knoxville."

"That sounds cool. I'd love to see him play sometime. I enjoyed meeting him tonight—he's nice people."

"Yeah—I love my bro."

Ty brushes his hair off his forehead. "So, um, want some company tomorrow at Mike's game?"

Holy shit. What an offer. But Knoxville is an hour and a half away. That's way too long to be alone with Ty and my parents.

"I'm riding to the game with my parents, Ty. Trust me, you'd rather go clothes shopping for all eternity than spend three hours in a car with them. Maybe some other time."

"I don't mind riding with them."

"I don't think that's a very good idea."

Ty frowns and stuffs his hands in his pockets. "Did I do something to make you mad? I'm sorry Coach put me in tonight, but I don't think that's any reason for you to be pissed at me. You were slaughtering that team."

I shake my head. "It's nothing like that."

"What is it then?" he blurts. He throws his head back and closes his eyes.

Shit. So maybe I haven't been the nicest person. But I can't tell him why he's distracting the hell out of me.

Ty turns, starts to walk away, and waves over his shoulder. "I guess I'll see you around then."

"Wait, Ty—how are you getting home?"

"I can take care of myself. I don't need you to arrange rides for me."

Tears rush to my eyes. "Um, I was going to offer to take you home. And, to ask if maybe you, I mean, if you aren't doing anything on Sunday…"

He stops, turns, and raises his eyebrows. "Yeah?"

"Um, would you want to go to my dad's preseason game with me? In Nashville? He's playing the Patriots. I always go when he plays New England because Tom Brady's awesome, but don't tell my dad I said that."

Ty smiles. "A Titans game? An actual NFL game? I've never been to one before."

That surprises me. It's strange that someone as good as Ty has never been to a pro game. "Yeah," I say, "JJ, Carter, and I are going together. And maybe Henry, if he can drag himself out of bed in time. That's doubtful, though."

"Do I need to get a ticket?"

"Of course not—we'll sit in the owner's box."

"Damn. Yeah, I definitely want to come."

"Cool. I'll call you about details. Oh—and wear a suit or something nice."

"I can do that. Thanks for the invite."

I smile. This is great. I get to hang out with Ty under the supervision of JJ and Carter. They'll keep me sane. "Did you want a ride home tonight?"

"Thanks for the offer, but I think I'll check out this party."

"Gonna hang with Kristen again?"

"Hell no," he says, laughing. "I like being with girls who have actual brain activity. Girls like you."

Oh. My. God. I quickly say, "Have fun. I'll call you tomorrow. Bye!" I jump into my truck and drive away. I don't bother looking in the rearview mirror this time. I know he's watching me.

• • •

At home, I run upstairs to Mike's room and pound on the door.

"Come in." I open the door to find Mike lounging on the floor playing a football video game. I sit down next to him, and he passes me the second controller. "What are you doing home so early?" he asks. "No parties or anything? No hot date with Ty?"

"If you want to play ball tomorrow, you'd better shut your mouth, because I'll kick your ass, bro."

"Yeah, right." Mike laughs as he immediately scores a touchdown. Man, do I suck at video games.

"So tell me what the Alabama coach said about me already!"

"We're going to talk about Ty first. He's really cool, Jordan. And even though he's not starting this year, he'll have his pick of colleges."

"Great," I say, throwing the controller down. I stand and shuffle across the room and fall onto Mike's bed. "Tell me what the Alabama guy said."

"Well, on the down low, since I stretched the rules a bit by talking to him about you, if you keep playing like you did tonight, they'll offer you a full ride."

"You're kidding me!"

"Nope," Mike says. "Keep up the good work and you're a shoo-in for Alabama. Just don't get distracted, don't get hurt, and don't do anything stupid."

"But isn't it kinda weird that they're willing to give me the full ride even though I didn't make any big passes tonight?"

"Hell, don't question it," Mike says, laughing. "Just roll with it. I would."

"It would be awesome if I went to Alabama—we'd be rivals!"

"Tennessee would totally kick your ass."

"Sure, keep telling yourself that."

Mike rubs his jaw. "But there's one thing I don't think either of us has considered. The coaches of any school you go to are going to use you as a recruitment tool. Alabama will be showcasing you all the time, and they'll want you to help with advertising."

"Ugh," I say. "Like that time *Sports Illustrated* wanted to do an article on me? Thank God Dad stepped in and said no."

"Yup," Mike says. "I don't think your life will be so private anymore. Everyone's going to know everything about you."

"As long as I can play college ball, I don't care."

"Cool. Now, on to more important issues—tell me what's up with Ty. I like him."

"Me too. I invited him to Dad's game on Sunday. Are you going?"

"I can if you want me to. Don't you want some alone time with Ty?" Mike asks, grinning.

"Please come. Please help me act normal. I really like Ty and want to be his friend, but I keep pushing him away. He sat next to me on the bus tonight and I ignored him most of the time."

Mike suddenly drops the controller. "He sat next to you on the bus? In the back row? In front of all those guys? Oh sis, he totally wants you bad."

"What are you talking about?" I say with a sigh.

"I can't even imagine having the guts to sit with a girl in front of all those guys. Henry and JJ will kick Ty's ass if he hurts you. And even if they don't kick his ass, they'll make fun of him for it in the locker room. Hell, I'd never stop mentioning it," Mike laughs.

Enough about Ty. "I'm going to bed. Thanks for the help with the coach."

"No prob. Wait—Jordan," Mike says, standing and putting a hand on my shoulder. "Give Ty a shot. I don't want you to go through life never taking a chance on a guy."

"I don't know if I can," I whisper.

"Why not?"

"I don't know how to kiss or anything like that."

Mike chuckles. "Sis, if he kisses you, you'll figure out how to kiss back pretty quickly."

"What if we get together, and then he breaks up with me? That would suck. And then we'd be stuck on a team together."

"He wouldn't risk anything if he wasn't serious. Trust me. I can tell he's a good guy."

I nod. "Yeah, I know."

But is a good guy worth the risk of losing sight of my goals? My dreams?

only father

Watching my favorite sport
Watching my favorite brother
    (okay, my only brother)
Watching my only father cheer for Mike
    Smiling
    Laughing
    Shouting
    Telling Mom how proud he is
    Saying no father could have a better son
And I'm sitting right there
Ready to drown myself in nacho cheese
'Cause all I have is football
And the person I want to share it with,
    more than anything
Hasn't even asked if I won last night…

henry

the count? 17 days until alabama

In his game, Mike totally kicked the Florida Gators' asses, 21–10. I screamed so much for my brother that I got hoarse.

Now I'm back at home, sitting in the kitchen, texting with Henry.

I text: How did party go?

Henry texts back: Carter got trashed & made out with freshman from lunch.

WTF! Carter really got drunk? He never drinks. I hope nothing's wrong.

Yeah, it was crazy. I was counting on him to give me a ride & I ended up lugging him home. He's a heavy SOB. LOL.

I know. He killed me with that sack on Wed. JJ?

After crazy fight, JJ & Lacey went upstairs to bedroom.

Shocker. Was Carrie there?

Yup.

And?

I hung with Marie again.

Was Ty there?

Kristen spent entire time throwing herself @ Ty

When I read that text, I throw up in my mouth. I text Henry back: Does Ty like Kristen?

Don't think so. Carter, JJ & I will be at su casa in hour 4 fantasy draft

K

Mom comes into the kitchen, carrying a bundle of sunflowers, and arranges them in a vase. "What are you doing tonight, Jordan?"

"The guys are coming over. Is that okay?"

Mom nods, pulling a bottled water from the fridge, and takes a seat.

"Thanks for coming to my game last night, Mom."

She smiles. "Wouldn't have missed it. So…tell me about Ty Green. I haven't seen a high school quarterback like him in years. Maybe ever."

"I know."

"He's better than your brother was at seventeen."

"Yeah, but we can't tell Mike that!"

Mom laughs lightly. "Were you upset with Coach Miller for taking you out?"

"Oh, hell yeah."

"Is Ty coming over tonight?" Mom asks. Glancing up at me, she starts peeling the label off her bottled water.

"Nah. But I invited him to Dad's game tomorrow."

"Ah, well I can't wait to meet him. He looks like a cute young man."

"Yup," I say before thinking.

"Oh?" Mom's grinning now. "Do you like him as more than a teammate?"

I shrug.

Mom folds her hands together and lifts them to her chin, and her smile brightens even brighter, like how the sky gets when the sun starts dribbling over the horizon during early morning runs.

Before I embarrass myself even more, and before Mom can start talking about feelings and shit, I dart out of the kitchen and run downstairs.

• • •

Later that evening, the guys and I are finishing up our fantasy draft while eating enough Chinese food to feed all of China itself.

Henry lies down on the rug and clutches his stomach. "Remind me not to eat two orders of General Tso's chicken ever again."

"Hey, Henry," I say.

"Yeah?" he replies with a grin.

"Don't eat two orders of General Tso's chicken ever again."

"This egg drop soup is complete crap," Carter says, kicking the egg snot stuff around with a spoon. "Not enough salt. And the eggs are rancid."

"When I turn eighteen, I'm getting a tattoo," JJ announces.

"Of what?" Henry asks.

"I'm thinking of getting a Chinese character, like right above my butt," he says, pointing at his lower back.

"You *would* get a tramp stamp," I say, biting into a fortune cookie as Henry and Carter start laughing. "What would it say?"

"I was thinking *thunder*, or *ripple*, you know, something deep like that."

Henry hoists himself up onto an elbow and leans over to whisper in my ear. "Maybe we could pay the tattoo artist off, and get him to write the Chinese word for *exit*."

I crack up. "Totally."

"What are you talking about?" JJ demands.

"We think you should go with *thunder*," Henry says, biting his lips together.

JJ thinks for a moment. "Yeah, you're right. *Thunder*, it is."

"I'll get a tattoo too," Henry says, flexing his left arm. "Of a hula girl, on my bicep."

I grin before asking, "What are you gonna get, Carter?"

"Um, maybe, like, flames? What about you, Woods?"

"Maybe the Alabama logo?" I point at my hip bone and say, "Right here?"

Henry coughs into a fist as JJ's cell rings.

"Yo, how's my favorite girl?" JJ says, grinning lazily and reclining against the couch as if he's the Greek god in charge of pleasuring the women of Hundred Oaks High School. Hell, he's probably waiting on some girls to jump out of the closet and start fanning him with palm leaves while feeding him potato chips. "I'll be there in ten minutes," JJ continues, standing up.

"Who was that?" Henry asks. "The redheaded chick from the cafeteria?"

"Nah. Lacey wants me to come over." JJ winks. "She *needs* me."

Henry laughs. "Have fun, man."

"Gag me," I mutter as I start cleaning up trash, picking up used chopsticks and fortune cookie wrappers.

JJ says, "Later," and runs up the stairs and out the basement door.

Carter stands up and throws a few take-out cartons away. "I'm gonna jet too, Woods. I need to get home before my dad freaks out."

"Why would he?" I ask, throwing Diet Coke cans into the recycling bin.

Carter shrugs, but he looks sad. "He thinks I'm not getting enough sleep."

I nod, understanding completely. I can't imagine what it's like to live in casa de Carter, where protein shakes and stomach crunches start the day, and pushups and being in bed by 10:00 p.m. end it.

Is that why Carter got drunk last night? Did he need a release or something?

"That's cool," I say, not wanting to push Carter into talking if he doesn't want to.

"Are you sure you're not secretly meeting up with that hot freshman from last night?" Henry says, a smile stretching across his face.

"No," Carter blurts out. "Shouldn't have done that…I mean, I'm not even into Stacey." He seems seriously torn up. "She's a nice girl."

"I get it," Henry says, slapping a hand on Carter's back. "After practice on Monday, let's go to the batting cages, okay?"

"Cool," Carter says, knocking fists with Henry and me before heading upstairs.

So now it's just me and Henry. I flop down on the couch and grab the remote, fully expecting him to leave in a few seconds. I'm sure he's got gobs of nameless chicks waiting for him.

Flipping through the channels, I stop on ESPN as Henry sits down on the sofa cushion next to me. He slumps down and closes his eyes, and even though he was acting normal a couple of minutes ago, I can feel sadness radiating off him like steam rising from hot asphalt in summertime.

"Can I stay over?" Henry asks finally.

"Sure. You're not going out?" I'm surprised, and glad, when he says he'd rather stay in than go out with the cheerleader du jour. I feel better when I know he's safe and not out doing anything crazy or reckless, like driving his truck at eighty miles an hour through a mud pit.

"Not tonight." He looks over at me and runs a hand through his hair. "You're not going out either?" he asks.

"What could I possibly have to do? JJ and Carter just ditched us. You're all I have left," I say, laughing.

"What about Ty?"

I feel myself blushing, my face ripening up like a strawberry. "Eh…I dunno. He's coming to the game with us tomorrow."

"Oh really?" He sighs, picks up the remote, and starts flipping through the channels.

"Henry—what's up? Please talk to me."

"Nothing's up."

"I'm worried about you."

"Can we go to sleep now? I'm tired."

I have nothing better to do, so I might as well get a good night's sleep. I've gotta try to make myself pretty for Ty tomorrow, and if I only get a couple hours of sleep, I'm sure I'll look like a gremlin. So I stand, put out both hands, and pull Henry up from the couch, and we go upstairs to my room. He takes off his shirt and jeans and puts on a pair of my mesh shorts as I change into sweatpants and a T-shirt. In my bathroom, we brush our teeth together, then drop our toothbrushes into the holder.

Just as I head to bed, he picks up the tiny canister of shea butter from the counter and flips the lid off. Takes a whiff of it. "Yum. So that's why you've been smelling better lately," he says, his chest filling with laughter.

Ripping it out of his hand, I say, "Give me that," but he snatches it away again. He takes some of the shea butter and slathers it on his hands and arms, smiling and smelling himself. I roll my eyes and head to bed.

I yank the covers back and crawl in, and Henry lies down next to me, reeking of shea butter. "Ugh. You smell," I say. "Turn around. We have to sleep head-to-toe. Mom's orders."

"We can't tonight. I heard a rumor that you have athlete's foot, and I can't risk getting it in my nose."

Laughing, I hit him with a pillow. "If you don't behave, you'll have to go sleep in Mike's room."

"No!" Henry blurts. He quickly scoots around and moves to the other end of the bed.

"Are you still scared of Mike's room?" I say, giggling.

He falls face first onto the pillow I just threw at him. In a muffled voice he replies, "No, I'd rather just stay with you."

"I bet you're still scared of his room because of your whale dream."

"We're not talking about that spooky whale. That haunted house thing was so fucked up."

"Dude—it wasn't a haunted house. It was a church Halloween bazaar."

Henry laughs. "Whatever it was, it was fucked up."

It's been nine years since Carter invited us to that Halloween bazaar at his church. Instead of creepy people in Freddy Krueger masks chasing us with chain saws, or people reenacting Blair Witch shit, all the booths were Bible-themed. The church had converted this long dark hallway into a replica of the inside of a whale's stomach, so people could experience what it was like for Jonah after he was swallowed.

Walking down that almost pitch-black hallway, I felt the walls and found they had hung plastic bags covered in Jell-O and Spam to simulate whale innards. A soundtrack of whale songs and crashing waves played over a cheap stereo, and pudding-filled water balloons littered the floor. Miniature internal organs?

I thought it was the lamest thing ever.

Henry? Well, Henry freaked out. He must have some deep fear of whales or something because he clutched my elbow and whimpered. Whimpered. I didn't make fun of him—I just covered his hand with mine and pulled him through the whale's stomach. Instead of three days, we were in there for about thirty seconds.

Later that night, Henry slept over at our house. He had always stayed in Mike's room, but in the middle of the night, Henry sneaked into my bed because he'd had a horrible dream he'd been eaten by a whale.

He's stayed in my room ever since. "You're definitely still scared of Mike's room."

He looks up from the pillow and grins. "Please let me stay. I promise I'll behave."

"Fine," I say, but as soon as we're lying down head-to-toe, he shoves his socked feet right in my face.

• • •

My alarm clock wakes me up at 9:00 a.m. I move to turn it off and realize that Henry's arm is draped across my stomach. How did he get turned around in my bed?

"Henry, getoffame," I mutter, pushing him away so I can hit the snooze button. Then I roll back over onto my pillow, and he moves back in closer and drapes an arm across me again. He nuzzles up against my neck. I'm starting to get more and more worried about him.

I run my hand through his curls for a few minutes until I absolutely have to get up. Climbing out of bed, I pull the covers up over him. It's obvious he's too down and out to go to the game today, so I don't even bother trying to rouse him.

After a quick shower, I pull on some black underwear I found in my dresser, courtesy of Mom. Walking out of the bathroom, I spend about thirty seconds in my closet. Though I hate wearing anything involving a skirt, I have to dress up if I want to sit in the owner's box, so I put on a simple black dress and slip on some silver flats.

Before I leave, I sit down on my bed and pat Henry's head. He barely opens his eyes, gives me a slight smile and buries his face in the pillow again.

"I'll call you after the game," I say. "Stay as long as you want."

"Thanks, Woods. Have fun with Ty," he says into the pillow. "Show him that underwear you're wearing—it'll make him wild."

I smack Henry on the shoulder. Considering we've been hanging out since we were seven, I'm sure he's seen me in my underwear a bunch of times, but he's never mentioned them before. "Why were you watching me change?" I exclaim.

"Uh, 'cause I'm a guy?" He flips the pillow and slaps it, fluffing it. Then he rolls over and closes his eyes again.

nachos grande

the count? 16 days until alabama

When I get to JJ's trailer, I honk my horn about ten times. I told Ty to meet me at JJ's because I don't want him to see where I live yet. Judging by the fact that Ty doesn't have a car and doesn't want Henry to see where he lives, I don't want him to see my house and think I'm some stuck-up snob.

JJ comes running down the rotting wooden steps, his extra weight flopping all over the place underneath a white, button-down shirt and tie. "We're coming. Stop your honking."

Walking behind JJ, Ty looks cute in his own button-down shirt, tie, and khaki pants. He cleans up well. He hops into the backseat and JJ sits up front next to me.

"You know, some people have manners and ring the doorbell," JJ says.

Ignoring JJ, I say, "Hey, Ty."

"Hey," he replies. Through the rearview mirror, I watch as he looks at me and takes a deep breath. He pushes his sandy hair off his forehead.

"Carter?" JJ asks.

"It's his grandmother's 70th birthday," I reply.

"Henry?" JJ asks.

"Asleep in my bed."

"What?" Ty exclaims.

"It's no big deal, dude," JJ says. "He sleeps there more than he does at his own place."

"Oh," Ty says as he fiddles with the buttons that open my truck's sunroof, opening it up and closing it a few times.

Somehow I'm able to drive my truck to Nashville without crashing it. Every time I glance at Ty in the mirror, I get distracted and start thinking about how great he looks in a tie.

An hour later, we walk into the owner's box. Mom's already here, boozing and schmoozing with the Titans' owner, but when she sees me come in with Ty and JJ, she comes over.

"Hello, sweetie," she says, giving me a kiss on the cheek. Then she turns to JJ and kisses him too.

Grinning broadly, JJ says, "Hey, Mrs. Woods. You're looking beautiful, as usual." I roll my eyes. JJ's such a flirt. No wonder all those silly cheerleaders swoon over him regardless of the fact that he's as big as a sumo wrestler.

"Thank you, JJ," Mom replies. "And who's this?" she asks, gesturing at Ty.

Ty stretches out a hand. "I'm Ty Green. Nice to meet you, ma'am."

"It's a pleasure to meet you, Ty," Mom says, smiling at me and Ty. My face must be as red as a stop sign. "Great job in the game on Friday night. It was like Jordan was the opening act and you were the headliner."

"Gee, thanks Mom," I say, laughing. I'm not mad—she's just trying to make Ty feel comfortable here at Titan rich-people central.

Mom winks at me and continues, "Ty, I can tell you have a great future ahead of you. Come on, you should meet Mr. Taylor, the owner." She puts a hand on Ty's back and leads him away.

Over his shoulder, he glances back at me and gulps. I take the opportunity to breathe and grab a bottled water. It's official: I'm into him.

JJ pulls me aside. "What the hell's up with you, Woods?"

"What do you mean?"

"I mean, what's going on with you and Ty?"

"Nothing."

JJ sniggers. "Like I believe that. He can't keep his eyes off you."

"Really?" I exclaim.

"Duh. Look, Jordan, you're my best friend. I don't know how much I trust this guy," JJ says, jerking his head at Ty, across the room. "I don't want him stealing your position away from you or using your family to get ahead. And Carter told me what he said to Duckett on Friday. That's not cool."

"I get what you're saying, but let's give him a chance, okay? Unless I have, like, ten interceptions in one game, Coach isn't giving away my position. And if he tried to use me, you and Mike and Henry and Carter would all kick his ass."

"True…so, uh, do you like him?"

Wow, I can't believe JJ just asked me about my feelings. Since this is such a momentous occasion, I can't lie, so I nod once.

"Hot damn! I thought you'd be single for life. Figured you'd run off and join a convent."

"You're such an ass," I say, laughing. "You know, Lacey's head over heels for you."

"Oh God, I'm never speaking to you again," JJ says, darting away. I watch as he builds the biggest plate of nachos ever, big enough to feed Rhode Island.

So JJ would still take me seriously, as a teammate and as captain, if I had a boyfriend?

I decide now's a good time to rescue Ty from my mom and Mr. Taylor. When I approach the group, Mr. Taylor smiles and says, "I hear you have some competition for your position, Jordan."

"Yes, sir. Thanks for inviting us today," I say. I always flatter him because I need to stay in Mr. Taylor's good graces. They serve these amazing ice cream sundaes, and JJ lives for that nachos grande bar.

"You're always welcome," Mr. Taylor says. "Your mom and brother tell me that Ty will easily be snatched up by a big Division I team."

Ty frowns and rubs the back of his neck.

I ask Mr. Taylor and Mom to excuse us, then I rescue Ty, grabbing his hand and pulling him to my favorite seat, this cushy leather couch on the other side of the room.

"Thanks," he says as we flop down on the sofa. "I was dying over there."

"Sorry about that. JJ distracted me with the nacho bar," I say with a laugh.

A waiter walks up and says, "Can I get you anything?"

"What do you want?" I ask Ty.

"Whatever you're having, I guess," he responds, shrugging. He coughs.

"We'll take two Cokes, two of those awesome hot fudge sundaes, hot wings—not the mild sauce, I mean the 911 sauce, the stuff that tastes like you're eating lava, and a large cheese pizza," I say.

"Ugh," Ty says. "Are you really a girl?"

I freeze. I want him to think of me as a girl, not one of those people in a professional eating contest, like Joey Chestnut—the guy who ate sixty-eight hot dogs in twelve minutes. "The food's awesome. It's the only reason I sit in the owner's box instead of at field level."

Ty chuckles and pats my thigh. He lets his hand linger there for about two seconds, but then pulls it away and folds his hands.

"You know," Ty says, focusing on the massive Titans scoreboard, not meeting my eyes, "I didn't want to come to Hundred Oaks, and I was worried about being on a team with guys I don't know, but you've made me feel like I'm part of something. So, thanks."

"No problem." I wipe my sweaty palms on my dress.

"No, really. You're a good leader. I like that you're serious. I like that you're different."

"Thanks," I reply, grinning at him as he continues staring at the scoreboard, keeping his strong, tan hands clasped together.

Just as Ty turns to smile at me, Mike's friend Jake comes over and sits on the other side of me. Of all days, why did Mike have to bring his horndog friend to the game?

Jake puts his arm around me. "Hey, Jor. Who's your friend? I hope he's not your boyfriend."

Ty is staring at the field, but I can tell he's listening to Jake because he's leaning closer to me and because the game hasn't started yet. Players are stretching and doing final drills. I spot Dad swinging his arms around and bouncing up and down. He looks pumped.

"Did you need something, Jake?" I ask.

"Just wanted to sit with the prettiest girl in the room," Jake says. He leans over and plants this wet sloppy kiss on my cheek.

"Ugh!" I exclaim, wiping slobber off my face.

Luckily, Mike comes over to rescue me. He grabs Jake's arm and pulls him away from us. "Sorry, Ty, there's a reason we don't let this guy out much."

When Mike and Jake are gone, Ty whispers, "Who the hell was that tool?"

"That tool will probably be a first-round pick in the NFL draft next year," I say, shaking my head.

"*That's* Jake Reynolds?" he says, turning to stare. His eyes are opened so wide, he looks like one of those poison dart frogs. "Holy shit. He's so awesome."

I laugh. "Trust me, he's not."

"Seems like he likes you. Don't you want to date a first-rounder?"

"Excuse me while I go vomit."

"So you're not interested in him?" Ty asks, smiling.

"Hells no. I'd rather date O. J. Simpson."

Ty laughs. "I'm glad to hear that…I think."

God, this is awkward. Lucky for me, the game starts and Ty goes nuts. I love that he's having a great time. We totally pig out on all the food I ordered, and I can already feel my dress getting tighter. I hope Ty won't think I'm fat.

I'm so focused on Ty that I don't pay any attention to my mom, my brother, or JJ. That's okay, though, because JJ only has eyes for the Titans' cheerleaders and his nachos. I also haven't paid attention to the game, which I don't realize until Ty tells me how cool it was when Dad ran for a touchdown from the ten-yard line right before halftime. I can't believe I missed that. Dad's almost too old to scramble for a touchdown.

At halftime, Mike comes over and squeezes in between me and Ty. "Hey, guys," he says, putting an arm around each of us.

"Why are you acting so weird, bro?" I ask.

"I'm acting weird because I have an incredible piece of gossip," Mike says in a low voice.

"Mike, I think you should forget an NFL career and become my agent. You shouldn't waste your schmoozing skills."

Mike laughs. "The thought's crossed my mind. So aren't you interested to hear my news?"

"Of course!" I say.

"You know who Mr. Taylor's brother-in-law is, right?"

"No."

"He's the head coach of Notre Dame."

"So?"

"Mr. Taylor asked if you might be interested, sis, but I told him that Alabama's your first choice. But I said that it would be worth it for his brother-in-law to come take a look at Ty."

"Thanks so much, Mike," I say, hugging my brother.

"Thanks," Ty says. His eyes are darting around from the field to Mike to me to his ice cream sundae. Why's he so nervous?

"Cool—well, I'll leave you guys alone. I've got some more chatting to do," Mike says as he stands up and shuffles back to the bar.

Ty rubs the back of his neck again and stares down at the field. "This has been a weird couple of days, Woods," he mutters.

"Tell me about it," I reply before thinking. Why the hell did I say that?

"After the game today, can we go somewhere to talk? Alone?"

Me and Ty alone?

"Of course," I reply, calm and professional.

But inside?

My heart and stomach are bouncing around like yo-yos.

ty's place

It's not destitute.

It's not Trump Plaza.

It's a cute house

    white paint chipping off its sides

        the lawn overgrown but

            nothing a lawn mower couldn't cure.

Wildflowers litter the yard

    morning glory and goldenrod exploding like Skittles,

    but

        white clover in spring is my favorite

            (when I was little, Henry made me necklaces

            out of it).

All in all,

    JJ and Henry live in squalor compared to Ty.

But the look on Ty's face

    tells me something is very, very wrong here.

he knew...?

"What did you want to talk about?" I ask as I put my truck in park. He grabs my hand and in silence, we sit here holding hands for a few minutes. He keeps opening his mouth as if he's about to say something, then shuts it again.

"My dad died six months ago," he says finally.

Surprising myself, I reach over and draw him into a hug. He lets his forehead rest on my shoulder. "I'm so sorry. What happened?"

"Awful car wreck. Drunk driver."

"Is that why you moved here?"

He pulls his body away, but keeps his arms around me. "Sort of."

"You said you live with your mom and sister? And grandfather?"

"Yeah—you should come in and meet Papa. He's great."

"Do I get to meet your mom and sister too?"

He shifts in his seat and starts playing with my sunroof again. "My mom was in the car too."

But if she was in the car...and didn't die...? "What happened?"

"Um, well, she's, um, paralyzed?" Ty buries his eyes in the heels of his hands. "And I mean, I really tried my best to take care of everything so my sister and I could stay in Texas...but I couldn't..."

"Why are you telling me this?"

He drops his hands and turns to stare into my eyes. "We're friends, right? I hope we are…I left everything in Texas."

I grab his hand. "Of course we're friends."

"Well, my dad didn't have as much life insurance as I thought he would…well, we didn't have much money to begin with. But Mom needs a lot of care…like, care I can't give her? She needs a nurse."

"So you moved here so your grandfather could help out?"

"Yeah…I had to sell our house in Texas…so we could afford Mom's care. Plus my grandfather already had a job here working in a pajama factory."

"A pajama factory?"

"Didn't you know that Tennessee is, like, the pajama capital of the world?" Ty grins slightly.

"No—I don't wear pajamas," I say without thinking.

Ty coughs. "What?"

"Uh, I meant I wear, like, workout clothes to bed—you know, T-shirts and mesh shorts and shit."

"Right…" Ty says, smirking. Ty's signature smirk is about the sexiest thing on the planet.

"I wear clothes to bed!"

"That *sucks*."

I slap Ty's shoulder. "So…your grandfather is taking care of everything then?"

Ty rubs the back of his neck, sneaking a peek at me. "No. Not exactly. He can't afford it either 'cause he doesn't get good health insurance, and it's not like his insurance could cover Mom's care anyway. My mom's parents died really young, so my dad's father was nice enough to take us in. I mean, he doesn't have to help take care of Mom at all.

"So…um, we're living off the money from selling our house right now. And yesterday, I found a job doing dishes for a restaurant on Thursdays, Saturdays, and Sundays. They were nice enough to work around our football schedule, but I don't know what the hell I'm gonna do."

"What do you mean?"

"Even if I get a job after high school, I'm not going to be making enough money to support my sister and get Mom the care she needs at the same time."

"Job? What about college?"

"Woods…I *can't* go to college."

"You have to go to college. What about Notre Dame? You're NFL material!"

"You don't think I know that?" Ty says quickly. Then he jerks his head, as if he's mad at himself. "I'm sorry…I didn't mean to say it like that. What I meant to say is that I want to go to college, and I want to play ball more than anything, but I can't just take four years off and leave my sister and mom to fend for themselves. Papa doesn't make much money at all…he's already taking on more than he can handle by feeding my sister and me."

"But there's gotta be something. You'll get a scholarship."

"Scholarships don't put food on the table."

"Then why are you playing ball now? Why aren't you working more than three days a week?"

He takes my hand again, caressing it. "I love football. When I was a kid, my dad and I would throw a ball around for hours. We did that almost every day…up until, well, you know, the wreck."

"So you just want to play ball?"

"This season is kind of like my last hurrah, because after this, I have to get a real job and stop dreaming."

I squeeze his hand. "You know what I think about dreams?"

Ty smiles slightly. "What?"

"That if you spend too much time dreaming, you'll stop actually doing. And when you actually do stuff, there's a good chance things will work out. We make things happen by attacking, not by sitting around dreaming."

"This is gonna make me sound like a jerk, but what exactly would you have to dream about anyway? Your life is, like, perfect."

I laugh loudly. "You're kidding, right?"

Ty shakes his head.

"Okay, well my problems are nothing compared to yours, but my dad doesn't believe in me at all and hates the fact that I play football."

"Really? But your dad seems so cool on *SportsCenter*."

"He's very cool...as long as you don't bring up my playing football."

"Your dad's wrong." He goes back to caressing my hand.

My body feels so hot. "Thanks."

"Can you come in for a few?" Using his thumb, Ty points over his shoulder at the house.

"Yeah," I say with a smile.

Hell, I'll come in for the rest of my life

Will I get to sit on his bed? Does he have graph paper bedding?

We hop out of my truck and go up to the porch, and as I approach the door, I start to freak a bit. How could I be so self-absorbed to obsess about being in his bed when his mom is here, paralyzed?

When Ty opens the door, he reaches back and grabs my hand, leading me inside. Everything seems meticulously clean. Would I find any dust in this house? The living room is totally 1970s, complete with a brown plaid couch. I love it. Maybe I can buy the couch off them and then they'll have more money. But from what I know of Ty already, he would never accept handouts.

A beautiful girl who could only be Ty's sister is sitting on the couch reading a magazine and watching television. She must be thirteen or fourteen and must be breaking all the boys' hearts at her new school. When she sees Ty, she jumps up from the couch and hugs him.

"How was the game?" asks his sister, a tall girl with sandy blond hair. She's wearing makeup and a cute top with a skirt. Yup, definitely breaking hearts.

"Great! Did you watch it on TV?" Ty replies.

"Uhh…no."

Ty laughs, then says to me, "Vanessa *hates* football. Vanessa—this is Jordan Woods, and Woods, this is my sister, Vanessa."

We shake hands and his sister beams at me. "Ty's told me so much about you! I love that dress—can I borrow it sometime?"

Ty groans. But which statement freaks him out more—the fact that his sister asked if she can borrow this lame dress? Or the fact that I know he's been talking about me?

"Vanessa, that's rude," Ty says.

I shrug. "You can have it if you have something else I can wear home. I hate dresses."

"Omigod! I'll go find something right now," she says, darting out of the room.

Ty rolls his eyes but smiles. He puts a hand under my elbow, leading me out of the living room toward the kitchen, where an older man is sitting at a table with his feet propped up, reading the newspaper.

"Papa, I'd like you to meet Jordan Woods," Ty says, glancing from his grandfather's face to mine.

The man stands up, extending a hand. "Jim Green."

"Nice to meet you," I reply.

"It's such a pleasure, Jordan. I've been reading about you in the papers for years."

"Really?" I say, not surprised. My name is constantly in the papers during football season, as football is the only thing to do around here.

"Yeah, before he moved here, I even sent Ty some of the articles in the mail," Mr. Green says, patting Ty's back. "I told him it would be hard to get on the team at Hundred Oaks, what with you there and all, so I was thrilled the coach let him on the team. Bob Miller is a good guy."

Wait, so Ty knew about me? He knew I was a girl? Then why the hell did he act so surprised when I pulled off my helmet?

"Now that you're back, I've gotta get to the factory. Lucky break—I got a Sunday overtime shift," Mr. Green says to Ty. "Nice to meet you, Jordan."

"You too," I reply as he leaves. I'm totally confused. Ty knew about me? My thoughts are interrupted by Vanessa's reappearance with a bunch of outfits. Ty starts digging through all the clothes, which include miniskirts, a leather jacket, and a pair of camouflage pants. Smirking, he lays a hot pink miniskirt, a jean jacket, and a tube top out on the table.

"No. Hell no."

Ty laughs, handing me a pair of mesh shorts and a Nike T-shirt. "Just kidding. You can change in the bathroom." Ty points to a door, and I go in, change into the workout clothes, and walk back to the kitchen barefoot. After handing the dress over to a squealing Vanessa, I notice that Ty's frowning, so I decide to make an exit. I haven't asked where his mom is, but I figure if he wants me to meet her, he would introduce us. Can she even talk? Or is she paralyzed to the point where she's, like, this is horrible of me, a vegetable? I'd never ask.

"I'd better get going," I tell Ty. "I need to check on Henry."

"Oh?" Ty replies, raising an eyebrow. "How come?"

Henry's breakup with Carrie is very public knowledge, like the whole Jennifer Aniston–Brad Pitt–Angelina Jolie thing, so I'm not betraying him by saying, "He's been sort of a wreck since Carrie Myer dumped him."

"Ah. Well, I'll walk you out."

Vanessa throws her arms around me. "It was so great to meet you. And thank you so much for the dress! You have a great fashion sense! Can we go shopping sometime?"

Ty chuckles. "I don't get the feeling Jordan likes shopping."

Vanessa's jaw drops. "I don't believe it. All girls love shopping."

I shake my head. "Nah, not me. But my mom would take you shopping. Lord knows I won't go with her. I bet she'd love the company."

Vanessa smiles and bites her lip. "I'd love that. Thanks, Jordan. I can tell we're going to be, like, great friends."

Somehow I force a smile. I'm sure Vanessa feels desperate for a mother figure of any kind, even a six-foot-tall, football-playing tomboy.

"I'll be back inside in a bit," Ty tells Vanessa, and he starts to follow me to the front door when Vanessa says, "By the way, Nate called—" and Ty stops.

"Jordan," he says, furrowing his eyebrows, "can you wait in the living room for a minute?"

I nod, walk into the other room, and stare up at a picture of Ty and his mom, dad, and sister hanging next to the front door. I'm thinking how beautiful his mother is and how handsome his father was, when I hear Vanessa exclaim, "Nothing bad is going to happen to me!"

Ty speaks in a hushed tone. "No. You are never going to any guy's house. He can come here, but you're not going anywhere. And that homework had better get finished."

"God! It's like being in prison!"

"I don't care, Vanessa. You're not going out."

Then Ty comes into the living room and sighs. "Woods…let me walk you out."

What's his deal? He must be terrified something will happen to her, like his parents. But you can't confine a teenage girl—that will just make her rebel. On the other hand, I can't imagine how Ty feels, knowing that his sister is his responsibility. She's all he has left.

I head outside in the borrowed workout clothes and my silver flats. It's like a late-afternoon walk of shame. Ty follows me out to my truck, loosening his tie. I hop in, and Ty surprises me when he climbs back into the passenger seat.

I stick my keys in the ignition, but I don't turn the engine over. I find Ty's eyes and ask, "So if you knew about me already, why did you act so surprised when I took my helmet off the other day?"

Ty pulls his tie the rest of the way off. "Um…I admit I knew you were a girl…"

"And?"

"I, uh, just wasn't expecting you to be…so…not butch?"

"What the hell does that mean?"

Ty leans toward me and runs a hand through his hair. "It means…I didn't expect you'd be so gorgeous."

still in the truck

He leans across the center console
brushes my cheek with a hand
glances down at my lips
runs a finger along my jaw
presses his forehead to mine.
He starts to move in.
    This is too much.
        I'm too scared to kiss.
            What if he thinks I'm awful?
                I don't want to get rejected.
                    He's on my team!
So I tell Ty I need to go.
Other than seven minutes in heaven with Henry
this is the closest I've ever come to a kiss
    and I tell him I need to go.
What the hell is wrong with me?
Ty pulls away
    glares at me
        and begins to get out of the truck.
"See you at school tomorrow."
He slams the door
    heading toward the house
        he doesn't wave or even turn to look.
Now it's *me* staring as *he* walks away.

• • •

FROM: Tucker, Mark (Athletics, University of Alabama)
TO: Woods, Jordan
DATE: Monday, August 30, 12:46 p.m.
SUBJECT: Opportunity

Dear Jordan:

We are so pleased you are considering joining our athletic community at the University of Alabama. Coffee Calendars, a company affiliated with our booster program, produces an athletic calendar that our boosters sell every year. While a certain portion of the proceeds go to support our sports programs, most of the proceeds go to charity.

Coffee Calendars is in the process of taking photographs for next year's calendar, and our boosters would like you to consider posing for the September picture. Members of the volleyball, softball, and swim teams have agreed to be featured.

If you plan to join our program, which we most sincerely hope you do, we'd like to schedule a photo shoot before your home game this Friday evening. Production schedules require us to begin this process as soon as possible.

Please let me know if you're available for a photo session.

Yours truly,
Mark Tucker
Director of Athletics

jerry rice

the count? 15 days until alabama

Monday at school. Last class of the day, home ec.

Along with music appreciation and auto mechanics, this is another one of the stupid, easy classes Henry and I are taking together.

"Okay, everyone," Ms. Bonner says, "Pair off into groups of two—husbands and wives."

Henry's the only guy in the class, so all the girls automatically turn to him. He puffs out his chest and grins broadly, looking around the room at all the girls he has to choose from. A sophomore sitting in front of us gives him a little wave and a smile.

Henry raises his hand. "Ms. Bonner?"

"Yes, Sam?" the teacher says with a sigh. She taps a forefinger on a textbook.

After slipping a pencil behind his ear, Henry folds his hands in front of him and gets this extremely serious look on his face like he's about to negotiate a peace treaty. "Before we can choose partners, I think we need a few more details on what we're going to be doing in these husband-wife pairs. Is, um…" Henry lowers his voice to a mere whisper, "…sex involved?"

All the other girls start giggling as Ms. Bonner shakes her head. "No, Sam. Sex is not involved."

"Then I don't understand how we can be husband-wife pairs," he exclaims. "That's what husbands and wives do."

The girls giggle even more.

"We're just going to be pretending," Ms. Bonner says. "Now, everyone, find partners."

The smiling, waving sophomore comes slinking up and touches Henry's arm. "Want to be partners, Sam?"

"Nope, sorry," he says. "I'm already married to Woods."

The sophomore glares at me. What the hell is her problem? Like Henry and I would commit to doing a school project with someone else in this class. Honestly.

"Okay," Ms. Bonner says, going to a closet at the back of the room, "Now that we all have partners, all husbands should come pick up their projects."

Pick up our project? Shrugging, I stand up and stretch my arms. Henry also stands. "No way, dude," I say. "I'm the man in this relationship."

"Oh yeah, absolutely," he says, grinning. He sits back down as I walk to the closet to see this project, which turns out to be one of those fake electronic babies. Oh good God. Ms. Bonner hands me a fake baby boy. The doll has these creepy glass eyes that look like they're staring straight into my soul. I hold the doll out in front of me like it's a flaming bag of poo and carry it back to Henry.

"Congratulations, Mommy," I say, dropping the doll into his hands. "You could've told me I knocked you up."

"My bad. I thought you'd force me to get an abortion," Henry replies, taking the baby and cradling it as if it's real. "He has your eyes, Woods."

"And your hair." The doll is bald. "Can we name him Joe Montana?"

"Hells no, his name is Jerry Rice."

"No, his name is Joe Montana."

"I was in labor with him for fourteen hours!" Henry exclaims as he rocks the baby back and forth. "His name is Jerry Rice."

I grin. "Fine."

Then the teacher gives us all this shit, like blankies and strollers and toys and other things that babies need. First, Ms. Bonner says we have to carry this crap around all week! But then she explains the real assignment. Apparently these babies have computer chips that make them cry at random times, and it's up to us to feed them and change their diapers. Feeding them involves putting a metal rod in their fake mouths, which shuts off the crying. If we take out the metal rod before the fake baby is done eating, it will start crying again. We have to keep our babies happy and alive until Friday—for five entire days! So even if the baby cries in the middle of the night, we have to get up and feed the baby or change it. And cheating isn't an option, because the memory chip inside the baby takes readings that the teacher will check at the end of the week.

This assignment is so stupid. Like I'm ever going to have children. Like I'm ever going to get laid. I bet I could get my chiropractor to write a note saying the electronic pulses from these babies have been known to cause cancer, which would eat away at my bones, which would make me useless on the football field. Wait…

"But Ms. Bonner," I call out, "What are Henry and I supposed to do during football practice?"

Henry puts a hand on my shoulder. "It's okay, dear. That's what grandparents and the junior varsity players are for."

Ms. Bonner throws her hands up in the air. Lucky for her, the bell rings. Henry spends an inordinate amount of time getting Jerry Rice situated in our stroller. Then we leave the room, carrying our diaper bags down the hall toward the locker rooms. On the way, we run into Carter and JJ, who both just about die laughing.

"Shut up!" Henry says, "You're going to wake up Jerry Rice."

"Jerry Rice?" Carter says, covering his mouth with a hand. I don't think I've ever seen Carter laugh so hard.

"Carter, would you like to be the godfather?" Henry asks. "You know, in case anything happens to me and Woods this week?"

"Charming," Carter says. "I'd be honored. Does JJ get to be godmother?"

"Obviously," I say.

"Can I hold Jerry Rice?" JJ asks. "He's so cute."

"No way, man," I reply. "I don't want to wake that thing up before practice. We'll be late if we have to feed it."

"What does it eat?" Carter asks.

"I have to breast-feed, 'cause I'm the mom," Henry says, continuing to push the stroller toward the locker room.

"Actually," I say, "It eats a metal rod, made out of, like, lead. So basically, we're learning how to poison babies."

"Radical," JJ says as we approach the gym, where we find Ty standing with Kristen, talking and leaning against the wall. When Ty sees me, he pushes away from the wall and comes over, leaving Kristen standing alone. What were they talking about? God, why didn't I just kiss him yesterday? Then I wouldn't have to worry about why he was talking to the floozy that is Kristen Markum.

"Yo, guys," Ty says, peering down into the stroller. "What the hell is that thing? Satan's spawn?"

"You'd better watch it!" Henry says. He puts on a serious face, throws an arm around my shoulders, and pulls me in close. "That's our child you're talking about."

Ty smiles, then looks at Jerry Rice. "Its eyes are seriously creeping me out. And I knew something was going on between you two."

"You're right," Henry says. "Woods is my husband, and I'm her wife."

Carter and JJ start laughing again, and then walk off through the gym to the locker room, leaving just me, Ty, Henry, and Jerry Rice. Oh, and the awful Kristen Markum, who barely qualifies as a human being.

"Woods? Do you have a sec?" Ty asks.

"Sure."

"Alone?" Ty eyes Henry and Jerry Rice, and I jerk my head at Henry.

"Fine," Henry says, rolling his eyes. "Divorce me if you must, Woods. I can't believe I've only been married half an hour and I'm already a single parent." Ty holds the door to the gym open so Henry can get the stroller through. I giggle at the sight of him carrying those diaper bags across the gym. Kristen is still standing there glaring at me with crossed arms, looking mega-jealous.

"Kristen—I'll talk to you later," Ty says, brushing his hair off his forehead. "Woods and I need to talk football."

"Oh, okay," she says, suddenly smiling and bobbing up and down on her toes. "Bye, Ty!" She gives him a hug and takes off down the hallway.

Trying not to barf, I ask, "What's up?"

"I'm so sorry about yesterday...how I just slammed the door of your truck and all. And I didn't even thank you for taking me to the game. It was one of the best days of my life."

Stuffing my hands into the back pockets of my jeans, I nod a single nod. "No prob. Ready for practice?"

"Almost," he says, putting a hand up to my shoulder, stopping me. Is he going to try to kiss me again? "Um, are you and Henry, um...you know."

"Are we what?"

"You know, together?"

"Of course not. We've been best friends for, like, ten years."

"Oh...got it. Sometimes it just seems like you're more."

"Would it be bad if Henry and I were more?"

He brushes his hair away again, then rubs his neck. Motioning for me to follow him into the gym, he takes off toward the left, toward the guys' locker room, and I move right, toward the girls'. He calls out, "Yeah, it would be very bad."

• • •

After throwing on all my pads, practice uniform, and cleats, I grab my helmet and jog out to the field, looking for Henry and our fake baby, Jerry Rice. I spot Henry up in the stands, talking to Mom. He's holding the fake baby out to her. She starts laughing and takes the doll from his hands and holds it by an arm. I see him waving his arms at her, as if he's freaking out over how she's holding the fake baby. He takes the baby back from her and then motions for her to make a cradle with her arms. She laughs again, then makes a fake cradle, and Henry sets the doll down in her arms. She shakes her head.

As idiotic as this assignment is, I can't help but smile at their exchange. Henry is the funniest guy I know, the funniest person I've ever met. Only he would pretend to take this assignment so seriously. I jog up into the metal bleachers, taking two steps at a time until I reach Mom and Henry.

"Why, Jordan, you didn't tell me I was going to be a grandmother," Mom says, flashing a smile at Henry.

"I didn't know either," I say. "Henry hid the pregnancy from me. Do you mind watching that creepy thing during practice, Mom?"

Henry grabs his chest. "That creepy thing is our son, Woods."

"I don't mind," Mom says. She nods at something over my shoulder. "Looks like Coach Miller wants you two down there."

"Thanks, Mom!" Henry says. It seems that Jerry Rice has put Henry back in a good mood again. He throws an arm around me as we walk back toward the field. "So, what did Ty want?"

"To thank me for taking him to the game yesterday."

"That's it?" he whispers.

"No..."

"I'm your wife, you can talk to me, Woods."

"Yesterday, when I dropped him off at home, he, like, um, leaned in for a kiss?"

"And?"

"So, I, uh, told him I had to go."

"You didn't kiss?"

"Nope."

Henry grabs my elbow, stopping us from going farther. "Why'd you do that? Don't you like him?"

"Yeah...I was scared, I guess. I dunno." I stare down at a piece of gum that's melted onto the metal bleachers.

"De-nied," Henry says. "God, I can't even imagine leaning in for a kiss and getting rejected. Ty must feel like shit today."

Shrugging, I grunt.

"So did he try to kiss you again just now? Or talk to you about the non-kiss?"

"No—he wanted to know if we're together," I say, laughing loudly and using my thumb to point from Henry back to me.

"You and me?"

"Yeah, he wanted to know if you and I are dating. I told him we're best friends."

"Yeah, he definitely wants you."

I glance at Henry sideways. His face is blank, like no smile or anything. "You think?" I whisper.

"I know."

Henry looks from my face back to the field, and his eyes pop open wide. I turn to see why he's gaping: JJ and Carter are messing around, trying to shove a scrawny wide receiver into Jerry Rice's stroller.

"JJ!" Henry yells, "You can't fit a freshman in that stroller."

• • •

Later that night, after a couple hours at the batting cages with Carter and JJ, Henry and I are in my basement having a mad foosball tournament. It's best three out of five games. I've won two; he's won one. In the current game, game four, I'm kicking his ass. Jerry Rice, with his creepy eyes wide open, is sleeping quietly in his stroller. *Monday Night Football* is blaring on the big-screen television in the corner. We're watching the Jets/Dolphins game and rooting for the Dolphins, of course.

"Can I stay over tonight?" Henry asks. Light from the television bathes his blond curls, making them shimmer.

"Course."

"I figure it'll be easier for us to take care of Jerry Rice that way," he says. "We can alternate the middle of the night feedings." He twirls the bar, hitting the tiny white ball into my goal.

"Why are you taking this so seriously? We could leave Jerry Rice in my truck overnight so we wouldn't have to hear him cry."

"I want a good grade."

"You did totally botch that corn bread assignment." I hit the ball toward Henry's goal, and his little wooden goalie blocks it. "I can't believe you got an F in corn bread."

"Most people can make it through life without having to be good at making corn bread. Being a parent is different."

"Yeah," I say, knowing how much my dad can suck sometimes. Henry and I are both lucky to have such great moms. At least Henry's dad isn't an asshole—he's just never home. Like my dad, Mr. Henry hasn't been to one of our football games in forever.

I slam the ball into Henry's goal, winning the game. I throw my hands above my head and strut around the room, victorious. Cupping my hands around my mouth, I make fake crowd noises. "And Woods wins it all!"

"Quiet! You're going to wake the baby," Henry says with a laugh. He flops down on one of the leather sofas and picks up his glass of lemonade. I pour myself another glass, then grab a few chocolate-chip cookies, sit down, and prop myself up against him. He wraps an arm around me, leans over, and grabs a cookie from my hand with his teeth.

"Thief!"

"Pig!"

• • •

The middle of the night rolls around, and Jerry Rice is screaming. Henry's bare feet are in my face, so I knock them out of the way as I sit up. Jumping out of bed, I grab the stupid doll from its stroller and force the lead rod into its mouth. Then I plop back down on the bed. It turns out that you can't just leave the key in its mouth. You have to, like, hold the fake baby at the same time or it will keep crying.

I sit back against my headboard and hold the doll in my arms. If I didn't have the fake baby right now, I'd totally be writing in my journal about Henry.

He's fast asleep, curled up at the other end of my bed, looking peaceful. The expression on his face says he's not really sad, and he's not overcompensating for his sadness by acting all crazy or silly, he's just...content. And that makes me glad, because more than anything else, I want him to be happy. Part of me doesn't even want him to wake up, because I know he'll eventually go back to being depressed about Carrie, or whatever the hell he's depressed about. If only he'd talk to me...maybe I could help.

My head droops down, and I accidentally drop the metal rod and Jerry Rice starts crying again. Henry stirs. Sitting up, the bedcovers fall down to reveal the plastic football charm and his six-pack.

Is Ty's body that perfect? I wonder how many times Kristen has already seen his abs...

"What's up, Woods?" Henry says, rubbing his eyes with fists.

"I dropped the metal rod, that's all." I cradle the stupid doll again.

Henry crawls up and throws an arm around me, pulling me in tight. Closing my eyes as I lean against his shoulder, it occurs to me that Henry is going to be a great dad one day. Not unsupportive like my dad or nonexistent like his.

Just a really great dad.

opportunity

the count? 12 days until alabama

It's Thursday, and as is tradition, JJ and I are sitting at Joe's All-You-Can-Eat Pasta Shack. I'm playing the salt-and-pepper-shaker game and JJ is scribbling in his crossword-puzzle book.

"I can't believe you're already doing a photo shoot for Alabama," JJ says. "Crazy."

"I know, right?"

"I'm proud of you, Woods."

"Thanks, man."

JJ jots on the puzzle and asks, "Ready for the game?"

I shrug, yawning. "I'm tired from dealing with stupid Jerry Rice all week."

"Where is that baby of yours?" JJ asks, looking under the table, as if I'd actually put a baby down there.

"He's with his mother, who's probably sleeping with Marie Baird right now." I roll my eyes as I stack the pepper on top of the salt.

"She's a damn nice piece of ass."

"Don't be such a pig, JJ." I pull salt out from under pepper, which falls to the table perfectly.

"Yes, ma'am," he says, before burying his nose in the crossword puzzle again.

I'm so sick of Henry's mood swings and his sleeping around, but I won't mention that to JJ. Two nights this week, Henry showed up at my house past midnight and crawled into my bed. I told him that I'll kick his ass if we play like shit tomorrow night, because I haven't had a good night's sleep in over a week, thanks to Jerry Rice's constant crying and my being stressed out by both Ty and Henry.

It's like JJ knows what I'm thinking, because he looks up from his crossword-puzzle book, smiles wickedly, and says, "You hooking up with Ty Green yet?"

Stacking pepper on top of salt, I shake my head. "Nah."

JJ furrows his eyebrows. "Well, why the hell not? I thought you guys were gonna start going at it in the owner's box on Sunday. You couldn't keep your hands off each other."

Shit. It was that obvious?

Honestly, I've been avoiding Ty since Monday, and he's backed off. Hasn't approached me in days, which is kinda good, but kinda sucks ass at the same time.

I sit up straight and say, "Ty's already hooked up with Kristen, and he can get whatever he wants from 99.9 percent of the girls at school."

"So?"

"So why should I be any different? I don't wanna be another random girl to him."

"What's wrong with just fooling around?"

"First of all, we're on the same team, and second, unlike you and Henry, I'm not a man-whore and wouldn't want to be a one-night stand."

"Then I'll kick his ass if he does that to you," JJ growls, clutching his pen.

"I know, I know," I say, putting my hands up in the air as if I'm being arrested. "Look, I'm just going to focus on playing ball. Okay?"

"Whatever you want, Woods..." JJ grins slightly and shakes his head.

I fold my arms across my chest. "Getting a college scholarship should be my number one priority, not hooking up."

JJ keeps smiling at his crossword book, obviously trying not to laugh at me. "What's a four-letter word for a soothing plant?"

Shrugging, I say, "I dunno...weed?"

He points the pen at me. "Right on."

• • •

"Are you sure about this?" I ask, staring at myself in the mirror.

One of the Coffee Calendar makeup artists has completely straightened my hair—it falls down my back like a stream of water from a faucet. And now the lady's dabbing foundation all over my face. Another woman brushes some pink shit onto my lips.

"Perfectly sure," the woman replies. "You look great."

"What does it matter? Aren't you taking a picture of me wearing a helmet?"

"Not exactly." She passes me an oversized Alabama jersey and a pair of short shorts. "Wear these."

I burst out laughing. "You must be joking."

The woman purses her lips at me, obviously getting sick of dealing with a girl who doesn't want to play dress-up. Or in the case of these clothes, dressing down, meaning barely wearing anything.

But if this is what the Alabama athletic director wants, this is what he'll get.

I walk into the bathroom and put on the jersey and short shorts, and then walk back out into the locker room, where I find Carrie and Marie.

They both take a step back when they see me.

"Wow, Jordan," Carrie says. "Your face looks really pretty."

"What are you wearing?" Marie asks, staring at my thighs.

I shrug, feeling my face burn. I close my eyes and somehow resist the urge to pull my hair back up into a ponytail and wipe all this crap off my face.

"You're wearing that for your picture?" Marie exclaims.

I nod slowly.

"This is seriously messed up," Marie says, shaking her head. "It doesn't even look like you're wearing pants."

The Coffee Calendar people motion for me to follow them outside, and I dart after them, happy to get this over with. When I peer over my shoulder at Carrie and Marie, to make sure they aren't teasing me, I find them looking concerned and sad.

We walk out onto the field, where a camera is set up next to a goal post.

I hear whistling, so I jerk around to find its source and see some of my teammates coming out of the guys' locker room. I spot Ty looking at my legs.

"You look smoking hot, Woods!" a junior varsity guy shouts, and then another JV guy echoes that horrific sentiment before Carter and JJ step in front of them. Then the whistling stops.

My face must match our Red Raiders jerseys.

Henry jogs over to me and pulls me aside. "What the hell are you doing?" He stares down at my legs and back up at my face and hair.

"I have to do it, 'cause Alabama wants me to."

"You don't have to do anything," Henry replies. "You're a killer player. You shouldn't have to demean yourself for them."

"I'm not! I'm happy to do this for my future team."

Henry nods slowly and pats my shoulder. "Okay..."

He looks kinda down, so I say, "You look taller without a Baby Björn strapped to your chest, you know."

"I'm gonna miss that Jerry Rice. He made me into a chick magnet," Henry says, grinning. "And Ms. Bonner told me that you and I made the highest grade in the whole class. We were excellent parents." He nods seriously, and I shove his chest, shaking my head and laughing.

"Picture time," I say, nodding my head at the photographer.

He starts to walk back to the team, but then turns and says, "Your hair looks great."

I smile at him.

"Let's get this over with," I say to the photographer. I pick up a football and hurl it fifty yards downfield so he can get a great shot of my wind-up.

"No, no," the photographer replies. "Put one hand on your waist, and hold a football with the other."

I do what he says, and the catcalls start again.

"Sexy!"

"I want a piece of that!"

I clutch the ball as hard as I can and look down at my sneakers, trying to think of something happy to get my mind off the most mortifying experience *ever*. I'll do whatever I have to do to play ball for Alabama...but this feels so wrong.

I can't believe the guys are still whistling and disrespecting me like this.

But when I glance over at the team, I find JJ has taken his jersey off and is modeling for the guys. His extra weight flops around as he struts up and down the sideline with his jersey thrown over his shoulder.

I breathe deeply, so incredibly relieved that my team wasn't making fun of me after all.

I crack up when JJ calls out, "I'm ready for my photo op, Jordan!"

game #2

Hundred Oaks High versus Stones River High, our main rival.
Final Score?
    24–21 Hundred Oaks.
I threw three great passes
and Henry scored three great touchdowns.
Ty didn't get to play at all,
which made me feel horrible.
I seriously considered asking Coach to put him in for the second half
but my pride won the internal battle over my pity and guilt.
Michigan was a no-show
Henry yanked his hair.
Ohio State was a no-show
Carter acted relieved…?
The *great* Donovan Woods was a no-show
I threw my helmet at my locker.

truth or dare?

the count? 10 days until alabama

"Who the hell invited the cheerleaders?" I ask, glancing over my shoulder into the family room. It's the Saturday night after our game versus Stones River and my parents are out of town for my dad's game in Jacksonville on Sunday, so I invited JJ, Carter, and Henry over to hang out, and they freaking showed up with Lacey, Kristen, Marie, Carrie…and Ty.

JJ and Carter stuff their hands in the pockets of their jeans and turn to stare at Henry.

"You guys are such *great* friends," Henry says. "I can't believe you threw me under the bus *that is* Jordan Woods."

"Don't call me a bus! That makes me sound fat."

"Since when do you care if you're fat?" Henry asks. He smiles and glances from me to Ty and back to me again. "You know, Woods, I'll keep saying it until you believe it—you'd like Marie if you'd just give her a chance."

A little embarrassed at being called out by Henry, I shrug. "Yeah, she does seem pretty cool in music appreciation."

Henry moves close to my ear and whispers, "Why does it matter if the cheerleaders are here?"

"The giggling gets on my nerves," I reply, but the truth is, I don't want Kristen around Ty.

"If I ask them not to giggle, can they stay?"

JJ gives me a pathetic puppy dog face that's just screaming, "I need to get laid, please let them stay."

Carter mimics JJ's "I want to get laid" face even though he's not dating any of these girls, has never gotten laid, and has never once actually mentioned that he wants to get laid.

Ty looks at me and shrugs.

I don't want the guys to leave, especially Ty. "Fine. They can stay. But under no circumstances will anyone make out on my bed or touch any of my personal possessions."

"Shucks," JJ says. "I only came 'cause I thought I'd get to fool around on your bed."

"You're such an ass," I say, grabbing a soda from the fridge as Carrie comes into the kitchen.

"Jordan," she says, "Do you have any Tylenol? I've got a headache."

"Sure," I reply, gesturing for her to follow me upstairs.

"You okay?" Carter asks as he cups her elbow with a hand. "Need a ride home or anything?"

"I'm cool, but thanks," she says to Carter, grinning as she follows me. As soon as we're in the bathroom and I'm rooting around in the medicine cabinet, Carrie shuts the door and whispers, "I don't need any Tylenol."

"Huh?"

"I just wanted to talk to you alone. What's going on with Ty?" she squeals.

"Nothing."

"Jordan, come on. You like him, right?"

I shrug and nod, averting my eyes.

She looks up at me and rubs my forearm. "So what's wrong?"

Why is everyone so interested in what happens with me and Ty? I feel like I'm on one of those shitty reality shows like *The Bachelorette* or something. Unknotting my hair, I let it fall down my back. I grab a hairbrush, untangle my hair, and then pull it back up again as I decide what to tell Carrie.

"Uh, he tried to kiss me last week, and I didn't let him. What if he never tries again?"

Carrie's kind blue eyes shine as she smiles. "He will."

"And, um, if he does, what do I do?"

"What do you mean?" Carrie asks, raising an eyebrow.

I purse my lips, incredibly embarrassed at having to ask. "How do I kiss him?"

"Oh." She pauses. "Well, sit here," she says, pulling the toilet seat down and patting it, telling me to sit. I take a seat and look up at Carrie. "Pretend I'm Ty…so when he leans in, just sort of wrap your fingers around his neck like this." She takes my hand and puts it on the back of her neck. Jesus, this must be the weirdest thing that's ever happened to me.

She leans in as if she's going to kiss me. "When his lips touch yours, just start touching him everywhere. His back, his jaw, his neck, his cheeks, his hips. Move your hands slowly, but keep him guessing."

"Got it," I say, taking my hand off her neck.

"And then use lots of lip, not so much tongue." She kisses the back of her hand, demonstrating for me.

"Got it," I say, but skip the part where I make out with my hand. "That's it."

"That's it?" I exclaim. It seems so much more complicated on TV.

"Yup, now go get 'em," she says, sounding just like Coach when he gives us pep talks before games. I'm surprised she doesn't slap my ass too.

Carrie and I walk back into the family room, where I sit down in my dad's favorite armchair and pop open my Diet Coke.

"I love your house, Jordan," Marie says, looking around. "Thanks so much for inviting us."

"You're welcome," I reply.

"I can't believe I'm getting to see your dad's Heismans," she says, gawking at the trophies on the shelf. She walks over and peers up at them. "My dad and brother will be so jealous."

I raise my eyebrows at Henry, who shrugs and smiles. All right, Marie does seem nice and sweet. Henry sits down on the floor and pulls her onto his lap. He whispers in her ear and kisses her cheek, and she giggles. He seems happy tonight, so that makes me happy. Carrie smiles at them, but I can tell she's still hurt. I'm dying to know why they broke up.

JJ sits with Lacey, and Carter sits with Carrie, probably because she's the only option left besides Kristen, who's still eyeing Ty with a shitload of interest. When Ty picks a seat, I notice he sits as far away from Kristen as possible, but she crawls over next to him anyway.

With everyone else paired off into couples, I feel like a ninth wheel.

"Who wants a drink?" Lacey asks, pulling these lame piña colada wine coolers out of her bag and passing them out to the other girls.

JJ moves to grab one, but I shake my head at him. I don't care if my team drinks, but they're not drinking on my watch.

"Couldn't you have brought something good?" Carter asks Lacey. "Like a nice Pinot Grigio or a Chianti?"

"I love Pinot Grigio," Carrie replies.

"What the hell are you talking about?" I ask Carter. "Chianti? How could that possibly compare with a Slurpee?"

"Hear, hear," Marie says, and we grin at each other before she takes a sip of her wine cooler. I laugh when she grimaces.

Ty's leaning up against a leather sofa with Kristen nestled up next to him. She's beaming, but he's staring at his fingernails. Then he peers over at me and I turn away as fast as I can and focus on the clown fish in our tank.

JJ and Henry are looking at me with eyes wide open, shaking their heads. Carrie whispers something in Carter's ear, and he starts nodding and laughing.

"Truth or dare time," Carrie says. She tucks her hair behind her ears.

"What the hell..." JJ says. "This isn't seventh grade."

"I still haven't recovered from seven minutes in heaven with Woods," Henry says. He sticks his tongue out and pretends to gag, then smiles.

"What?" Ty blurts, looking from Henry's face to mine and back again.

"It was awful, man," Henry says, cracking up. "Woods beat the shit out of me in the closet. She gave me a black eye."

Ty starts laughing and grins at the carpet.

"Okay, okay," Lacey says, holding up her hands trying to calm us down. "Carter—truth or dare?"

"Dare."

Staring at the ceiling, Lacey cocks her head. "I dare you to hump the Heisman Trophy."

"Sacrilege!" Henry yells.

"That trophy is not on the table!" I say.

"Over my dead body!" JJ exclaims, glaring at Lacey as if she's just killed Peyton Manning.

"Geez, sorry, guys," Lacey replies. She scoots away from JJ, putting a good foot between them. "It's just a trophy."

"No, it is *not* just a trophy," Ty says, glancing up at my face.

"Pick a different dare, honey," JJ says. Grinning, she unscoots and moves to sit on JJ's lap. He gives Lacey's hip a quick squeeze.

Honey?

Obviously he knows he's not getting any tonight unless he's nice and supportive, but honestly? So what if her waist is the size of a green bean and her breasts are like cantaloupes? Her brain is the size of an M&M.

"Hump the Heisman Trophy, my ass," I mutter.

"Okay," Lacey says, tapping her lip with a finger. "Carter, I dare you to make out with Carrie."

Carter raises his eyebrows at Henry, who shrugs. This surprises me, because even though he says he's not upset about Carrie, I totally thought he was depressed because she broke up with him. So why would he be okay with her kissing one of his best friends?

Then Carter turns to face Carrie. She smiles and lets out a short burst of laughter, then leans back on her hands and crosses her ankles in front of her. Carter coughs into a fist and kisses her quickly on the lips. When he pulls away, they smile at each other for a few seconds. It's actually kind of cute, and I wonder if Ty would smile at me like that after a kiss. If I had just let him kiss me last week, maybe I'd know.

"That wasn't making out!" Lacey squeals.

"My turn," Carter says, ignoring Lacey. "JJ—truth or dare?"

"Truth."

"What is your favorite NFL team?"

Lacey snorts. "Oh God."

JJ strokes his chin and pretends to take a long time choosing an answer. A minute later, he folds his hands. "Uh, I guess I'll have to go with the Titans."

Lacey throws a pillow at Carter, who puts his hands up in a gesture that says, "What?"

"Kristen—truth or dare?" JJ asks.

"Dare," Kristen replies, gazing at Ty.

"I dare you to go in the kitchen and make me a steak and mashed potatoes, woman. Medium-well, please. Steak's in the freezer!"

Henry dies laughing, rolling over onto the floor, clutching his stomach.

"Jerks," Marie and Carrie say, shaking their heads.

"You chauvinist pig," I say to JJ, who starts laughing just as hard as Henry, which makes me laugh, which makes Ty laugh.

Then he and I stare at each other, laughing.

Kristen clearly sees this and sighs loudly. She glares at me and then stands up, puts her hands on her hips and stalks toward the kitchen. I hear her banging around in there, rattling pans and opening and shutting the fridge.

"Jordan—truth or dare?" Kristen calls out from the kitchen. I hear her slamming a pan down on the stove. Then I hear drawers and cabinets opening and slamming shut.

Truth is always God-awful, but what if she dares me to spend the rest of the night alone in my room, or dares me to leave my own house so she and Ty can be all alone? Shit.

"Dare," I reply.

Kristen, now wearing an apron, pokes her head back in the family room. "I dare you to jump into the lake."

I stand up. This dare is a cinch.

"In your underwear," Kristen adds, pointing at my body with a spatula.

Crap. Which underwear am I wearing? Do they even match my bra? Do they look…gross? I think I'm wearing plain white underwear. God, I don't want Ty to see me in ugly underwear. I cover my face with my hands. I just need to get this over with, so I sprint out my back door to the dock.

• • •

I jump into the freezing water, which reeks of algae and fish. I love it. The cool water lowers my temperature and makes my racing heart slow down.

I look down at my plain white tank and boy shorts, which are sticking to me like a wet paper towel clinging to spilt Coke on a kitchen floor. Why can't I just wear pretty underwear like the cheerleaders? It's not like the team would ever have to know…

I submerge my body in the water up to my neck so no one can see me. Hopefully everyone will take my clothes lying on the docks as proof that I'm in my underwear. A minute goes by, but no one comes out. Then, illuminated by light from my house, darting through the trees, I see him walking toward me. Just him. Just Ty.

"Hey," he says. "How's the water?"

"Freezing. Where's everybody else?"

"I told them that if they want to keep their arms, they wouldn't come out here."

I laugh. "You told them you'd pull their arms from their sockets?"

He grins. "Yup."

"And how do you, Mr. Measly Quarterback, expect to do anything to JJ?"

"I imagine I could do some damage if I were mad enough."

I chuckle. "Keep telling yourself that. Thanks for scaring them off. Turn around so I can get out and get dressed."

"No."

"No?"

"No." He stares straight into my eyes. "I didn't scare them off for you. I did it for me. I'm coming in with you." He pulls off his shirt and kicks off his flip-flops. His body is perfect, chiseled like a statue. He begins to unbuckle his belt and unzip his jeans, and I twirl around in the water. I gaze across the lake at the distant shore, trying to focus on the trees, the sand, the rocks, anything.

I hear a splash. The water moves toward me.

Suddenly I feel his hands wrap around me from behind. He rests his forehead on my back. "God, it's cold," he says. "Warm me up."

"I'm cold too."

"Why have you been avoiding me?"

Trembling, I take a rattled breath. "Ty, I need to stay focused."

"Am I causing you to lose focus?" He laughs.

"Maybe."

"What if I told you I've already lost all focus because of you?" He rests his chin on my shoulder and glances at my face.

"I'd say you're screwing with me."

"It's true. Being around you is like drinking a shot of whiskey."

"You feel drunk when you're around me?"

"That's an understatement."

"Ditto."

He drags his hands across my stomach, dipping a fingertip into my belly button, and I feel his mouth on my shoulder. My brain tells me to run—to forget about this. But my body tells my brain to shut the hell up.

"Jordan," he mumbles.

"Yeah?"

He turns me around, causing ripples in the water, and then his mouth is on mine. Our first kiss explodes like mixing soda and pop rocks. His soft lips feel better than I ever imagined. I don't know what I'm doing with my lips or my tongue, so I try to follow his lead and let him do the work. I hope my lips don't feel like limp spaghetti.

Soon, I'm figuring out how to kiss—he runs his tongue along my lips, so I bite his lower lip in response. He laughs. I inch my fingertips across his shoulders and elbows as I move my mouth to his throat.

He whispers, "You're beautiful."

"Thank you." I'm not so scared anymore. If he likes me for who I am, it doesn't matter what kind of underwear I'm wearing. Or that I'm not wearing makeup. Or that I'm over six feet tall. "You're really cute too," I say, giving him another kiss on the lips, digging my fingertips into his abs.

"I've never wanted anyone so much in my life."

I moan softly as he kisses my neck, right beneath my ear, in return. "You want me?"

"Every bit of you," he mumbles. Taking my hands in his, his eyes find mine. He caresses the tops of my hands with his thumbs. He says, "Race me across the lake?"

All I want is to feel his body against mine, but I can't resist a challenge. "You're on." I take off swimming, having done this a hundred times in my life. I know I can swim the length of the lake in about two minutes. I easily beat him, pull myself onto the banks, and lie down on a soft mossy patch, so green it's almost like lying on Astroturf, only without the rug burns.

"You could've told me you're a female Michael Phelps before I made an ass of myself," he says, smiling as he drags himself out of the lake. He shakes the water out of his hair.

He lies down next to me, leaning on an elbow, his eyes scanning my body. He doesn't seem to have a problem with my soggy underwear. Has a teenage girl ever felt less sexy than I do now?

I shiver when he runs a finger across my bare stomach, right above the elastic of my boy shorts, before exploring my body with his lips. I weave my hands through his hair, then pull him up so he's facing me, and he smiles. He nudges my nose with his. "I want you."

We kiss some more, and while gasping for breath, I reply, "I'm all yours."

rumors

the count? 8 days until alabama

I'm hiding out in a bathroom stall at school on Monday morning. Except for Ty, I haven't seen anyone since Saturday night, and I'm not looking forward to all the questions that are undoubtedly coming. Like, where did Ty and I disappear to? And what's going on between us? I don't even know the answer to that one. Do "I want you," and "I'm all yours," mean we're officially dating now? Or was I just a random hook up?

Right as I'm about to stand up and leave the bathroom, I hear the door opening and shutting.

"Don't worry about it, Kris," says a girl.

I peer through the crack in the stall and see Lacey and Kristen staring in the mirror as they start to apply lip gloss and fluff their hair.

"How can I not worry about it? Of all girls, he ditched me for Jordan Woods. Well, if you consider her a girl. Gross," Kristen says.

"I don't think he likes her," Lacey replies. "He just can't."

"Maybe he just wants to screw her because she's a virgin."

"Yeah...maybe."

I take a deep breath. Kristen's going to tell the whole school that I disappeared with Ty on Saturday. It's seventh grade all over again.

Wait, what if they're right? What if Ty only wants to devirginize me? But how would he even know? It's not like Lacey and Kristen know everything. I could've screwed Mike's friend Jake Reynolds, and they'd never know.

"So what do I do?" Kristen says.

"Play it cool. I don't think he'll stay interested in Jordan for too long—especially not when he sees how much time she spends with Sam Henry. JJ told me that Sam stays over at her house all the time. Like in the same bed!"

Kristen gasps. "What? That's so weird. Maybe she's not a virgin, after all. Maybe she's a slut."

Damn it, Henry's like my brother—don't they know that? Rather than deal with these awful girls face-to-face, I decide to stay in the stall until they leave. And then I'm getting the hell out of here. I'd rather skip school than deal with the aftermath of Saturday night.

When they're gone, I tiptoe out of the bathroom and head for the front doors of the school. Halfway there, I see Marie, who rushes up to me, smiling. "Jordan! Oh my God—you and Ty? You're so lucky."

I feel bad for ignoring her because she's actually nice, but I can't deal. Seriously.

Other girls in the hallway stop moving when they see me, giggling and whispering to each other.

Bates and Higgins walk up. "Yo, Woods," they say.

"Great game Friday," Bates adds, knocking fists with me.

"You're a shoo-in for Alabama," Higgins says, resting his arm on my shoulder. "I hope you'll put in a good word for me."

Thank God—they don't mention the hideous photo shoot either. Then a few other guys pass me and say hi, acting normal. But all the girls stare.

Then I see JJ, who walks right up and grabs my elbow. "Are you okay? Because if you aren't, I'm gonna kick that pretty boy's ass. Right now."

What? JJ, Mr. "If You Share Your Feelings with Me I'll Snap Your Head Off," is concerned about my love life?

"I'm fine," I tell JJ, "But I don't feel good. I'm gonna go home." I take off again, and then I see him. Ty. Coming toward me and smiling. He waves. And I sprint for the front door.

• • •

Now I'm hiding in the potting shed, alternating between writing in my journal and repeatedly tossing a football up in the air and catching it. I like it in here. Makes me feel like a kid again, without any of these problems.

After throwing the ball up and catching it for the thousandth time, I wedge the flashlight under my chin and begin to write:

The whole school knows about Saturday night
  Saturday, disappearing with Ty was the right decision
  Right as eating peanuts at a baseball game
  Right as the sound of coffee grinding on Saturday morning
  Today? Confused as hell

I can't believe how much I'm beginning to love writing. Not just getting thoughts out of my head, but the challenge of finding creative words and rhythms and fun descriptions.

Right as the smell of smoke following fireworks

Still, writing's a weak thing to be doing. At least compared to playing quarterback. Or eating those scalding 911 wings that made me and Ty cry at the Titans game.

The door to the shed suddenly slams open and Henry crawls in next to me, watching as I hide my journal behind a watering can.

Running a hand through his curly blond hair, Henry hip-checks me and presses his shoulder against mine.

"Yo, Woods—how could you miss practice? You have the plague or something?"

"If I do, you've got it now too."

"Why'd you skip school?"

We lean back against the shed wall, and I curl up under his arm and drop the football onto his lap. Faint sunlight shimmers through the grimy window.

"'Cause people were talking about me in the hallway."

"So?"

"So that's never happened to me before."

Henry pulls me in closer and rubs my arm as I go on. "I don't want to lose the team's respect. If I lose my confidence, I'm going to play like shit, and shitty players don't get offered spots on Division I teams like Alabama."

His eyes focus on mine and we stare at each other for a while. With his tan skin and emerald eyes, Henry is an extremely cute guy, and it occurs to me how many girls at school would love to find themselves in a potting shed with him. Then he says, "Want to play the hand-slap game?"

I sit Indian-style and Henry mimics me. He puts his hands out toward me, palms up. I place my hands on top of his. A second later, he yanks his hands out from beneath mine and tries to smack the tops of my hands, but I jerk away.

"Winner gets the football charm, right?" I ask, nodding at his chest.

"Hell no," Henry replies, not missing a beat. He puts his hands back out, and we play several more times before he speaks again. "Today, in music appreciation class, Mr. Majors said we all have to choose an instrument and write a five-page paper about its origins. We also have to discuss the instrument's relevance in today's society. But don't worry, I signed you up for a great instrument."

"What?"

"The harpsichord."

"What the hell is a harpsichord?" I exclaim.

"I dunno," he says, smiling. "I saw it on a poster in the classroom."

"You must be kidding. How could an instrument I've never heard of have any relevance in today's society?"

"These things wouldn't happen if you didn't skip school."

"What the hell, man? What instrument did you pick?"

He shrugs. "An instrument that has a lot of relevance in today's society. The guitar."

I grin, slapping his hands hard. We play several more times, and I win more often than he does, which makes me happier.

"Woods, it's okay to get involved with someone. You can date, you know." Instead of smacking Henry's hands again, I smack him upside the head. "Damn it," he exclaims, laughing. "Stop beating me up. Look, I'm gonna tell you something, because you're my best friend. Underneath that crazy knot you call hair, all us guys know you're really a girl, and we want you to be happy."

I knock him in the shoulder.

"I'm being serious, Jordan. I don't know what you're so scared of. I know you like Ty, and it's obvious he likes you, and you're all pushing him away…you're finally acting like a girl."

I glare at Henry.

"And it's not a bad thing," he adds.

"Ty and I are on the same team, Sam."

"I don't care."

"Dating him will cause drama."

"It seems to me that *not* dating him is what's causing the drama... you not showing up for practice, my ass...Coach was worried and pissed, to be honest—he tried calling, but got your voice mail." Henry stretches his palms back out for another round of the hand-slap game. I put my hands beneath his and two seconds later, I swiftly jerk my hands out and slap his hands hard.

"So what do you think?" Henry asks.

"Sam...if I date him, no one's going to think I'm, like, a slut or anything, are they?"

"Of course not...because I think you have to sleep with more than one person, possibly several, to be considered a slut."

"You would know," I reply with a laugh.

He clutches at his chest, but then says, "I'm proud to be a man-slut."

"Why do you guys have to sleep around all the time? Why can't you just stay with one person?"

Henry slaps my hands, then runs his hands through his hair and stares at a bag of mulch. "I dunno...maybe I just haven't gotten with the right person yet. It's kind of hard to stop."

"To stop sleeping around?"

He nods.

"I just don't get that, Henry."

He keeps focusing on the mulch. "Why would you ever think you're a slut?"

I grab his hands and hold them tightly. Biting my lip, I find his eyes. "I, um, heard Lacey and Kristen talking bad about me in the bathroom today. They wondered if I'm a slut..."

"They're just jealous of you, Woods. Why would you care what those girls think?"

I take a deep breath. "They also said the only reason Ty's interested in me is 'cause he wants to take my virginity, and that scares me...'cause I almost gave it to him the other night."

Henry shuts his eyes for a sec. "That's a lie. He cares a lot about you."

"How do you know?"

"You don't think JJ, Carter, and I had a talk with him?"

"You didn't."

"Did."

"Oh Jesus..."

"Woods, answer me...are you going to give Ty a chance?"

I feel scared. I don't want the whole school talking about me and Ty. I don't want anyone calling me a slut. As captain of the football team, I can't lose the respect of the guys I lead. But my brother and Henry are also right—a vision of me as a thirty-year-old virgin has-been quarterback flashes in my mind. I shudder.

There must be a way for me to be both Ty's girlfriend *and* the star of the football team. Can't I have both?

I mean, the guys watched me do that ridiculous photo shoot and still respected me afterward.

"Okay," I whisper. "I'll give him a chance."

"That's all I needed to know," Henry says. He kisses my forehead, jumps to his feet, and stretches out a hand. "Come on."

We walk outside the potting shed, into a warm pink dusk, and I see Ty standing over next to the tire swing that hangs from an old ash tree. A breeze whips through the grass as I start making my way over to him.

"See you, Woods," Henry says, pulling his keys from his pocket.

"You're not staying for dinner?"

"No, I have a *study date* with Savannah Bailey. But Ty will stay."

Henry disappears around the side of the house to the driveway, and I head over to Ty.

Smiling, he pushes the tire swing toward me, and I catch it and force it away from us. Then I hurl myself at him and he pulls me into his arms beneath the dripping green leaves.

I let him kiss me.

I'm losing myself again, losing track of everything that's important to me. And the thought of that scares me too. I don't want to become one of those girls who loses all control and perspective because of a guy, but even this thought, this warning to myself, is being pushed out of my mind by Ty and his hands and his lips.

He whispers, "Let's go to your room."

• • •

Our clothes are starting to come off.

Mom's volunteering at the hospital, and Dad's still at practice, but I'm not taking any chances. "Ty, hold up," I say, hopping out of bed.

"What's wrong?"

Not answering, I shuffle across the room in my underwear, lock the door, and then rejoin him in my bed.

Things start getting even more intense, so intense we just know it's going to happen, so I say, "Do you have something?"

"Yeah."

He leans over the side of my bed, reaches down to the floor, and grabs a condom from his jeans pocket. I'm a bit scared, but this feels so right. He actually likes me for me. And I just have to have him. Every bit of him. Now.

A little while later, we're still clinging to each other under the covers.

"Want to make this official?" he asks.

"What? Like be a couple?"

"Yeah."

"Sure," I say, smiling.

He brushes the hair out of my face with his pinky finger and cups my chin with his hand. I can't believe we just did it. *It!* It did hurt some, but it wasn't scary…it was…fun and sweet.

Now we're staring at each other and he keeps giving me little kisses. "I've never felt like this before," he says.

"Me either. So why me?"

"You're strong and in control and different and mature. Why me?"

All I can think about is how hot he is, but then I say, "You're smart and cute."

"That's it?" he replies, tickling my stomach. "*That's it?*"

"What more do you want?" I reply, laughing as I squirm.

"Well, Kristen Markum gave me a long handwritten note saying how much she wants me. Along with a picture." He raises his eyebrows at me and laughs.

"Ugh. I hate that girl."

"Why?"

I take a deep breath. "Well, besides the fact that she called me a dyke and a slut and accused me of sleeping with JJ and Henry…"

"What else?"

"Kristen and I were okay friends growing up…and then in seventh grade, we were really excited about going to the Christmas Dance."

I couldn't wait—I had these cool, red New Balances I was going to wear, and Kristen and I bought these matching red cashmere sweaters. I thought I might get to dance with this eighth grader who was kinda cute. Maybe even get my first kiss.

I go on, "And then Carter asked Kristen to the dance, and she sort of laughed in his face."

"Yikes."

"I know. He felt awful, so I got all the guys on my football team to boycott the dance, and I threw this awesome party in my basement instead. We had, like, a slasher movie marathon, and Dad made chili dogs and gave us root beer and told all the guys these epic football stories from when he played with Emmitt Smith and Michael Irvin…and, well, all the guys went back to school on Monday saying my party was better than any dance could ever be."

Ty laughs. "You're hilarious."

"And all the girls at school were really pissed at me 'cause I'd ruined the dance for them, and Kristen told *everyone* that I'd boycotted the dance because no guy would ever want to dance with me."

Because I was taller than all the guys…and huge.

Ugly.

"Ouch," he says, turning to look at the ceiling.

"And I've still never been to a dance."

I don't tell Ty about how after Kristen said that, I decided being a guy was better, because none of my teammates would ever say anything so horrible to me. And none of them ever have.

"Well, I would've gone to your slasher-movie chili-dog party, 'cause you're beautiful," Ty says, smiling.

A knock sounds on the door, and I hear someone fiddling with the knob. Shit! I didn't think my parents would be home for another half hour! Then I roll over and look at the clock—I totally lost track of time. I quickly start pulling my clothes back on. Ty does the same and we're laughing at each other as we struggle with shirts and jeans and underwear.

I hear Mom say, "Jordan, what are you doing in there?"

"Nothing…hanging out with Ty."

I don't hear her say anything else for a few seconds, but then she says, "Well, come on down for dinner. Ty? Can you stay? Mr. Woods wants to meet you."

Crap. I bite my fist and shake my head furiously at Ty, which doesn't deter him at all because he says, "I would love that, Mrs. Woods. Thanks for inviting me." He has this shit-eating grin on his face, so I punch him hard on the shoulder, and he falls back onto my bed. "Damn it, Woods. That hurt!"

I smile at him as he puts his jeans on. After pulling my hair back into a knot, we head downstairs, and I pray that Mom doesn't question why Ty and I were in my room with the door locked.

Sure enough, when she sees us come into the kitchen, she gives me a knowing look, but doesn't say a thing. I'll be in for it later, though. She tells me to carry the roast to the table and asks Ty to grab the gravy, which takes just about everything we've got because we're giggling so hard.

But Ty stops giggling when we walk into the dining room, where Dad is already sitting with his signature bottle of Gatorade. Ty straightens up, seeming to grow by several inches, and wipes the smile off his face. After setting the gravy down on the table, Ty stretches out his hand to Dad and says, "I'm Tyler Green, sir. It's nice to meet you."

Dad smiles and returns the handshake. "Donovan Woods. I've heard a lot about you." Dad gestures at the seat to his immediate right, then points at Ty to sit in it. I sit down to Ty's right, poised to butcher the roast.

"So," Dad says to Ty, "my son tells me you've got a cannon for an arm."

Ty smiles slightly. "Oh, I'm nothing compared to you and Mike."

What? No mention of me? Believe it or not, I can throw just as far and as hard as Mike. Doesn't Ty know that? Between me, Mike, and Ty, Ty's the obvious football prodigy. Maybe I shouldn't be so proud, but it would've been nice to get some recognition from my new boyfriend.

Mom finally brings the corn and bread to the table, and we dig in.

"What are your plans for college?" Dad asks Ty as he grabs some roast.

"No plans yet," Ty replies.

"What colleges are you looking at? Which schools have contacted you so far?"

"None so far, sir."

Dad bites into a piece of bread, chews, and narrows his eyes. "I find that hard to believe."

Ty glances at me and takes a deep breath, so I say, "Just drop it, Dad."

Dad glares at me. "Jordan, just because you have some competition for your position doesn't mean you should be selfish and ruin Ty's college aspirations. If he's better than you, like everyone's saying, you should be helping your teammate to get a good scholarship. Maybe you should tell Coach Miller to give him more of your playing time."

Dad says these horrific things as easily as if he's buying a book of stamps at the post office.

I choke on my lemonade. Tears rush to my eyes as Ty pats me on the back.

"Donovan, please," Mom says, pinching the bridge of her nose. "Jordan has earned her spot on that team. She deserves every second of playing time she gets."

Dad keeps chewing his bread. "Doesn't Ty deserve a chance to play too?"

"Dad, you have no idea what you're even talking about. You don't even know Ty. And you never come to our games anyway." I turn to face my mother. "Mom, thank you for dinner. May I be excused?"

Mom seems on the verge of tears. She nods slowly. Before I leave the room, I steal a peek at Dad, who is chewing on his roast. Does he even have a clue how much he just hurt me? He just embarrassed me in front of my brand new boyfriend. When I find Ty's face, it's impassive. Blank as a bed of snow. Is blank how he really feels about me?

After running upstairs, I throw open my closet and pull out my trainers and put on some running clothes. I storm back through the house, peering into the dining room, and see that Ty's still sitting there with my father, eating as though nothing just happened.

Running down the road in twilight, winding around the little curves near my house, jogging past the cow pastures and a rustic red barn, I keep waiting for Ty to sprint up behind me, announcing that he punched Dad in the face or something. I run for an hour, but Ty never comes sprinting after me.

I can't help but notice that, unlike Henry, Ty didn't tell my dad to shove it or stick up for me in any way. I get that Dad intimidates people, but how could Ty not say *anything*? I'm his girlfriend! I just slept with him, and he just absorbed Dad's attack on me, acting like it didn't happen.

Shouldn't he be out here chasing after me?

revelations

the count? 7 days until alabama

After practice, I leave the locker room and I'm heading to the parking lot when Carrie rushes up to me. I can see Ty standing next to my truck waiting on me, but I stop to find out what she wants.

"Carter told me you and Ty are dating now—I'm so happy for you."

"Thanks."

"Is he, like, an amazing kisser?"

I smile and, without thinking, I blurt out, "He's great." Okay, okay, it's kind of fun talking about Ty. It's not like JJ, Henry, or Carter would want to know how Ty's tongue feels.

Carrie returns my smile. "See, kissing's not that hard."

"Yup."

"He's got a great body too."

"Yup."

"Jordan? You know you can talk to me, right? I'd never repeat anything you say."

I glance at her and nod. It would be great to talk to her about everything, maybe even get some more pointers on what guys like. "Thanks, Carrie. Um, yeah, I had one question, but you can't tell a soul."

"Lips are sealed."

"Um, well, *it*, you know, sort of hurt. Does it always hurt? Because JJ and, um, Henry, say it feels great."

She smiles, shifting her bag on her shoulder. "The first time?"

I nod.

"Sure, it hurts. But they're guys—it always feels good to them. So you've only done it once, then?"

I nod.

"It won't be so bad next time."

"It wasn't *bad* the first time!" We both crack up.

"I'm glad you're happy, Jordan."

"What about you? Are you and Carter…?"

She shakes her head. "He's cool, but I miss Sam, and I need to get over him before I try dating again."

The shock of this statement causes me to drop my bag. "What? But you broke up with him."

"I know…I had to."

"Why?" I say, putting a hand on my hip. I can't believe I trusted her and she doesn't seem to have any clue about anything.

"Jordan…I think you should talk to him about this."

"Why? It's your fault you broke up!" I'm tempted to push Carrie to the ground and punch her face. Henry hasn't been himself at all since she dumped him, and here she is, saying she's still into him! What. A. Skank.

She tightens her ponytail, then peeks at me. "He wants to get back together with me, and you should know that I love him very much…but I can't be with a guy who doesn't love me back."

"What are you talking about? He loved you."

"Is that what he told you?" Carrie says, frowning.

I scan my memory, but now that I think about it, I don't remember him ever saying anything about loving Carrie. But he seemed so happy with her! "No, he never told me that in so many words, but I'm sure he does."

She nods, biting her lip and examining her fingernails. "I can't be with him if he's in love with someone else."

"Who?" I exclaim.

"You don't know?" Carrie says slowly.

I shake my head.

"Think about it. You'll figure it out." She raises her eyebrows, letting me get a good long look at the tears in her eyes, and walks away. Wow, my first attempt at girl talk was pretty shitty considering I made Carrie cry and all. What sucks? I actually liked talking to her about Ty.

Will she ever want to talk to me again?

But what *was* Carrie talking about? Who's Henry in love with? If he's in love, he would tell me. He definitely would tell me.

And then I realize who *she* is.

Me.

• • •

All those nights of sharing a bed
All those times he put an arm around me
All the things he's done to make me happy
...encouraging me to give Ty a chance
He must really love me if he'll watch me date another guy
just to ensure I'm happy
But he's like my brother
And Ty is my boyfriend now
My dream boyfriend

The guy I just lost my virginity to
What's scary?
I'm so hot for Ty
but Henry makes me feel whole
in a totally different sort of way
even if I've never considered jumping him
Fuckety, Fuck, Fuck

• • •

I gave Ty a ride home. Now we're sitting in my truck in his driveway, making out, but all I can think about is Henry. No, it's not like I'm pretending to make out with Henry while kissing Ty; it's that I'm wondering why he never told me about his feelings. Why didn't anyone tell me until after I got my first real boyfriend?

"Ty?" I mumble.

"Yeah?" he says, running his lips on my neck. It feels amazing. He goes up my shirt, and instead of losing myself in Ty, my mind wanders back to Henry again.

"I've gotta go over to Henry's house for a little while, but can I come back over here afterward?"

"Why do you have to go?" He crawls on top of me and pulls on the lever that makes the seat lean back. There's a cracking sound, and we fall back along with the seat, laughing. I kiss him again.

"I'm worried about Henry," I say.

"Why? Is everything okay?" He runs his hand over my hair. His eyes are so blue…I love them. I remember when I thought I would drown in them, but then I suddenly start thinking of Henry's green eyes.

"He left practice without saying anything today and that's weird, and he didn't pick up his phone when I called."

"Can I go with you?"

"It's okay—I can go by myself."

Ty grabs my hand and squeezes it hard. "I'd feel better if I could go along."

I pull my hand from his grip. "Why?"

"I like knowing where you are."

"I'll have my cell."

"I'll go along, and I'll just wait outside for you."

"Ty, I'm fully capable of driving myself to my friend's house."

"Fine," Ty says, kissing my forehead. He crawls off me and climbs out the driver's side door. Then he sticks his head back in the window and kisses me again. "Don't stay gone too long. If you're not back here in two hours, I'm coming after you with a search party."

"Deal," I say.

"Listen," Ty says, shoving his hair off his forehead, "I'm so sorry about yesterday…at dinner."

One big difference between Ty and Henry is that Henry will always say what he thinks when he thinks it, but Ty always comes back to apologize later.

"Whatever," I say.

"No, not whatever. After you left, I was so angry. I explained my entire situation to your parents and let them know I just want to play football and hang out with you, but I'm not going to take your position away from you." Ty strokes my jaw with a fingertip.

"What did my parents say?"

"Your dad seemed furious about the wreck, and your mom seemed sad. She offered to pay for my mom's care, but I refused it."

I love my mom. She acts so selfless. "Why did you refuse?"

"I don't need handouts, Woods. I just need to work hard and stay organized. But I do need a great girlfriend." He kisses me again, but my body doesn't melt or turn to rubber.

Is Ty right for me?

• • •

Before I go to Henry's trailer, I call Mike on my cell. When he answers, I yell, "Crisis major!"

"Calm down, Jordan. What's goin' on? Is Dad acting like an asshole?"

"No."

"Is it Ty?"

"Uh...no. Well, sort of."

"I heard you guys are dating."

"From who?"

"JJ called me. And Mom thinks you're dating him, even if you haven't told her yet. She's hurt you didn't mention it."

"I'll tell her later."

"So what's this major crisis?"

"Carrie Myer just told me that Henry's in love with me!" I only hear silence coming from the phone. "Mike?"

"Well, duh. Didn't you know?"

"What the hell are you talking about?" I say, sighing.

"Jordan, he's loved you forever. It's obvious. Have you not seen how he stares at you?"

"No...he's just...Henry."

"Mom and I always thought you knew but weren't interested. Do you honestly think Mom and Dad would let him spend the night at our house if they thought you were into him?"

"No, I didn't know." I'm shocked; this feels crazy. How could I not have noticed? I thought we were just friends, that this is how our friendship is—very touchy-feely and supportive. My friendships with JJ and Carter are different, because they aren't emotional. They aren't like Henry, who's full of love and loyalty and sweetness. God, I sound like a girl.

"So," Mike says, "now that you know, what are you going to do? Do you like him at all?"

"I'm not sure."

"He's a great guy, Jor, and a great friend. Don't mess with his heart. You have to be up-front with him."

"I will. I'm going to see him right now."

"Call me after, okay?"

"'Kay," I reply. Then I bang my head on the steering wheel.

• • •

I ring the doorbell, and Henry's youngest sister, who's only four, opens the door. When she sees it's me, she yells, "Jordan!" and grabs my leg. Mrs. Henry smiles and after detaching her daughter from me, she gives me a hug and smooths my hair. I always get the feeling she's dying to grab a hairbrush and a curling iron and give me a makeover.

"What's up, Mrs. H.? Where is he?" I say, waving at his other sister, who's twelve.

"In his room. I don't think he's feeling well." She stares down the hallway; her face is a shadow of concern and sadness. I know she and her husband do their best for their kids, but it's definitely been tough for Henry, what with me and Carter, two rich kids of NFL players, for best friends.

Without another word, I go to his room and stand outside the door. I have no idea what I'm going to say, or how to find out if he's actually in love with me. How long has this been going on anyway?

Finally, I decide to go in. I knock, open the door, and find him lying facedown. It's like his head is being swallowed by the pillow. He turns to face me and his blond curls flop all over the place.

"Yo, Woods," he says, rolling over to make room for me on his twin bed. It's tight quarters for two buff football players, both over six feet tall. I have no idea what I'm doing, but I lie down next to him and examine all the glow-in-the-dark stars stuck to his ceiling.

I cough. "Sam?"

"Yeah?" He rolls over, propping himself up on an elbow, and focuses on my face. Usually when he does this, I think it's sweet and friendly, but today when he does it, it kind of makes me all warm, all over my body. His gorgeous green eyes bore into mine, and a curl swings back and forth across his forehead, and I reach up and brush it away. I let my fingertips linger on his temple. He narrows his eyes, then lies down on his back again.

"So how'd things go with Ty last night?" Henry asks.

"Things are fine. I guess we're dating now."

"Cool—I'm glad you're cutting loose, Woods."

I swallow. "Um, so I had a talk with Carrie today after school."

"Oh?" He runs a hand through his hair, then props himself up on an elbow again.

"Why did you never tell me?"

"Tell you what?"

"You know…why you and Carrie broke up."

Falling back down onto his pillow, he rubs his eyes. "What did she tell you?"

"She told me she's still in love with you, and then I about punched her lights out for hurting you, but then she told me she couldn't be with you…because you're in love…with, um, someone else?"

"I'd say that's about right," he whispers. He rolls over to face the wall. "I can't believe she fucking told you that."

"Well, maybe she said that so I wouldn't beat her up."

Henry laughs lightly. "Yeah. Good point."

I roll over and prop myself up on an elbow, looking down at him over his shoulder. "You haven't answered my question. Why did you never tell me?"

He glances in my eyes for a second, then shuts his own. "It would've changed everything, Woods. And I don't want anything to change."

"Yeah, I get it."

I have no idea what I'm doing, but I have this overwhelming urge to hold him, so I curl up against him, spooning him. It's weird, because part of me feels so right right now. The other part wants to be with Ty. I wish Carrie had never told me about why they broke up, because now? I keep thinking about the barrier between Henry and me, the barrier that can't be crossed, the barrier I never even thought about.

Something is stirring inside me. Have I loved him, as more than a friend, all along?

What the hell is wrong with me? I'm used to knowing what's best for me. I guess it's a big decision. Choosing whether to take it to the next level. But it wasn't that hard to decide with Ty. I wanted him, so we did it. It's not so simple with Henry, with someone who has filled ten years of my life.

And what about Ty? He's sexier than Tom Brady, but he's no Henry.

When I'm nestled in tight, Henry flips over, takes his arm out from between us and puts it around my shoulders, squeezing me to him. I rest my chin on his chest and find his eyes, taking everything in.

Then I feel my lips dragging me up toward him, toward his mouth, and right when I'm about to kiss him, just to see how it feels, he puts a restraining hand on my chest.

"We can't, Woods. I'm sorry…"

"Oh. Okay." Embarrassed, I drop my head back onto his chest. Birds chirp outside the window, and I hear his sisters laughing and playing out in the living room as we lie here in silence. I feel tears welling in my eyes. I reach up and drag the back of my hand across my face.

"You have a boyfriend now, Woods! You can't just go around making out with every guy you see," he says with a laugh. After squeezing my shoulder, he sits up, grabs a deck of cards from his bedside table, and starts shuffling. "Let's play some war." He starts dealing the cards into two stacks.

Another tear falls from my eye, but I don't have the strength to wipe it away. All my energy is being used by my heart, because it's having to pump twice as hard just to keep working. Why wouldn't he kiss me?

Henry keeps dealing. When all the cards have been separated, I pick up my stack and shuffle my cards again. Then I look up into Henry's eyes, and he's staring back at me, at my tears, and I see all these tiny wrinkles around his eyes—sadness wrinkles. He frowns, biting his lip.

"What the hell just happened?" I say, staring over Henry's shoulder at his Jerry Rice poster.

"I don't want anything to change." He throws down a card, a five. I throw down a nine. I sweep both cards away and back up into my stack. He throws down a king, I throw down a four. He sweeps the cards away.

Should I tell him that everything already *has* changed?

I throw down a seven.

a debate

Ty:

Damn, he's fine.

Damn, he's a good quarterback.

Damn, he's nice and sweet.

Damn, he's a good kisser.

Damn, he's buff.

Damn, he's great to his family.

Damn, now that I know about Henry,

I'm not sure Ty and I are right for each other.

Henry:

I love the way his curls flop around and hang across his forehead.

I love how he never just lets me win. I have to earn it.

I love how he touches me just because.

I love his loyalty.

I love how when we sleep head-to-toe,

he always finds a reason to sleep head-to-head instead.

I love his unconditional support.

I love his spontaneity and crazy sense of humor.

I love his stupid dances.

I love…him.

carter

the count? 6 days until alabama

Ten thirty a.m.

In the potting shed, sitting up against a bag of fertilizer.

I just can't go to school today. I write in my journal:

Love hurts worse than getting slammed by a 250-pound linebacker

After playing war in silence yesterday afternoon, and except for saying, "I don't want anything to change," Henry didn't give an excuse for why he didn't kiss me. In his defense, I didn't ask again either. I just sat there hoping he'd change his mind.

Since I never skip, Mom came in to check on me this morning.

"Is it your father?" she asked. "Because he feels horrible about how he behaved at dinner the other night."

I shook my head.

"Is it Ty?"

"No," I replied, burying my face in the pillow like Henry does. Remembering what Mike said yesterday, I blurted out, "Oh yeah, Mom, I'm dating Ty now, I guess."

She smiled and clasped her hands together. "Good. Your father and I like him very much. Come downstairs for some breakfast if you feel better."

I still don't feel better.

My cell rings. Before checking the caller ID, I try to guess who it might be. It's either Ty or Henry. Please be Henry. Please be Henry. I look at the screen. It's Carter.

"Yo," I say.

"Woods, what the hell are you doing?" he says. "Get your ass to school or Coach won't let you come to practice this afternoon."

"I don't feel good."

"What's wrong?"

"Everything."

Carter doesn't respond. We're great friends, but like with JJ, we don't spend a lot of time talking about hopes and dreams and puppy dogs and shit. We're just good friends who hang out, eat, and play ball together.

"Want me to get Henry?" he says finally.

"No!"

"Woods, what's going on? Do you need me to come get you?"

"Yes, please come get me. Let's go to Waffle House," I say.

"You got it. I'll be there in twenty. You owe me, though. I'll have to skip cooking class, and I was gonna learn how to make dumplings today."

"I'll buy you a lifetime supply of dumplings," I say, hanging up before Carter can change his mind.

I run back inside, take a quick shower, and put on the underwear that Henry liked—the black ones. It's not like I think Henry will see the underwear today; I just hope they'll be good luck. God, clues were all over the place, and I didn't pick up on any of them. When a guy notices your underwear, that means he's looking, Jordan!

Henry said he didn't want anything to change, but does he actually mean that? How can you be in love with someone for forever and not be willing to take a chance when it finally hits you in the face like a linebacker?

• • •

After Carter and I have ordered enough food to feed ten people, I slide the salt and pepper shakers over in front of me. I stack salt on top of pepper, then yank pepper out. Salt falls straight down onto the table, not spilling a lick. Carter takes the shakers and stacks pepper on top of salt. He pulls salt out, but pepper comes down at a weird angle, spilling all over the table.

My phone buzzes. Ty texts me: Where are you?

I don't answer him.

Instead, I take a sip of Diet Coke and say, "What's going on with Ohio State?"

"They're still interested," Carter replies.

"And you're not?"

"I'm going to sign with them—my dad's got it all set up."

"But?"

"Um, you know, I love playing ball, but I don't know if I want it to be my life."

Nodding, I stack pepper on top of salt.

"It's kind of like it's not my life. I mean, it's my dad's life. It's what he expects me to do," Carter says, running his fingertips through the mess of pepper he spilled on the table.

This is huge. Carter never opens up like this. "What do you want to do?" I ask.

"I dunno…cook?"

"Cook."

"Yeah, I want to cook, like I want to become a chef."

This is just insane. No doubt, if he wants it, Carter has a future in the NFL. And he wants to cook?

Is this how people think of me? Jordan Woods is a girl and she wants to play football? Shouldn't she be playing with makeup and clothes and strutting around the mall? *What the hell is wrong with her?*

So I guess I shouldn't judge Carter. No wonder he's always talking about stuff like Chianti and L'Auberge Wherever.

Thinking about how much I'm beginning to enjoy writing, and how hard this must have been for him to bring up, I say, "Carter, if you want to become a chef, you should become a chef."

Carter's gaping. "Really?"

"Yeah—I play football 'cause I love it. You don't need anyone's permission to do what you love. You should just do it."

Carter pouts his lips and clenches a fist. "Okay, I will. I just have to figure out a way to tell my dad and not give him a heart attack."

"Good luck with that. But can't you play football *and* take cooking classes at Ohio State?"

"I guess. I mean, that's probably what I'll do, but I just feel like it's not me, it's not my decision, it's not me living my life. I've never gotten to figure it all out."

"Sometimes you have to do things you don't want to do. To get something better, you know?"

"Yeah. So you gonna tell me what's up with you, Woods? You've been weird for like two weeks."

"Well, most of that was Ty."

"I kind of figured that. You're together now, so why skip school?"

"How's Henry today?" I ask as the waitress brings plates of hash browns and eggs and waffles to our table.

"Fine, I guess. Tired. He said he was out late with Kristen Markum."

Kristen? Is Henry freaking kidding me? He went out with her knowing what she said about me on Monday?

Hearing this makes my eyes tear up again. I grab the plastic ketchup bottle and squeeze it as hard as I can, spraying ketchup all over my hash browns. I try to bust the bottle, squeezing harder and harder until there's nothing left but hash browns drowning in a mound of ketchup.

Feeling the empty bottle disappear from my hand, I glance up and see Carter placing it on the table and putting his hand into mine where the bottle was. He squeezes my hand and moves around to the other side of the table to sit next to me. "Talk to me."

"I thought he loved me."

"Who? Ty?"

"No...Henry."

"Of course he loves you...I love you too. And so does JJ."

I look up at Carter, who puts an arm around me. "Not like that."

"Oh." Carter starts to fidget, squeezing my shoulder unnecessarily hard. He doesn't say anything else—we just sit here for the next hour, picking at the waffles and hash browns and playing the salt and pepper game. I'm glad he's here with me, even if he's not saying anything. Sometimes friendship is just that, just being with someone.

Then Carter's cell phone rings. Peeking at the screen, he takes a deep breath before answering. "Yo...yeah...yeah..." He focuses on my eyes, puffy and stinging from all the tears. "She's okay...we're at the Waffle House out on the highway...yeah...bye."

"You did *not* just tell him where we are?"

"You need to talk to him." Carter picks up the check and goes to the cash register, then comes back and drops several dollars on the table. "Henry's gonna come pick you up. And I shouldn't be here." Carter pats my back one last time and leaves.

trades

I hop into Henry's truck, and he drives. I have no idea where we're going. In silence, he winds alongside stacks of hay and beneath tree branches that hang over the back roads. Which one of us is going to speak first?

I know he saw my puffy eyes when he first pulled up, but he chose to focus on a Dumpster instead. It's bad if your best friend in the world would rather look at a Dumpster than at you.

Ty texts me: I need to know where you are.

I don't text back.

Finally, Henry parks out by the Cumberland River, and we get out and walk toward a dam. Now that it's September, the weather is turning cooler. I like it. I can smell the leaves—they'll change color soon. I want to get rid of this tension, so I run down along the banks of the river, heading nowhere. I expect Henry to jog after me, to race me, but he just keeps walking slowly.

Henry doesn't want to race?

I run for five minutes, then take a seat on a fallen log. I look down into the shallow water at the tiny fish and tadpoles swimming around. When we were little, Henry and I used to go out to the creeks near Lake Jordan. There, we'd spend all day trying to find crayfish, or as we called them, crawdaddies. The trick to catching a crawdad is to grab him right behind the neck like you'd catch a snake. If you don't, the crawdaddy will nick you with his pinchers. We got pinched all the time, but it was always worth it when we finally caught a giant four-inch-long crawdad.

Now I'm wishing we had never grown up, because I don't know what's going to happen today, but it can't be good. My tears fall into the shallow water, hitting the rocks and fish.

Henry finally sits down next to me on the log, but we don't touch.

"Jordan?" he says.

"Yeah?"

He picks up a small, flat rock, then stands and skips it twice across the surface of the water. What a poor showing—I can skip a rock more than two times. I dig around next to the log and find a heavy, flat stone, dimpled with grooves and peppered with black specks. I stand and skip it three times. I rule.

"How are you?" he mutters.

"Remember when Nomar Garciaparra got traded from the Red Sox to the Cubs?" I start.

"Yeah," Henry says, picking up another flat stone. He skips it across the water three times.

I scowl. Oh, it's on. Bending down, I scrounge beneath the log for another flat stone. "So later, when Nomar started playing for the Oakland As, he came back to Boston for a game, and it was like he was still a player for the Red Sox. Everyone at Fenway gave him this mad standing ovation that lasted, like, a whole minute."

"Yeah?"

"Yeah, it was like nothing had changed. The Red Sox fans still loved him, and he got all teary-eyed and shit."

"Yeah."

I take my newfound stone and skip it three times. Crap. There must be a stone here that's capable of doing four skips. "But you know, things *had* changed. He wasn't really a Red Sox player anymore. He was an Athletic."

Henry sighs. "What are you trying to say?"

"I'm trying to say that, even if we aren't both Red Sox players anymore, we can, uh, still give each other standing ovations when we visit each other."

Henry flicks another stone, but it only does two skips. Then he laughs, wiping curls off his forehead. "Woods, I don't speak Shitty Sports Metaphor Language. I have no idea what you're talking about."

I go over to him and touch his arm. "If you had told me you liked me as more than a friend, I totally would've agreed that the feeling is mutual."

Henry nods. "But you didn't know that before," he whispers. "Until you heard how I felt."

"Yeah, I'd just never considered it. You're like my brother…well, you *were* like my brother."

"And now?"

"And now…" I pick up a big rock and throw it into the water, causing a huge splash. That felt great. "You're a lot more than a brother." I turn to stare at him again.

Henry picks up an even bigger rock and throws it into the river. It makes a much larger splash than mine. Damn it.

I search for a bigger rock, find one and pick it up, launching it into the river. My splash totally kicks Henry's splash's ass.

"Woods, I just want to stay Red Sox."

"What?"

He laughs. Turning to face me, he puts a hand on my hip, rubbing it softly with a thumb. "I love you..."

"I love you too," I blurt.

He smiles, but it's not a happy smile—it's like a resigned smile. "I really do love you, Woods, but I like what we have now. And if we go off to different colleges, it'll be horrible. We'd be apart all the time. I couldn't handle that. I'm already dreading it."

"Me too..."

"And if I'm already dreading it, and we're just best friends, imagine how bad it would be if we were more...what if we broke up? We'd never get over it. Well, I never would." He picks up another rock and feeds it to the Cumberland.

"I get it. But Kristen Markum?"

His face goes all red, and he kicks some rocks into the river. "Won't happen again."

"You mean, you're not going to screw around with girl after girl anymore?"

"I dunno. I gotta cope somehow."

"Your *coping*," I say, making finger quotes, "is fucking with my heart. You were breaking it long before I even knew how you felt. I've been worried about you."

"You don't think your being with Ty has just about killed me?"

"Dude!" I laugh. "It's been three days or something."

Henry grins, stretching out his hand toward mine. "Friends?"

I take his hand. "Red Sox forever." And then, thinking of Kristen Markum, I shove Henry into the river, creating a much bigger splash than any of my rocks.

• • •

That evening, as I'm writing, Ty comes into my room without knocking. I barely have time to hide my journal.

"Why haven't you been answering my calls?" he asks in an agitated tone.

"I'm sorry—I've had a rough day."

"I don't care, Jordan," he shouts. "When I call, you need to answer the phone."

This is all too much. I close my eyes. Through clenched teeth, I say, "Excuse me? Don't talk to me like that. Ever. Understand?"

When I open my eyes, I find Ty curled up at the end of my bed, tears rolling down his face. "I thought something had happened to you," he whispers. "I thought—"

"You thought what?"

"You might be hurt. Or dead. I didn't know about my parents for hours…I couldn't reach them on their cells."

I crawl down and pull Ty's head into my lap, stroking his hair. "It's okay. I'm okay," I whisper. "I'm sorry."

Ty stays in my arms for the next hour. What causes the worst pain I've ever felt? Watching a quarterback, who prides himself on maintaining control, fall apart.

stupid fish plaque

the count? 5 days until alabama

After our weekly gorging at Joe's, JJ and I are hanging back at my place, playing some Nintendo Wii. JJ's kicking my ass at the game where, riding a cow, you race around a dirt track and knock down scarecrows for points.

"Woods," JJ says, as he pummels a few scarecrows with his cow, "you'd better not miss any more practices. I hate snapping to your pretty-boy boyfriend."

"Shut up, man," I say as I totally miss a line of five scarecrows. Why do I suck so bad at video games?

"Ty's so picky," JJ continues. "Like, if I don't hike the ball at just the right speed and angle, he gets ticked off."

"I'll talk to him."

"You'd better. Or Carter and I are going to kick his ass."

"Please don't kick my boyfriend's ass," I say, exasperated. Why are all the men in my life acting like total boneheads?

The door to the basement squeaks open, and I hold my breath, waiting to hear who opened the door. Is it Henry? Please God, let it be Henry. At school today, we didn't speak at all, which is strange considering we have four classes and the same lunch period together.

How are we supposed to be Red Sox forever if, after one day, he's already acting weird again? I wish Carrie had never told me why they broke up.

"Jordan?" Dad calls out from upstairs. "May I see you in my study please?"

I drop the Wii controller on the floor and trot up the stairs to the study, where I stand in the doorway.

"Come on in."

Dad's sitting at his desk, shuffling through paperwork. He never invites me in his study—it's like his inner sanctum of football. He might as well have a "No Women Allowed" sign on the door because Mom hasn't been in here in ages. I don't even think it gets cleaned—it's full of empty pizza boxes and Gatorade bottles, coated in layers of dust.

"Take a seat," he says, gesturing at the leather sofa where he and Mike watch film of past games. My head says there's no way he'd ever watch film with me, but my heart is hoping that's why I've been invited here. Doubtful. When I sit down, I hear a crunch, so I stand up and find that I've just sat on a Cheeto. Gross.

"Jordan," Dad says as I wipe orange dust off my butt, "I was wondering if you'd like to go to the go-kart track and out for milkshakes tonight. You know, like we used to?"

"Like when I was ten?"

Dad nods.

I lift a shoulder. "Not really."

"Okay," he mutters while staring at his paperwork. "Listen, I'm so sorry about what I said at dinner the other night. You're right—I didn't know anything about Ty or his family."

I shrug.

"Can you forgive me?"

This is about Ty? I'm so mad at Dad right now, I could easily smash his flat-screen TV. I want to grab his stupid football-shaped lamp and hurl it out the window. And though it's sacrilege, I'm considering smashing his Joe Montana autographed picture.

"I can forgive you about Ty, but how could you say I'm selfish? I'm just trying my hardest to do what I love. You compliment Henry and Ty, but you never ever mention me! You'd support every other football player on the freaking planet before me!"

I can't believe I said that out loud. I throw my head back and peer at a trophy case, realizing he has one of those plastic singing fish plaques on his shelf. I thought Mom threw that out years ago! He's gonna be in huge trouble with Mom for keeping that dumbass fish.

Dad turns to see what I'm looking at. "Oh hell," he says, rubbing his head as he looks at his fish. "You're not gonna tell Mom, right?"

"Depends," I say.

"On?"

I pull a deep breath. "I want your support. I want you to come to my games."

"Jordan—I love you, but I've seen what this game can do to people..." Dad stands up and stares out the window at Lake Jordan. "I don't want that for you."

"Why's it okay for Mike, but not for me?"

"I've seen the concussions, I've seen knees wrecked, I've seen legs broken in four places." Dad exhales deeply. "Mike can handle all that."

"So can I! You've always gone to his games. You never come to mine. And I've worked so hard." I'm tempted to stand up and smash that stupid fish plaque over his head.

Dad's eyes meet mine. "I know you work hard and I know you're a great player…but I get scared. I don't want to see anything bad happen to you…I couldn't handle it." His voice trails off.

"But I love football and have a chance at playing for Alabama!"

"Why do you want to go to Alabama so bad?"

"It's the best football team in the country." Duh.

Dad picks up a pen from his desk and clicks it a few times. "I don't think they'll ever let you play."

"What are you talking about? Of course they will."

"Don't you find it a bit weird they invited you to visit campus and basically offered you a full ride before seeing you in person?"

My head droops a bit. I wondered the exact same thing. "Maybe they saw some of my tapes from last year."

"And then they make you pose for a calendar? It's like they want you to be their trophy. And I would've said the same thing if this had happened with your brother, you know."

"Dad, I'm one of the best football players in Tennessee. Did you ever think Alabama may actually want me to win some games for them?"

Dad shakes his head and clicks the pen some more before chewing on the end of it. "You understand the long hours? The hard hits you'd take at the college level? Dealing with sixty Jake Reynoldses *all the time*—the jerks who will constantly degrade you?"

"Yes, Dad. I understand all of that."

Dad looks at me for a long time, then picks up a football from the floor and tosses it to himself.

Twirling the ball as he goes over to stare out the window again, he says, "Jordan, I love you and I'm so proud of you. I'll try to be better."

I feel a snag in my throat and swallow hard. "I love you too, Dad."

"So, I called down to Texas to speak with Buddy Simpson about your boyfriend."

Buddy is one of Dad's old friends. He used to play for the Cowboys and now just hangs out in Texas not doing much of anything except following the football circuit. If something's happening in Texas regarding football, Buddy usually knows about it.

Dad tosses the ball up and catches it. "A bunch of schools were interested in him after last year, but he's been ignoring all their calls and emails," Dad says. "Even Florida showed some interest."

"So he lied to us?" I reply, tracing the lines of my palm with a fingertip.

"Yup."

I take a deep breath. "I'm not surprised. He's really only concerned with what happened to his parents…and making sure his sister is okay…"

"I'd like to help him—and his sister. I'm worried about him."

Thinking of Ty crying last night, I say, "I'm worried too."

"Taking care of a sister and a sick mother is not something a seventeen-year-old should have to do."

"Yeah. I don't know what I can do, though. He doesn't like being taken care of. He likes being in control."

Dad tosses the ball to me. I catch it and toss it back to him. "Well, let's give him some control then. Tell him I'll loan him whatever money he needs to take care of his mom. But he has to pay me back with interest."

I smile. "I like that idea."

"Think he'll go for it?"

"Maybe. I'll talk to him about it."

"Good. You know, Jordan, even if he was just some guy on the math team, not some great football player, I'd still want to help him out."

Sometimes the *great* Donovan Woods can actually be pretty cool.

it gets worse

the count? 4 days until alabama

As I pull into the school parking lot before our third game, my cell rings. Mike.

"Hey, bro, guess what?"

"What?"

"Alabama's athletic director sent me another email. He said a friend of his, an Alabama alum, is coming to look at me tonight." Since recruiters are technically only allowed to watch a player once during the season, sometimes college coaches ask boosters or alumni to come see the rest of the games. It's kinda shady, but that's just the way things work. "And he thanked me for doing the photo shoot," I add.

"Great."

I shut off the truck's engine. "Are you coming with me to visit campus Tuesday?"

"Can't. Big history exam that day." As I get out of the truck, Mike says, "Listen, you need to dress up when you go. Wear a dress and fix your hair, okay?"

"Why?"

"Remember when I talked to the coach at your first game?"

"Yeah."

"He told me that if you join the team, the coaches will expect you to act like a lady."

"What? Why?"

"I dunno. Probably 'cause they want to give off a certain impression."

"Oh."

"Well, if you want to play for Alabama, you'll have to do what they say. You might as well go ahead and start now."

"Okay," I reply with a shaky voice. "I guess I can do that." Even though it's not me at all. What does acting like a lady have to do with rocking on the football field?

I remember when I decided to play ball. I actually started out as a cheerleader, for a Pop Warner team, the Hornets. Mom dressed me up in skirts and ribbons and handed me pompoms. Henry played quarterback, and instead of cheering, I was searching for crickets behind some trees, because good bait is always important. The ball went out of bounds—I ran to grab it, and hurled it, and the ball flew farther than any of Henry's passes. He caught the ball, ran back to me, and said, "Darn, you're good," with this big smile on his face, his two front teeth missing. "Wanna come out for pizza and air hockey after the game? With me and the team?"

That day, I traded my pompoms in for cleats. And Henry became a wide receiver. And part of my heart became his.

I go to the locker room and get changed into my pads and uniform, and then head out to the benches. I see Henry chatting with Carter, beneath the moonlight and the starry sky. I'm about to go tell him about Alabama and the talk with Dad and Ty freaking out on me, but Coach takes me aside.

"Coach, Alabama's sending someone to watch me tonight!"

Coach doesn't smile, just clutches his clipboard to his chest, and stares out at the field where some of the guys are warming up.

"Woods, I don't know what's going on with you, but you can't miss two practices without saying a word to me."

I focus on my cleats and mumble, "Sorry, Coach."

"If it weren't for Alabama, your ass would be on the bench, and Ty would be playing. Got it?"

I look up into Coach's eyes. "It won't happen again. Promise."

"It'd better not, or Ty will be our starting quarterback. You're the leader of this team, Woods. These guys expect a lot from you. If you don't care enough to show up at practice, or at least talk to me about whatever the hell's going on in your life, then you don't deserve to be captain."

I've fucked so much up.

I just need to get this game over with. Prove to Alabama that I'm such an awesome player, it doesn't matter how I dress. So good that I could even wear kilts and play bagpipes all over the place, and they would still love my football skills.

"I'm sorry, Coach."

"Get going on drills," he demands, gesturing at the field with his clipboard.

I jog over to Henry and pull him away from everyone, but instead of being all loose and playful like he usually is, he seems stiff.

"What's up?" he asks, with his hands on his hips.

"Remember when I first started playing ball? And I was looking for crickets and then I threw the ball back to you?"

"No."

What? We used to joke about this all the time. How I destroyed his future career as quarterback of the Titans.

"What do you need?" he asks, focusing on the cheerleaders, who just came out of the locker room and are getting set up on the track surrounding the field. The crowd starts waving and cheering as Carrie does a back-handspring.

"Just need to talk about some stuff," I reply. Is he okay? He won't look me in the eye. "Want to come over after the game? To watch a movie?"

"I can't." He waves his arms around in a circle, warming up.

"Oh. What are you up to tonight?"

"Nothing."

"Then why won't you come over?"

He stares down at the field before saying, "Because I don't want to, Woods."

I stuff my helmet on my head and bite into my cheek. He's never done this to me before.

"I need some time alone," he says.

"Captains," a ref yells, and Henry jogs to the sidelines without speaking to me again.

Tears trickle out of my eyes as I slowly buckle my chinstrap.

All I know is, without him as my friend, I'm just a shell. Just a playbook without any plays.

• • •

"Woods," Coach shouts, waving his clipboard. "The coin toss."

I look up, my eyes blurred from tears, and find Carter and JJ jogging over to me. JJ takes my elbow in his hand and leads me toward the center of the field, whispering, "What's wrong?"

"An Alabama alum is here to watch me," I mutter.

"Awesome," Carter replies, patting my back.

"I feel sick," I reply.

"You'll be great," JJ says. "Northgate's got nothing on us. Not with you playing."

"Carter—can you do the toss?" I whisper, and he nods and pats my shoulder.

Carter calls heads. It lands on heads, and he chooses to receive.

"Thanks," I mumble as we head back over to the benches. Henry runs out to receive the kickoff, and while I shake my shoulders out and drink some Gatorade, Ty comes over.

"What's going on?" he asks, focusing on my eyes.

"Nothing."

He puts his helmet under an arm and rubs the back of his neck with his other hand, peering at me. "You've been weird ever since, you know, we slept together. I'm sorry if you felt pressured, or anything..."

I so don't need this right now. "It's nothing like that. I just need to get in the zone for the game."

Northgate's set to kick off, and Henry's bouncing around in the end zone getting ready to receive, and my knees are shaking. Partly because of the Alabama alum, partly because of Henry, but mostly because I feel like my entire life has changed in the past month.

I'm used to being in control, and even that's gone. I gave up what I had left when I missed practice.

"You sure you can play?" Ty asks. "We can't afford to lose if we want to make it to district finals."

"I'm fine," I say through gritted teeth.

"Good. Watch out for the corner blitz."

"I know."

He shakes his head and looks at the crowd for a few seconds. "After the game, we need to talk," he says before walking over to stand next to Coach.

"Fanfuckingtastic," I whisper to myself.

I scan the bleachers, looking for Mom—she's sitting with Mr. and Mrs. H. I bet Henry's glad his dad finally showed up at a game. Must be nice.

Mom stares down at me, concern etched on her face. "I love you," she mouths.

I wave at her, thinking how much I needed that.

Northgate kicks off, and Henry makes it to the thirty before getting slammed to the ground. The team and fans erupt, screaming and clapping, and the marching band plays the fight song. I run out onto the field with JJ, who slaps my back before we get into formation. My hands shake.

"Z-spread eighteen," I shout, and JJ hikes me the ball. I pedal three steps backward, scanning the field, then zip a short pass to Higgins. He jumps to catch the ball, but it sails right over his head. Incomplete.

"Damn it," I mutter. I wipe my sweaty palms on my towel.

Back into formation.

JJ hikes the ball again. Keeping it simple, I hand off to Bates, and we gain fifteen yards. Nice.

Next play? I hurl the ball downfield to Henry, but he sidesteps a cornerback at the last second, and the ball lands directly in the cornerback's arms.

Interception.

The cornerback darts down the field toward our end zone, and I sprint over and throw myself at him, but I miss the tackle, flip, and crash onto my back in the grass. Ow.

The cornerback scores. Because of me.

Because I'm playing like complete crap.

When I run back over to the benches, Carter says, "It's okay."

"It's not." I only had one interception all last year, and that's when I blew it at the state championship.

I can't blow it again.

JJ and I hustle back out after Northgate kicks off. "You've got this, Woods," he says.

On the first play, I hand off to Bates for ten yards, but then on the next snap, I fumble the ball and as I'm scrambling after it, I get slammed and my helmet smashes into the ground. My nose feels like someone hurled a brick at it.

Thank God JJ recovers the ball.

We lose the ten yards.

Breathing deeply, my hands keep shaking as I huddle with the guys. "Go route to Henry. I'm bombing it straight down the field."

We clap and break, and JJ hikes the ball again. I dash back several feet, avoiding the linebacker trying to sack me, and throw the ball to Henry, but it's way short. I don't get enough on the throw and he runs the wrong route—he was supposed to come back on the ball, but didn't.

Northgate intercepts again.

"Shit!" I yell. Higgins manages to tackle the safety who got the pick on me, but it's Northgate's ball again.

I can hear my teammates shouting from the bench, including Ty. "What the hell, Woods?" he calls out with his arms spread wide.

I want to yell, "It's not only my fault!" but captains don't do that.

Henry jerks his head, looking pissed at himself for messing up the play.

My eyes dart to the fence where all the recruiters and alumni stand, and locate the hat with the Alabama logo on it. The guy's writing in his notebook and shaking his head. Another guy wearing an orange Tennessee windbreaker is with him. Great. So now Mike will know I've screwed everything up.

I'm a total waste of Alabama's time.

I yank my chinstrap loose and storm over to the bench as shit-loads of cameras blind me like strobe lights. Damned reporters.

Coach walks up, while Henry stands as far away from me as possible, but I can see him panting hard as he glances at me. Good. He should know this is his own damn fault. Couldn't he have waited until the game was over to destroy my heart?

"What's going on, Woods?" Coach asks.

"Sorry, Coach," I say with a shrug.

He whispers, "I'm sorry too. Your head's not in the game. You're benched."

And right then, when I look up into the stands for Mom, I see Dad kiss her cheek and take a seat.

losing it

Ty ran the score up 28–7
Didn't even look like he was trying as
    he bombed the ball down the field over and over again
        to Higgins
The *great* Donovan Woods finally showed up
Sat in the stands
Signed autographs
Smiled and laughed
It's like he knew I'd get benched
It's like he knew Ty would play
So he came
A recruiter from Mike's school showed up
Gawked at Ty
Even worse?
Mr. Henry came
But didn't get to see Henry play for real
Ty didn't make one pass to Henry
I ruined my chances with Alabama
I threw my helmet at my locker

the daily special

will i still get to go to alabama?

After the game, Ty and I head to my truck. He still wants to talk.

In the parking lot, we pass JJ and Lacey, who are pawing at each other up against her mom's Ford Taurus. Classy.

Celebratory rap music rings out from Higgins's truck, and Carrie and Marie are encouraging Carter to start a bonfire.

"Nice game, Ty!" Kristen calls out, sitting on the tailgate of Higgins's truck, displaying lots of leg.

"Good job, Green," Higgins adds, slapping Ty's back.

And no one looks at me.

Then I see Henry sitting on the tailgate of his truck. With Savannah Bailey standing in front of him, in between his legs. He kisses her and pulls her hips up against him and digs his fingers into her brown hair, and I feel this pain shoot up my arm and into my chest.

"Is there one girl at this school he hasn't been with?" Ty asks, nodding at Henry.

"Good question."

When Henry comes up for air, he looks over Savannah's shoulder at me. He mouths, "I'm sorry."

Even though I'm pissed, I give him a slight smile.

"Give me your keys," Ty says, thrusting his hand in front of me.

"Why?"

"Give me the keys. You're not driving when you're upset."

"I'm not upset!" I snap.

"My dad died in a car wreck, you know."

I reluctantly pass Ty the keys; he rips them from my hand, and we climb into my truck and start to drive. A minute later, I get a text from Henry: I'm really sorry.

I text back, Okay.

But it's not that simple.

Thinking of Henry gives me this dull ache in my chest. How long will *that* be around?

Back at Ty's place, I wait in the living room as he visits his mother, who I still haven't met, then I watch as he checks on Vanessa, who's already asleep. He brushes her hair away from her face and kisses her cheek.

I sit down on Ty's bed, but he doesn't join me. He pulls out his desk chair, flips it around toward me and straddles it. Folding his arms across the back of the chair, he rests his chin on his forearms and stares at me.

"You okay?" Ty asks.

"I'm fine."

"So your dad actually came tonight..."

I roll my eyes. "Maybe it's karma for skipping practice for the first time ever."

"Um, after the game, your dad introduced me to a coach from your brother's school."

"Figures," I say, burying my face in my hands. But like with Henry, I won't be selfish. I'm not going to sacrifice Ty's future just because I have a horrible relationship with my father. Looking up, I say with a smile, a real smile, "I think it's great."

Ty focuses on the carpet. "Are you sure you're okay?" He moves to sit with me on the bed, taking my hand in his. "I'm so sorry I yelled at you the other night."

"I'm fine…wait. I talked to Dad about his offer to help pay for your mom's care so you can go to school." Ty sighs and falls backward onto his pillow. I lie down on the pillow too, taking in its scent of soap. "And I know you don't want to accept a handout—believe me, I wouldn't either—but would you be willing to consider a loan? To be paid back with interest after college?"

Ty stares at me. "Interest."

"Yeah, like once you're on an NFL team."

"There's no guarantee I'll end up in the NFL."

"You'll never know unless you try. And you can do that with my parents' offer. Even if my dad is the biggest asshole on the planet to me, I think you should take advantage. If not for you, for Vanessa. You'll be able to provide so much more for her if you go to college."

"Woods, before I can accept this, I need to know if you really want this."

"Of course I want you to take the money and focus on college."

"I meant us. Do you want to date me?"

I do have feelings for him, even if they aren't as strong as my feelings for Henry. He's cute and sweet and he totally gets what football means to me. "Yes, I do."

"I really like you. And with everything that's happened to me in the past few months, I can't handle much more."

"What do you mean?"

"When I moved here, I didn't know what would happen. I didn't care about much of anything except for making sure my mom got taken care of and my sister got to school. Once I got that figured out, for now anyway, I thought I could be selfish for a little while. I could play some ball, make some friends…and then I met you."

I'm biting my fingernails, feeling that dull ache making way for a much deeper pain. Who ever knew Jordan Woods was capable of being such a heartbreaker? I'm plundering the hearts of football players, left and right. It must be the new pushup bras.

He continues, "And I'm falling for you—I love how driven and serious you are. I can't believe everything that's happened between us. But if you're not going to be mature and serious about me, like I thought you would be, I want out now."

"You want out?"

"Yeah. If you're going to keep running off with Henry, doing God knows what, I want out. I don't like it when I can't reach you on your cell. I *need* to know where you are."

I must be awfully important to him since he's freaking out like he did with his sister. Picking up a phone isn't a lot to ask. "I'll pick up from now on. I'm sorry about the other day. I left my phone in the car." Lie.

"Good. And I can't stand how Henry gets to stay over at your house at night. So can you not…?"

Um, okay. Allowing Ty to have a say in my friendship with Henry is *a lot* to ask. I've been dating Ty for what? Five days? And he's already questioning my friendship with Henry? I guess he has a point. I mean, two days ago, I was totally ready to end this for Henry. But if Henry and I can't be together, and if he's going to act like a jerk, and if he's going to kiss another girl in front of me, I'm not putting my life on hold.

I won't give up my boyfriend for the best friend who said, "I need some time alone."

"Ty—I'm serious about me and you. Henry's been my best friend for ages, and I can't imagine not hanging out with him, but he won't be sleeping over anymore. And just so you know, nothing has ever happened between us. You're the first guy I've ever wanted. You're my first everything."

"*What?* Why didn't you tell me? Jordan…"

I grab his hand. "I'm fine. But what's not okay is how you played tonight. Why didn't you pass to Henry?"

Ty glances at me sideways. "Um…I dunno…I guess I'm a little pissed at him. I heard he disappeared from school on Wednesday, just like you. And since you didn't answer my calls…I thought…"

I cut him off, leaning in for a kiss. With this kiss, I'm telling Ty I'm serious, that I will continue being serious.

When unrequited love is the most expensive thing on the menu, sometimes you settle for the daily special.

having cake

the count? 1 day until alabama

After practice on Monday, Ty and I are leaning up against my truck, making out in full view of the junior varsity football team. I open my eyes slightly and see a couple freshman guys gawking at us. I grin, continuing to kiss Ty. When I open my eyes for a second time, I see Coach staring at us, pulling off his cap and scratching his head. He focuses on his clipboard but looks up at us again several times before finally going back into the school. This must be the weirdest thing a football coach has ever seen: two quarterbacks making out.

When I open my eyes for the third time, Henry, who must've finally come out of the locker room, is staring at us. I stop kissing Ty the minute I see Henry, because the last thing I want is to hurt him.

"Woods, would you please get a room? Seriously," Henry says.

Ty pulls away from me and grins, staring into my eyes as he says, "What do you need, Henry?"

Henry looks only at me. "Can I have a minute?"

"Go ahead," Ty says, but he doesn't move. He turns and puts an arm around my waist, as if to protect me. As if to tell Henry he's not leaving me alone with him.

"Alone," Henry says.

"Anything you want to say to her you can say to me," Ty says, digging his fingertips into my hip bone.

"Ty," I intervene, "I can talk to my best friend if I want to." I jerk my head at my boyfriend, and he nods. After squeezing my hand, he shuffles across the parking lot to talk to Higgins.

"He shouldn't be acting like that," Henry says, glaring at Ty.

How Ty acts is none of Henry's business. "What's up?" I ask, leaning back against my truck.

"Can I stay over tonight? I need to get out of the house."

I stuff my hands into the pockets of my mesh shorts, pissed that he wouldn't hang out with me when I needed him, more than ever. What happened to "needing a break"?

"Henry, we can't do that anymore. I have a boyfriend now."

"So? I thought nothing was going to change."

"That has to change. I can't share a bed with another guy if I have a boyfriend."

"I'm not just another guy, Woods."

"I know, but I promised Ty you wouldn't stay over anymore."

Henry seems furious. He's biting down on his bottom lip and he keeps kneading his palm like he's getting ready to punch something. "JJ and Carter were right. They told me Ty was going to start taking over everything. He already got your position. He's controlling the plays on the field. And now he's taking you away from me."

"That's not true! He got to play on Friday because I skipped practice and messed up."

"He didn't throw a single pass to me on Friday!"

"That's not my problem. Maybe you weren't open."

"I can't believe you just said that. You know I was open."

"I don't know what to tell you, Henry. You can't have your cake and eat it too."

"Like you even know what that means."

I'm crying now. "Excuse me? I'm not stupid. It means you can't expect everything to stay the same."

"We agreed that nothing would change between us!"

"Ty and I are dating now. He's asked one thing of me—he doesn't want you sleeping over."

"Jordan..." Henry grasps his curls with both hands.

"And if you didn't want him to take me away from you, maybe you should've talked to me when I needed you so badly on Friday." Tears slip down my cheeks. "Maybe you should've taken me when you had the chance."

"Look, Woods, we're not ever going to be together, so you need to get over me."

"I already was." Lie.

Henry glares at me. "I'm glad to hear I mean so little to you that you're already over me."

"This is all your fault, Sam. You control all the plays here. But you haven't even stopped to consider what I might want. You just tell me how it's going to be. Well, Ty doesn't control me, and you don't control me. I control myself."

Henry laughs a mean laugh, staring up at the cloudy blue sky. "What a crock of shit. You let everyone else control you and tell you how to feel. Ty, Kristen Markum, Alabama, your dad..."

"Screw you. If I lose my scholarship to Alabama, it's all your fault."

I get into my truck and slam the door shut and bang my forehead on the steering wheel. Through my tears, out of the corner of my eye, I see Ty come back, and he and Henry start yelling at one another outside my truck. I turn the ignition and drive off.

How could everything in my life fall apart in less than a month?

• • •

Later that evening before *Monday Night Football*, I'm in our exercise room, slamming my fists into the punching bag.

"Asshole," I yell, throwing a punch. "Moron," I say, kicking the bag, causing it to swing back a few feet toward the wall. "I thought you loved me! You screwed up my chance at Alabama." I throw a few more punches but stop when I hear a loud slurping noise coming from the doorway.

Peeking around the bag, I find Carter leaning up against the doorframe drinking a Slurpee through a straw. Glancing at the clock, I see the game will be on in a few minutes. Thank God, the Vikings and Chargers will be a great distraction from thinking about how mad I am at Henry.

"Hey," I say, ripping off my gloves, then wiping sweat off my forehead using my tank top.

"Hey," he replies, walking over and handing me a Styrofoam cup. "Thought a Slurpee might cheer you up. It's pink lemonade." He smiles as I start sucking it up through the straw. Damn, it's good.

"Thank you," I say as I take a seat on a weight bench and lean over onto my knees. "I've gotta talk to Dad about buying a Slurpee machine from 7-Eleven. We could put it out by the foosball table."

"But then JJ and I would never leave your basement," Carter says with a laugh.

"Fine with me. At least you guys haven't become total boneheads."

Carter lets out a deep breath, then starts slurping again.

"Is Henry okay?" I ask, though I'm not sure I want to know what happened after I left today.

"Well..."

"Just give it to me straight, man. Does he hate me?"

"Of course he doesn't hate you." Carter stares up at the ceiling, not looking at my face. "He loves you more than anything," he says quietly, then pulls the lid off his cup and starts shaking it, trying to get more Slurpee out.

"What aren't you telling me?"

Carter takes another deep breath. It's so weird for us to be talking about this stuff. I mean, shouldn't we be planning how we're going to beat the shit out of Cool Springs on Friday?

"Um, well," he says, "Henry sort of punched Ty in the jaw, so then Ty busted Henry's nose, and then Henry gave Ty a black eye, all before we could break them up. They're not really hurt, but they both got suspended from school for a week and can't play on Friday."

"Good."

Carter clears his throat. "Good?"

"Yeah, good," I say, getting up and kicking the bag again. The chains hanging from the ceiling groan as the bag swings around in circles. "That means I'll get to play the whole game, and I won't have to throw the ball to Henry. Jerk." As the words tumble out of my mouth, I immediately regret them. This must be how Jake Reynolds feels every time he speaks. A sob rises in my throat as I plop back down on the weight bench. I can't believe how much I've hurt Henry and Ty.

And Alabama will never want me now.

Sitting down, Carter slides up next to me, slipping an arm around my waist. I lean against his shoulder and say, "I promise I'm never gonna lose sight of football again."

Carter nods, then grins. "Yup, who needs a girlfriend when you've got good friends and football?"

JJ suddenly appears in the doorway, chuckling. "Should I leave you two alone so you can get it on with a football?" He yanks his wallet out of his pocket and finds some condoms, which he throws at us.

"Shut up, man," I say, dodging the condoms, "or I'll kick your ass out of here for good, which would suck for you because I'm gonna get Dad to buy us a Slurpee machine."

JJ has a hurt look on his face as he stares down at the cups in our hands. "Where's my Slurpee?"

Carter shakes his head and points toward the door. "Can we just watch the game and play some foosball already?"

"Let's do it," JJ says, clapping his hands together as if we're in a huddle. I love my friends—I feel better already. Now all we're missing is Henry. Even if we both acted like total jerks today, I want to know that he's all right and right here beside me.

After I kick JJ's and Carter's asses at a few rounds of foosball, the Vikings are winning by ten points, and Henry still hasn't shown up.

"Is Henry coming?" I ask JJ quietly. I bite my lip so I won't let another sob out.

After throwing a dart at the dartboard, JJ finds my eyes for a sec, then looks away. "I don't think so, Jordan."

trip to alabama

The plan?

I'm going to tell the athletic director and coaches that Friday night was a fluke 'cause I got food poisoning from Joe's All-You-Can-Eat Pasta Shack, that it won't ever happen again, and pray to the football gods to give me another chance.

The only reason they might is because my dad is the *great* Donovan Woods.

Can't believe I'm banking on my name to get me through today.

Mom and I have just arrived at the University of Alabama...with Dad. When he got into the car with us, I gasped so hard I'm surprised I didn't puncture a lung.

I hope I get to throw a ball around and meet some of the other players today, but mostly I'm excited to see the stadium.

Because of Dad and Mike, I've been on pro and college fields hundreds of times, but this is the first time it will be *my* field. Box seats and beer and VIP boxes for my fans are a big step up from the metal bleachers and cheap frozen pizza at the high school level.

Since Alabama expects me to act like a lady all the time, I'm wearing a new grey dress and heels, so I'm stumbling along as we enter the quad, which is covered in red and white Roll Tide flags. I'm drawing tons of attention to myself, including the stares of some hot guys. I mean, they're nothing compared to Ty, but I'm glad to know there will be more of a selection than at Hundred Oaks. Some of them smile at us.

I elbow Mom. "Dad better watch out. These college guys are totally into you."

Mom laughs. "That would certainly be a scandal. The wife of the Tennessee Titans' quarterback runs off with a twenty-year-old college boy."

Then a dark, tall guy with wavy black hair walks by us. He puts Ty to shame. "Uh, Mom, if you ran off with that guy, no one would blame you."

And then Dad gives me a noogie and says, "What did you say?"

"Dad! Stop," I exclaim, smoothing out my hair. "Everyone's staring!" I add, which makes him laugh even harder.

We find the athletic department, where the director greets us enthusiastically, offering us coffee and soda and food, and if we didn't cut him off, I'm sure Mark Tucker would've offered us a trip to a spa and a vacation and a new Ferrari.

I did my homework. Before Mr. Tucker became the Director of Athletics for Alabama, he was an Olympic skier. Then he totally wiped out in the final seconds of a race, blowing the gold medal. So he retired, vowing never to ski again or some shit like that. Afterward, he went back to college and got a degree in school administration.

"We're so glad you could visit," Mr. Tucker says, shaking my hand and patting my shoulder simultaneously. "Come on in my office." He ushers us in, and I can't help but notice all the people in the outer office gawking and pointing at me. What's that about?

Mom, Dad, and I take a seat, and then I hear Mr. Tucker raising his voice, so I turn and see he's speaking with his assistant. "Where is he?" Mr. Tucker says quickly, quietly.

"He said he doesn't have time for this," the assistant replies.

"I don't care what he says," Mr. Tucker exclaims. "Tell him to get over here. Now."

Who doesn't have time for what?

Dad furrows his eyebrows as he turns from watching the exchange. He glances at me.

Mr. Tucker shuts the door and sits at his desk, unbuttoning his suit jacket. "So, Jordan, what are you thinking of majoring in?"

I kinda want to say creative writing, but the last thing I need is my future teammates to hear that I'm beginning to like poetry. "I'm not sure yet, Mr. Tucker. Maybe physical therapy? I dunno."

Mr. Tucker laughs lightly. "No need to worry. You have a lot of time before you have to figure that out. So, I trust you know how excited we are that you're considering joining our program?"

"Yes," I reply. "Sir, about the game on Friday, I wasn't feeling well and didn't play my best, but it won't happen aga—"

He waves a hand at me. "Don't worry. Happens to the best of us."

I played like complete suckage on Friday night—how could he not care? Maybe he's sympathetic 'cause he flew off the Super G ski track and landed in some pine trees. "But—" I say.

"Your performance on Friday night isn't an issue," Mr. Tucker adds.

"But she threw two picks," Dad exclaims. Confusion and anger cloud his face.

Mr. Tucker waves his hand again. "So you know we want you to be part of our recruiting team here at Alabama?"

"Um, yes, sir. But I don't know what that means exactly. Would you want me to talk to potential players or something?"

Mr. Tucker fiddles with a paperweight on his desk. "Well…yes, but that's not all." The office door slams open to reveal a man in khakis, a windbreaker, and a baseball cap. Typical coach-wear. It's the head coach, Rob Thompson. He's one of the best coaches in the game; his specialty is rearing future NFL quarterbacks. Some of the best have come from this school.

I jump to my feet and smooth out my dress, but before I can introduce myself, Coach Thompson says, "You've got five minutes, Tucker. I have practice."

My mouth falls open. The coach doesn't have more than five minutes to speak with a potential quarterback? One they are prepared to give a full ride to? What the hell does that mean?

"Can you give us ten minutes, Rob?" Mr. Tucker asks. "And I'll give Mr. and Mrs. Woods and Jordan the tour of the grounds and stadium."

"You've got five," Coach Thompson says, shaking Dad's hand, then taking a seat on the other side of Mom.

She purses her lips and clutches her bag. She looks like she might just stand up and leave.

Does Coach Thompson have a problem with the Titans? Maybe he's acting like an asshole because my bro plays for Alabama's main rival, Tennessee. But wait, I would be an asset because I know how Mike plays and thinks. Coach Thompson must realize this. So what the hell is this dude's problem?

Dad sits back down in his chair and rubs his eyes with a thumb and a forefinger.

Mom speaks up first. "Mr. Tucker, you were discussing Jordan's role in recruiting? What exactly does that mean?"

"We'd like for her to speak at some events and do more photography work for us—like she did for our boosters' calendar. We'd also like her to be the face of our charity program. We encourage foster children to consider sports, showing them that a team can be a family too."

I feel confused. Mike doesn't have to do any of this stuff for Tennessee. Sure, they make posters of him, but it's not like he has to pose like I did. And I'm all for charity and helping kids, but with practice and school and traveling to games, how will I have time for the charity program, speaking at events, and recruiting?

"Okay. I can do those things," I say, peeking at Coach Thompson. "But it seems like all these extra activities might affect my practice time. Shouldn't I be focusing on playing ball?"

Coach Thompson crosses his arms and stares out the window. "You won't be playing football for me anytime soon."

"But she has the best QB record in the entire state of Tennessee," Dad replies, and my heart gets so excited I think it might stop.

"It's true—I threw for 2,653 yards and thirty-one touchdowns last year alone."

The coach laughs, but it's not a nice laugh. "I think my five minutes are up, Tucker." He stands and walks out of the office, letting the door slam behind him. I'm going to play for this jerk?

Glaring at the door, Mr. Tucker runs a hand through his hair and rises from his desk. "I'm sorry about Coach Thompson. He's under a lot of stress...you know, with the upcoming game against Florida. Let me show you around the school."

"I sure hope the coach won't be treating my daughter like that when she's a member of his team," Mom says, folding her hands in front of her.

"Oh, of course not," Mr. Tucker says, ushering us out of his office.

"Let's go home," Dad says to me.

"But I haven't seen the field yet."

"I think we've seen enough."

"Dad, come on," I whisper, bouncing on my tiptoes. He'd use any reason to get me to leave. So what if Thompson's in a grouchy mood today? "Alabama's my dream."

Dad rests a hand on my shoulder and, eventually, he nods. "It won't hurt to take a look around campus."

We get to see some of the classrooms and the new state-of-the-art gym and workout facilities, including a new pool. All of this bores me. I want to see the freaking stadium! It takes about an eon for us to go out there, what with these awful shoes I'm wearing, and with Mr. Tucker's need to point out every last little thing, from where the bike racks are located to where I could pick up a newspaper to where students are allowed to smoke. I would hope an athletic director would know better than to point out ashtrays to a quarterback, but whatever. I'll trudge through Mr. Tucker's show-and-tell as long as I get to see the field eventually.

Finally, when we get to the stadium, Dad says, "I'll stay outside." He drops to sit on a bench. "I've gotta make some calls."

He slumps, staring at the parking lot, and doesn't take his phone out.

Mom and I head inside Bryant-Denny, which is so beautiful, even better than on television. The lush green field reminds me of an Irish countryside, and I can even smell the freshly painted yard lines. The giant red scoreboard and the little tunnel leading from the locker room make me giddy. I can't wait to run out of it. Water coolers are set up on the benches and staffers are carrying balls and assorted equipment across the field.

I indulge in a few daydreams, including one where I run for a touchdown with only ten seconds left in a tie game, and another where I throw for a touchdown from the fifty-yard line. Okay, that would never happen, but it's a cool dream. I'm knocked out of my fantasies by some guys who jog up to me. Wearing red and white sweats, these guys are even hotter than the ones we saw on the quad. I recognize them from pictures on the team website—three wide receivers and two running backs.

They all smile at Mom and say, "Hello, ma'am." At first, I'm convinced they're southern gentlemen, but then one of them says, "And you must be Jordan Woods, our new poster girl!"

The other four guys laugh. So that's how it's going to be? Not only can I play quarterback, I can play this game too: sarcastic bitchiness. In my heels, I stumble up to the asshole wide receiver who just taunted me and say, "Yup. I'm the new poster girl. But only because you weren't pretty enough. Wouldn't want to scare the fans away."

"Oooh," and "Ouch," the other guys say, slapping the wide receiver, who bats their arms away.

"You're prettier than I thought you'd be," says one of the wide receivers. "I've changed my mind. I won't mind you being on the team one bit. I hope we get to be roommates." He sidles up next to me and wraps an arm around my shoulder. Ugh. Jake Reynolds's face flashes in my head. I shove the wide receiver away, hard, but immediately regret it because this is not how a lady acts. Hopefully none of the coaches saw that. The receiver stumbles away, laughing.

Mr. Tucker is fiddling with his cufflinks, glancing back and forth between me and the Alabama players. "Shouldn't you all be getting ready for practice?" Frowning, he points toward Coach Thompson, who is inspecting a player's knee and talking to a trainer at the same time.

The guys all say "Yes, sir" and jog off toward the benches.

I've been lucky for the past ten years, because everyone in Tennessee just accepted me. What should count is that I'm a great football player, a great person. It shouldn't matter that I'm not a boy.

But I guess that's how everyone sees me. Girl first, football player second.

Just like Henry said.

It gets worse when the wide receiver who groped my shoulder comes running back over, tossing a ball. He throws it at me so hard that when I catch it, I stumble backward because of these stupid shoes. He laughs at me. Kicking the heels off, I decide I'm not gonna let this asshole embarrass me. He's standing there, stretching his arms out and smiling, just daring me. So I run back a few steps, but instead of throwing the ball at the wide receiver, I draw my arm back and launch a thirty-five-yard bomb over the dude's head. Oh yeah, it goes exactly where I want it to. The ball flies right between two of the other assholes, hitting the water cooler. Ice and water explode all over the rest of the players who made fun of me.

They turn and gawk at me. Even Coach Thompson is staring. It takes every bit of decorum I possess not to slap my hips with my hands and yell, "Suck it!" at these fools.

The wide receiver gapes, then shrugs, saying, "Nice. But you've still got a lot to prove, little girl."

I glare back at him, wishing I had another ball, because I think his helmet needs a good dent in it. Considering I led my team to the state championship game last year, I *have* proven myself. Girl or not, I'm an awesome football player.

"Well, Mom, I think we've seen enough. Thank you, Mr. Tucker, for your time." I elbow Mom, who is smiling at the water cooler mess on the other side of the field.

"Oh, yes, thank you, Mr. Tucker. I'm glad there's at least one gentleman at this school," Mom says.

Hell, I don't think I've ever seen anyone act more embarrassed than Tucker. His face is red and sweaty and he's dabbing at his forehead with a handkerchief.

Dad's right. Alabama never wanted me to play in the first place. No wonder Mr. Tucker didn't care that I fucked up royally on Friday night.

So now what?

• • •

Later that night, I'm sitting on the dock, writing in my journal while watching the moon shine down on algae-covered Lake Jordan.

When I got home, I stripped out of that stupid grey dress and hurled it into the closet, where I found Henry's blue Converses nestled up against a pair of my cleats. And then I noticed his Super Mario Bros. T-shirt, so I sat down in the closet and cried into Luigi's face. And then I realized how psycho that was, so I ran out to the lake. (After putting clothes on, of course.)

As soon as my back was to the house, I started bawling. I don't know what's worse: me screwing up on the field and letting my team down, or knowing that Alabama never wanted me to play in the first place.

Now, I keep opening and closing my cell phone. I want to call Henry so much. But why bother?

And I can't call Ty to tell him about my trip to Alabama. I can't show weakness in front of him—he'll just question my ability to play, like he did on Friday night.

Carter and JJ just aren't good at talking about this stuff. Besides, I don't want anyone to know about what happened today. I mean, if Alabama isn't going to let me play, then why should I keep starting for Hundred Oaks? Might as well give Ty the chance so he can get a full ride to college.

He does deserve and need it…

I write in my journal:

> Even though Dad's always been kind of a jerk, at least I had my dreams and my best friend.
>
> Well, Henry's gone, and my dream school wasn't a dream after all. I have a boyfriend now, but the perfect boyfriend was right in front of me, and I didn't even notice.
>
> It's like I flew into a black hole, into a void where I don't know anything.

"Jordan?"

I look over my shoulder as I snap my journal shut and sit on it. Dad's standing behind me with his hands in his pockets.

"You okay?" he asks.

"Please just leave me alone…"

Dad comes and sits down next to me, pulls his loafers off, and dips his toes in the lake.

"You gonna say *I told you so*?" I mutter.

"Course not. Just came out to check on you—you haven't said two words since we left Alabama. Mom's worried." He jerks his head toward the house, so I turn and see Mom staring from the kitchen window, arms folded across her stomach.

Dad asks, "Why do you want to go to Alabama?"

I shake my head at him as I wipe my nose on my sweatshirt sleeve and repeat what I said the other day. "It's the best football school in the country." Duh.

He elbows me in the side. "Hey—what about Ole Miss? I turned out okay, didn't I?"

I let out a tiny laugh.

Dad swats at a mosquito before saying, "Alabama may have the best record ever, but that doesn't mean it's the right school for you."

"And what is the best school for me, Dad? One without a football team?"

He blows a bunch of air out and leans back on his hands, staring up at the clear sky. "I don't know what the best school is for you, but you should explore all your options."

I pull my knees up to my chest and wrap my arms around my legs, thinking how embarrassing it would be to admit to my teammates that I'm not going to Alabama. Maybe if I play harder and better than ever before, they'll have no choice but to let me play.

"Alabama's what's best for me, Dad."

He reaches over and rubs my back. "Your mom and I love you no matter what you choose, but I hope you'll seriously think about other colleges."

"Whatever."

Dad pauses for awhile. "How about we go fishing together on Saturday? Just you and me?"

So he can try to talk me out of Alabama again? "No thanks."

Pain washes over his face as he stares into my eyes and takes his hand off my back. Then he gets up and heads back to the house while I keep staring at the moon and slapping at mosquitoes.

When I turn to see if Mom's still looking at me from the kitchen window, I don't find her staring at me. But Dad is.

Maybe he does care, but I can't forget how he's tried to get me to quit for years. This is what Dad's been waiting for—for me to give up.

But I'm not going to.

• • •

FROM: Woods, Jordan

TO: Tucker, Mark (Athletics, University of Alabama)

DATE: Saturday, September 18, 07:32 a.m.

SUBJECT: Thank you

Dear Mr. Tucker:

Thank you again for inviting me to visit campus last Tuesday. I enjoyed meeting Coach Thompson and the players. While I look forward to helping with recruitment and working with charities that the University of Alabama supports, I'm very excited to play for the football team one day.

I've enclosed a video from our fourth game. Last night, we beat Cool Springs 42–14. I threw for 300 yards and ran for one touchdown. Please feel free to share my video with the coaching staff.

I'm looking forward to visiting campus again and to joining the team next year.

Sincerely,
Jordan Woods

• • •

FROM: Tucker, Mark (Athletics, University of Alabama)
TO: Woods, Jordan
DATE: Monday, September 20, 09:13 a.m.
SUBJECT: RE: Thank you

Hi Jordan:

I hope you enjoyed your tour of campus. It was great to meet you and your family. I'm sorry you couldn't stay longer.

We just received the proofs for next year's calendar, and we love your photos. We're most excited you're joining our community.

The University of Alabama Alumni Charity Ball is on December 4, and we'd appreciate it if you could attend. Several alumnae have expressed a desire to meet you.

Yours truly,
Mark Tucker

loneliness

the count? 21 days since the fight with henry

"For our next project," says Mr. Majors, the music appreciation teacher, as he paces back and forth across the classroom, "you and your partner will pick a classical composer. I'd like you to prepare a ten-minute oral report, including a biography of the composer's life and an analysis of how that composer's work has influenced current music. Also, I'd like you to play a recording of a piece of music written by that composer and tell us what it means to you. So now, please go ahead and choose your partner and your composer."

Even though he hasn't been speaking to me, I automatically look at Henry, who's sitting in the desk right next to mine. He glances at my face, and after frowning his perpetual frown, he turns away. "Yo, Bates," Henry shouts across the room. "You're with me."

Bates, who was already moving to sit with his usual partner, looks from Henry to me and back at Henry again. Shrugging, Bates says, "Sure, whatever."

"Henry," I say. "Come on."

He shakes his head. "I'm working with Bates on this one."

A bunch of other kids start looking at me and Henry, wide-eyed. The whole class is silent.

I pick up my pen and start clicking it repeatedly, hoping the noise will distract me, because I'm about to smash something. No other football players are in this class. Maybe I just won't do the project—I don't give a shit about this class anyway.

But if I get a bad grade, the principal could make Coach bench me for a few games until I bring my grades up. And I can't stand to miss a game—I've gotta prove to Alabama that I'm the best high school quarterback in the country, and that when I join their team, they should let me play.

As I put my head down on my desk, I feel a tap on my shoulder. I turn and find Marie, Henry's recent fling.

"Hey," she says softly. "I need a good grade on this, and since you did great on that disco project, I was hoping we could work together?" She smiles at me.

"Um, sure."

"Cool," she says, sitting down next to me. "I've been meaning to tell you I loved your flea-flicker play the other night. You don't see those very often."

My mouth drops open. "You know what a flea-flicker is?"

Marie shrugs and pulls a nail file from her purse, running it across her fingernails. "Sure. Who doesn't?"

• • •

After practice, I try to catch Henry before he drives off, but he leaves without saying anything. Leaning up against my truck, I pull out my cell and dial his number, but he doesn't answer. This must be the hundredth time I've tried to call him in the past two weeks.

Why oh why did I accuse him of not being open on the field? And why did I defend Ty? Why didn't I just let Henry sleep over anyway? How do I fix this? "Sam," I say to his voice mail, "I hope you're feeling okay. Can we please talk? I miss you so much."

As I'm flipping my phone shut, Carter walks up. "You okay?"

I nod. "Just worried about Henry."

"Me too," Carter replies as he shifts his bag from one shoulder to the other.

I'm sick of talking to my journal about this shit. "Do you think I should dump Ty? Do you think Henry would go back to normal if I did that?"

Carter focuses on his sneakers and clutches the strap on his bag. "I dunno…"

"I mean, I like Ty, but it's not like I'm in love with him or anything."

"Hmm…"

"And we've been having sex, and I worry that it's a mista—"

"Whoa, whoa," Carter says, waving his hands. "Too much info."

"Oh." I wish Carter could give me some advice, some answers. "I think I'm just gonna go over to Henry's place."

"Cool—good idea."

Carter and I knock fists, and then I get in my truck and drive over to Henry's trailer. But when I get there, his truck is gone. His mom's station wagon is here, though, so I jump out of my truck and jog up to the front door.

Mrs. H. answers after I knock and gives me a hug, smoothing out my hair with her fingers. "He's not here, sweetie," she says, looking up at me.

"That's cool. Know where he is?"

"I think he was going to lift weights and run at the gym with the personal trainer."

"Personal trainer?"

Mrs. H. keeps playing with my hair as she says, "Yes—I'm so

happy your father introduced Sam to that trainer. He'll be in such good shape for college and will have a much greater shot at getting a scholarship. I'm so glad Sam has your family—I don't know what we'd do without your father's support."

I smile. So Henry took Dad up on it? "Right," I say, acting as if I know everything. His mom clearly doesn't know about what's happened between Henry and me. "Well, I'll get going then. Thanks, Mrs. H."

She pats my back. "I'll tell him you stopped by."

I hop off the front stoop and start heading to my truck, but then whip around. "Mrs. H.? Could you also tell him that…I'm so proud of him and that I love him?"

She smiles. "Of course—but he already knows that."

• • •

Later that afternoon, when I get home, Dad stops me in the driveway.

"Let's go over to the drive-in tonight," he says.

"The movies?"

"Yeah."

If I didn't feel so awful about Alabama and Henry and every other thing going on in my life, a smile probably would've popped up on my face.

I love the old drive-in movie theater. In the summer, Henry, Carter, JJ, and I like to go buy a few tubs of fried chicken, and we sit in lawn chairs in front of the big screen and try to guess what the characters are saying on the screen, because we never turn the speakers on.

"I don't wanna go to the movies, Dad."

"Why not? You love it there."

"I do, but not with you."

Dad rubs his eyes. "Why won't you ever do anything with me?"

"Let's see. You'll get Henry a personal trainer, but the only thing you'll do for me is say that Alabama will never let me play, as if you're doing me a favor, and then you go along on the trip to campus so you can rub it in, and then you tell me to consider other options? You never even considered my first option."

"That's not wha—"

"Whatever, Dad."

I storm off to the backyard, looking over my shoulder to make sure Dad isn't following me, and then duck into the potting shed, where I lie down on the dusty ground and use a bag of mulch as a pillow.

Sunlight flickers through the window as I stare up at the cobwebs, looking for patterns like people do with clouds. I spot a section of web that looks like the state of Tennessee. One time Henry spotted a web that looked like a Snoopy Pez dispenser.

Several minutes later, I hear Mom speaking, so I get up and peek out the window. I wipe some dust from the glass. Mom's standing in her garden, surrounded by tall sunflowers, talking to Dad.

"I'm sorry, dear," she says, cutting a sunflower stem, "but Jordan's never going to let you in any part of her life until you start paying attention to what she wants."

"I don't want to see her get hurt. I watched one of my best friends die at thirty-eight because he'd had so many concussions..."

"I know, but football is what your daughter loves most right now. You can either share that with her, or you can share nothing with her. Probably for the rest of your life. Your choice." Mom turns around and heads back inside the house carrying a bundle of flowers, leaving Dad alone.

He rubs his eyes some more, then lifts his head, and touches one of Mom's sunflowers.

• • •

Three nights later, I carry the mac and cheese to the table and take a seat, glancing at Henry's empty chair. Ty's at work tonight and Mike and Jake are at school, so the dining room feels lonely with just me, Mom, Dad, and Dad's bottle of Gatorade.

I spoon some salad and macaroni onto my plate, then grab a few pieces of bread. I miss having to wrangle with the guys for food.

"So, Jordan," Dad says, wiping his mouth with a napkin. "How's school?"

"Fine, I guess." Lie.

"Where's Henry been?" Mom asks.

"I dunno…he's busy." Lie. I bow my head and push my macaroni around on my plate.

"I've been thinking I should call him," Mom says.

I don't respond. I sip my lemonade, which has recently lost its flavor. I don't even enjoy my favorite drink anymore because it only reminds me of Henry. God, what doesn't remind me of him? Even macaroni reminds me of Henry.

One time when we were about nine, we decided to open our own restaurant in the family room. We called it the *Bite and Tackle*. I was the chef and Henry played the waiter. We draped a tablecloth over the coffee table and set it with plates, glasses, and silverware from the kitchen. Using markers and glitter and construction paper, we drew up an elaborate menu that listed our offerings: fruit punch Kool-Aid, microwaved popcorn, fish sticks, and macaroni and cheese. Our only customers were Mom and Mike, but it was a hell of a lot of fun, and Mom left Henry a twenty-dollar tip, which we promptly spent on skee-ball at the arcade.

"Jordan—what's going on with Henry?" Mom asks.

I shrug. Out of the corner of my eye, I see Dad shaking his head at Mom, as if to tell her to drop it.

"So," Dad says. I hate all these awkward attempts at conversation. "Who are you playing tomorrow? It's Davidson County, right?"

I turn to stare at Dad. Did he just bring up a game? One of *my* games? Holy shit. I nod frantically. "Yeah—we're playing Davidson County. It's homecoming."

Mom smiles at Dad and pats his hand. Dad stares down at his plate, chewing on his salad. After swallowing, he says, "I'll be there."

"Cool," I reply. I take a sip of lemonade and notice I can actually taste the sugar now.

mom

Nothing like me—
Never direct—
Behind the scenes
Always behind the scenes
She asked what's going on with Henry
Surprising
She never intrudes
During dinner, Dad made me feel better
After dinner, the emotions all rushed back
Empty
Alone
Confused
Lost in the woods
I lie on my bed
Wishing I was looking up at glow-in-the-dark stars
Like in Henry's room
But my ceiling is bare
Like my heart
Tears are falling
Mom comes in
Curls up next to me
"Mom"
It comes out as a cry
"I know"

I bet Henry would find it hilarious if I knocked him out of the car. The old Henry would have, anyway. "So you're really taking Carrie to the dance?"

Carter grins a tiny smile. "Yeah, but it's not like a date or anything. We're going as friends."

I feel a smile edging on my lips, secretly hoping it ends up becoming a date. Carter deserves a nice girl.

I'm going to the dance with Ty, of course, and although he vehemently objected to "attending a suck-ass gym social," JJ is taking Lacey. But I don't know if Henry's going.

Finally, after what seems like a year, Henry and Carrie climb out of the convertible and join the rest of the homecoming court. Now the marching band is playing the Whitney Houston song, "I Will Always Love You," and I'm feeling like I could barf at any given moment. Everyone besides Henry, even the other football players, is dressed up in a tux. He chose to stay in his football uniform. I want to laugh, I really do, but I'm still so pissed at him. I'm sad too.

Because Kristen is still obsessed with Ty or something, the cheerleaders asked him to "preside over Carrie's coronation," meaning he gets to put the cheap-ass crown on her head. He kisses her cheek as she steadies her plastic tiara. Before he walks away, he and Henry glare at one another.

As head cheerleader, Lacey puts a stupid cheapo crown on Henry's head. She smiles at him, but he just frowns back at her. He glances over at me for a sec, but then pulls the crown off and starts twirling it on a finger. Shaking her head, Carrie reaches over, takes the crown off his finger and puts it back on his head.

Doing everything I can to ignore the marching band's rendition

who the hell was in charge of homecoming?

the count? 25 days since the fight with henry

As some sort of prank, God decided that Henry should be homecoming king and Carrie Myer should be queen. It's halftime, and I'm suffering through this horrible ceremony where they ride around the track in a scrambled-egg-colored convertible and wave at the crowd.

The marching band is playing the theme song from *Titanic*, "My Heart Will Go On."

"Seriously?" Carter says as he leans up against the fence surrounding the field. "Didn't that movie come out, like, decades ago?"

"Even I could plan homecoming better than this," I reply. "Yellow convertibles and *Titanic*, my ass." I toss a football up in the air and catch it. Taking aim at Henry, who's still sitting on the back of the convertible, I pretend to throw the ball at him.

"Don't even think about it," Carter says, laughing softly.

"I bet I can knock Henry out of the car," I say, taking a few hops back and rotating my arm as if I'm about to launch a long bomb.

"You definitely could, but I know you don't want to embarrass Carrie like that. Give me the ball."

Reluctantly, I drop the ball into Carter's outstretched palm, but of "When a Man Loves a Woman," I'm staring at the scoreboard, which reads 17–0 (Hundred Oaks, of course), when Carter says, "You're playing an amazing game, Woods."

"Thanks—so are you." I pause. "I've really been stepping it up, you know, to show people what I'd play like in college."

"Did Henry tell you that Western Kentucky and Auburn sent him letters about playing for them next year?"

I smile down at my cleats. "No, but that's great."

"So have any other schools called you or emailed or anything?"

I take a deep breath and peek at Carter out of the corner of my eye and twirl the football. "Um, not really. No."

"What?" he says, his eyebrows raised higher than a goal post. "Think it's 'cause everybody already knows you're gonna take Alabama's offer?"

I think back to when Mike was a senior, and just about every team in the whole freaking country called him. Everyone from crazy-big teams like LSU and USC to not-so-impressive teams like Appalachian State in Boone, North Carolina. Even after Mike made a verbal commitment to Tennessee, letters still flooded our mailbox and the answering machine filled up, like, three times a week.

"I don't know why no one's calling," I tell Carter. "But yeah, probably 'cause of Alabama." Lie.

It's because I'm a girl. Just like Henry said.

Feeling tears welling in my eyes, I wrap my arms around my waist, clutching my red and black jersey, and lean back against the fence, soaking up sappy marching band music until Mrs. H. comes rushing up to me.

"Jordan, sweetie," she says, "I need a picture of you with Sam. Come on." She grabs my hand and pulls me over to where the homecoming court is standing. Mom and Mrs. Carter are there too, oohing and ahhing over Carrie's pink satin dress.

"Let's get a picture of the four of you," Mom says, pointing at me, Henry, JJ, and Carter. As Henry rips the crown off his head, I stand between JJ and Carter as our moms get camera happy. They make us trade places about a billion times and encourage us to smile while passing their cameras back and forth to each other, showing off their shots.

Finally after about fifty freaking photos, a teary-eyed Mrs. H. says, "Sam, Jordan, I want one of just the two of you."

Carter steps away, leaving a gap between me and Henry. We simultaneously take a step closer together, but we don't touch. "Smile!" Mrs. H. says, so I put on a fake grin, but when I look out of the corner of my eye, Henry's face is blank.

This is the closest he's been to me in three weeks, so I take my chance. "Sam, I'm so, so sorry."

"Me too," he replies softly.

"Can we talk about all this?"

"Jordan, I just can't right now," he whispers, glancing at my face once before walking to the bench, where he pulls his helmet on over his blond curls and starts reading a playbook.

• • •

Standing in the locker room after the game, which, of course, I rocked, I'm getting ready for the dance. I'm actually excited.

I've never been to a dance, and I've certainly never worn a girly evening gown dress thing. Mom and Vanessa took me to the mall and while I played video games in the arcade, they picked out this awesome black number with a slit up the side. It had better drive Ty crazy, because I can't breathe in this damned thing. I have to admit it looks really pretty, though.

Looking in the mirror, I brush my hair, trying to make it look good, but I can't seem to do anything with it.

The door to the locker room slams open and Carrie walks in. I haven't spoken to her since that day at practice.

I don't say anything; I just keep brushing my hair, hoping that maybe some sort of fairy godmother will pop up and make my hair respectable, and maybe turn my Gatorade into a Ferrari like Cinderella's fairy godmother turned that pumpkin into a horse-drawn carriage.

"Love your dress," Carrie says softly. Using the mirror's reflection, I watch as she eyes me. She drops her bag into her locker and then rubs her elbows.

"Thank you. I like yours too," I say, glancing at her pink dress. Only she could make that color look good.

Biting her lip, she starts to leave.

"Carrie—wait."

"Yeah?"

"Um, do you think, maybe, you could?" I lift a clump of hair.

She licks her lips, looking at the ratty black and red carpet, but then comes back over to me, takes my hand, and leads me to a bench. She sits me down and starts fiddling with my hair.

In the mirror, I watch as she brushes my hair and pulls it back. She lets little wisps of hair out of the bun so that it almost looks like one of my knots, but somehow this seems softer, daintier. It looks good.

"Thank you," I say.

Carrie takes a deep breath. "I'm so sorry I told you, Jordan…this is all my fault. I don't know if Henry will ever forgive me. I hope you can."

Standing and smoothing my dress, I smile. I prefer being around guys, but I need this friendship too. It's not like Carter or JJ could talk about girl stuff, like hooking up with guys. Or fix my hair when I'm desperate. If I asked Carter to fix my hair, I'm sure he'd muss it and slap a hat on me.

"Yeah—definitely. I'm really glad we're friends."

She beams at me. "Thanks. Ready to hit the dance? Ty's outside waiting for you and he looks so damned hot I almost jumped him."

I laugh. "Yeah, it's hard not to do that," I say as we leave the locker room, where we find Ty and Carter waiting for us.

"Holy crap, Woods," Carter says, looking me up and down. "You can't wear shit like that. It's, like, against the nature of the universe or something." Chuckling, I walk up and shove him, and he laughs too. "Just kidding," he whispers. Pulling me up close, he continues, "Seriously though, you'll be the most gorgeous girl at the dance tonight."

"Thanks," I reply, giving his shoulder a punch.

Ty's holding a red rose and he's wearing a button-down shirt and khakis with no tie. Carrie was right—he looks rugged and hot. I take the rose from him and give him a kiss.

"Who said the rose was for you?" Ty whispers into my neck.

"Who's it for? Carter?"

"Uh, *yeah*." Ty grins.

I bring the rose to my nose, to smell it. "Thank you anyway. You look nice."

Ty eyes my dress. "You look sexy." He pulls me away from Carter and Carrie, heading away from the gym and toward the parking lot.

"Uh, Ty, the gym is that way."

He turns around, moving backward as he keeps pulling me. "I know. But after seeing you in that dress, I want to rip it off you."

Laughing, I drop his hand. "No way, man. I've never been to a dance. We're going." I turn and march toward the gym, making him chase me. From behind, he jogs up and slips a hand around my waist.

Inside the gym, red and black balloons hang from the walls and crêpe paper is everywhere.

"Über-cheesy," I tell Ty. "Even I could do better than this."

Still, I'm glad to experience this before I graduate.

A slow Tim McGraw song is playing as Ty grabs my hand and leads me to the center of the gym. He whirls me around, then pulls me in close. I rest my chin on his shoulder and gaze around at the darkened gym, taking in the scene.

JJ and Lacey are standing in the corner, fighting. Carter and Carrie are dancing, smiling at one another. I sure hope she's able to get over Henry, because it seems as if Carter actually likes her, and he never seriously likes anybody. Kristen is dancing with Higgins, but she keeps glancing at me and Ty, then quickly looks away. Jealous much?

I lean my forehead against Ty's for a minute, but then move my chin back to his shoulder, taking in the scene again. Now, JJ and Lacey are standing in the corner, making out. Ridiculous. Then Henry comes into the gym. He certainly didn't dress up for the dance. He's wearing holey jeans and an old T-shirt, but he still looks damned hot.

He's twirling that stupid cheapo crown on his finger and gazing around the gym. A couple of girls hustle up to him, probably asking him to dance, but he waves them away. Leaning against the wall, he keeps twirling the crown. As the slow song ends, Henry's green eyes find mine, and I pull away from Ty and begin walking toward my friend. Henry stares at me, then stares at my dress. And then he just turns around and leaves the gym, dropping the stupid crown.

What the hell?

• • •

FROM: Woods, Jordan
TO: Tucker, Mark (Athletics, University of Alabama)
DATE: Saturday, October 9, 06:47 a.m.
SUBJECT: District finals

Dear Mr. Tucker:

I hope you are well. I'm looking forward to attending the Alumni Charity Ball in December. Thank you for the proofs of the calendar. I love it.

I just wanted you to know that we won our final game of the season last night. We beat Davidson County 31–7. I threw for 320 yards. I've attached a video of the game for you to share with the football coaches.

Next week, we head to district finals, and if we win, we'll go to the state championship. I hope you and Coach Thompson can make it to the game.

Thank you again for everything.

Sincerely,
Jordan Woods

party at carter's, saturday night

Loud music

Low lights

Lame cheap beer

Ty's at work

JJ made me come

Don't know why I did

Carter and Carrie sit out by the pool

    deep in conversation

JJ and Lacey sit on the couch

    deep in each others' throats

I sit in the kitchen, surrounded by junior varsity guys

    sucking up

        fishing for compliments on their game

            asking what chicks like

                (as if I'd know)

The back door opens—

Carrying a whiff of chlorine and fall

And Henry being dragged by Samantha Milton

She says, "Let's find a room"

He sees me

Stops

Swallows

I run outside

Start my engine

When I look up

He walks out

We wave, we stare

I drive away

dad

the count? 30 days since the fight with henry

Ty and I are throwing a ball around in the backyard. We're playing burnout, a game where we throw the ball at one another as hard as we can, and the first person to drop the ball loses.

Ty is standing about thirty yards away as I launch the ball at him. He catches it and throws it back to me. He's a damned good quarterback—I have red stinging hands to prove it. I jog back a couple steps and hurl the ball at Ty, and surprisingly, he actually drops it.

"Damn," he shouts. "That one had some heat on it, Woods."

"Want to play again?"

"Nah," he says, walking toward me, tossing the ball up and catching it. Then he grabs my side and pulls me up against him, and we kiss. "So guess what?"

"What?"

"I might sign to play at Tennessee."

I squeeze his biceps. "That's great!"

"It's good that I'll be living near Mom and Vanessa. It's no Alabama, but it's still a damn good team," he says, laughing.

I rest my chin on his shoulder and wrap my arms around his waist. "Yeah, it's no Alabama."

"And since your brother is graduating next year, I'd be starting as a sophomore."

"I'm really excited for you." *I'm also really jealous of you.*

"When do you think you'll start at Alabama? As a sophomore? Or a junior?"

I hug Ty harder and close my eyes. "Not sure," I lie, thinking about how Mark Tucker never even discusses my skills on the field, and probably never will. This embarrasses me so much, that deep down I know the truth, that Alabama is probably never gonna let me play, that unless I look for another college program that might take a girl, my football career will probably be over at the end of this season. But what if Alabama ends up giving me a shot? Why should I give up now when I've worked this hard?

"Let's see who can throw the farthest," I say. "After each pass, step back about five yards."

"'Kay." Ty throws the ball at me and I catch it.

I go back a few yards, and toss it to Ty, who catches it and steps back a few feet. Then he throws it to me again. We keep hurling long bombs until we're about fifty yards apart.

"Go to the other side of the lake," I yell.

Ty smirks. "You really think you can throw a ball across the lake? It must be at least sixty yards at the skinniest part."

"Come on! I wanna try."

"Fine. But if it goes in the water, you're the one fishing it out."

"Deal."

Ty jogs down to the lake and sprints around the banks toward the other side. While I'm waiting for him to get in position, Dad comes outside and stands next to me.

"Damn, Ty sure has an arm on him," Dad says.

I didn't figure Dad would say anything about my arm, but I still feel my body sagging a bit. I guess I'll never stop hoping he'll want to support me.

Dad cups his chin with his hand. "I was watching you guys throw the ball around. It's amazing that, out of the entire United States, the NFL can't find thirty-two good quarterbacks. Yet you and Ty can both throw perfect spirals at age seventeen."

"I know, right?" I toss the ball in the air and catch it.

"You really think you're gonna throw that ball across the lake?" Dad says with a smile. "I doubt even your brother could make that pass."

"Watch me." I jog back a few steps and hurl the ball as hard as I can. It flies over the water, and like Dad and Ty suspected, it doesn't land in Ty's arms. It hits the water right before the bank and bounces up onto the grass.

"That was incredible!" Ty yells from the other side of the lake as he picks up the wet ball and wipes it on his shirt.

"Nice," Dad says, patting me on the back.

I turn and smile at Dad. Not to taunt him or anything, but because I'm glad he at least said, "Nice."

"I wonder if I could make that pass across the lake. What you just did was pretty amazing," Dad says, squeezing my shoulder. He takes a deep breath. "Can I throw the ball around with you?"

I stare at the gleaming water for a sec, my pulse racing as I turn to look at Dad, who's wearing that same expectant look he gives me when he asks to go fishing, or to race go-karts. I find myself wrapping my arms around his neck, letting him pull me in for a hug, for the first time in forever.

"You can throw the ball around with us as long as you take me out for milkshakes later."

"Deal."

"Jordan," Ty calls out. "Catch!" He runs back a few steps, winds his arm and hurls the ball. It doesn't come anywhere near me and lands about ten feet away, right in the water. It splashes and just floats there like a cork. Ty bows his head as Dad bursts out laughing.

I crack up too. "You're fishing it out, Ty!"

game #8

Dad made a call
Michigan came to look at Henry
I didn't play favorites
And alternated my passes
One touchdown for Higgins
Three for Henry
He's an awesome wide receiver
He's the biggest asshole ever
The *great* Donovan Woods showed up
After the game
Dad hugged me
Patted my back
Kissed my forehead
Didn't mention how I played
But did say of all the kids on the team,
Henry has the most potential and heart
Hundred Oaks–31
Tullahoma–24
The district title's in the bag
Poster girl or not
I'm going to Alabama
My dream school…
So why do I feel so empty?

first date

the count? 39 days since the fight with henry

The week after the district championship, which, by the way, I rocked, we have Friday night off, so Ty's taking me on a date. Our first real date. Since he spends his Thursdays, Saturdays, and Sundays washing dishes, and every other day is devoted to practice and games, we haven't had a chance to go out, just the two of us. Usually, he comes over after practice for a couple hours, we make out, and then he goes home. At school, we eat lunch and walk down the hall, but it's not like we've gotten to spend a huge amount of time together. In some ways, I barely know him.

What's his favorite color? Favorite band? Favorite vacation? Mustard or mayo? Both? When the hell is his birthday?

In some ways, I do know him. Does he like my hair up or down? Down. Boxers or briefs? Boxer briefs. Does he like it when I dress up? He prefers my jeans and T-shirts. Joe Montana or John Elway? Elway. (Blasphemy.)

Henry? Favorite color? Silver. Favorite band? Led Zeppelin. Favorite vacation? A cross-country trip with his dad to the Grand Canyon. Mustard or mayo? Ketchup. Birthday? December 1.

Ty picks me up and we're off to some undisclosed location.

Wearing jeans and a sweater, he's borrowed his grandfather's car for the occasion, and he brings me a bouquet of red roses. It's 5:30, which is early for a date, so we're driving into a lilac-and-bubblegum-colored sunset when he reaches over and rubs my thigh.

He smiles and it reminds me of the first day I saw him, how just seeing him made my body crazy. Practically catatonic. Even if he's not perfect for me, perfect like Henry is, it's easy to like Ty.

Soon I notice we're heading away from town and out into the country, aka nowhere. "Ty, where are we going? There's nothing out here."

"That's what you think," he says with a wicked grin stretched across his face.

"Where are we going?"

"It's a surprise."

"I hate surprises. And how can you like surprises? You like being in control."

He chuckles. "Yeah, but I'm in control if I'm the one doing the surprising."

He parks the car and we get out and walk across a vast green field, overrun with hay and weeds, until we come to a path that leads down to a little waterfall, where Ty has set up a picnic. I bet 99.9 percent of all women would absolutely swoon if they saw this setup, and I'm in the majority.

Gaping, I grab his elbow. "How did you find this place?"

He smiles, gesturing for me to take a seat on the blanket he's spread out. "My grandfather told me about it." He lights a couple of lanterns.

Water is lapping over rocks and crickets are chirping as Ty reaches into a backpack and pulls out sub sandwiches, potato salad, and chocolate-chip cookies, my favorite.

"You really know the way to a girl's heart."

He piles some potato salad on a paper plate and passes it to me. "Well, not every girl's heart. Just yours." My face heats up. If I had never heard that Henry loved me, would I still be completely crazy over Ty? Probably.

"So," I say, biting into my meatball sub, "what do you like to do when you're not playing football or washing dishes or controlling Vanessa's social life?"

Ty wipes his mouth with the back of his hand. "Well, controlling Vanessa's social life is my whole reason for being, but when I'm not doing that, I like reading."

"Reading? What do you like to read?"

Ty laughs. "Books...they're these things with paper and words."

I flick a forkful of potato salad at him, which he dodges. "I know that, asshole. What kinds of books?"

"I like reading about history, you know, the Civil and Revolutionary Wars. I'm thinking about being a history major."

"Cool," I say. Hell, I know nothing about wars, and I barely pull a B in history class. How smart *is* he?

"What do you like to do when you're not playing football, Woods?"

I'm shoveling potato salad in my mouth as I think about my journal. But if I don't even feel comfortable telling my best friends about it, how could I tell Ty? "Um, I like to play games. Like cards and foosball. I like running, and I like challenges and races too."

"I can see that."

"What's your favorite color?"

"Clear."

"Clear?"

"Yes, as in women's bathing suits."

"Hardy har har," I say, giggling. "For really though, what is it?"

"Blue. And you?"

My first reaction is to say blue too, but then thoughts of Henry's green eyes pop into my head. Ugh. I mean, here I am, sitting in my own personal Eden with Ty as tempting as Eve's apple, and I'm thinking about a guy who I thought was my best friend. A best friend who ditched me the moment things got rough.

"I like blue too," I say, rebelling against green. I don't care how much my heart wanted me to pick that color.

"Cool."

I focus on my sub sandwich, demolishing it, then I move on to the cookies.

"It's a beautiful night..." Ty says.

"Yup. I love fall..."

"Me too. It's my favorite season..."

"Mine too..." I eat another cookie.

Do we have *anything* to talk about?

When we're hooking up, it seems like we have lots to talk about, but maybe that's because we're too busy kissing. This lack of conversation, this isn't what love is supposed to be like, right? But what happens when you don't find that right person? Do you just spend the rest of your life in a relationship where the conversation isn't great, everything isn't perfect, but *it is* nice and sweet?

Knowing how much I'm missing Henry, should I even be with this guy?

Maybe I could deal with unrequited love, but since I know Henry does love me, it's not really unrequited. It's...unaccepted love? Avoided love? Abandoned love?

When the cookies are all gone, I lie back on the blanket and stare up at the emerging stars, trying to think about nothing but Ty and waterfalls and blue eyes.

prepping for the state championship

the count? 45 days since the fight with henry

The day before the state championship, I'm feeling down. Isn't senior year of high school supposed to be the best year of my life? What a bust.

"Woods?" JJ says, knocking me out of this pity trance I've been drowning in for a week. We're sitting at Joe's. "You gonna eat that?" JJ points at my untouched plate of spaghetti, then leans across the table and feels my forehead with the back of his hand.

"Stop it, man. I'm fine," I say, batting his hand away.

"Eat. You need your carbs for the game."

I salute JJ, then dig in, forking up some saucy noodles and lifting them to my mouth. "You nervous about the game?" I say through a mouthful.

"Hell yeah." Using his non-fork hand, JJ clicks his pen incessantly. "But as long as you're the one playing, I'll be fine."

I sigh. Sure, Ty's a tad controlling, but he's a quarterback! "What's your problem with Ty?"

JJ shrugs. "I've told you. He's picky. You don't see what he's like in the locker room, looking down on all of us, nagging us about how we don't tuck our jerseys in right, or how Carter made a block using the wrong part of his shoulder. I mean, what's that about? I honestly don't know what you see in him."

I focus on my pasta. "He's sweet, he's nice to me, he's hot. Let's be honest, there aren't a lot of options around here." I use my fork to point at him. "Like you said, Lacey's a good lay, right?"

JJ bows his head toward me, obviously conceding. "Hey, if the sex is good, what else do you need, eh?"

"Well, um, I bet sex might be better if you're actually in love, you know?"

He shrugs. "Pass the Parmesan, will you?"

I pick up the cheese and pass it to JJ, feeling deflated. With Henry gone, I have no one to talk to except my journal, and it can't ever talk back.

"Look, Carter and I don't care if you date Ty. But Henry…"

This surprises me, because this is the first time JJ has brought up Henry since this stupid feud started. "Why? What did he say?"

JJ clicks his pen, hesitating. "Just that he can't stand being around you while you're dating Ty and he thinks you've chosen Ty over us."

I drop my fork. "Oh, that's total bullshit, JJ."

"I know."

"Did you tell Henry that?"

"Sure…but I think he's gotta work this out for himself. And that's all I'm gonna say."

"All I'm gonna say is that first, Henry told me to date Ty. Then he got mad about it. Then I gave Henry the choice of whether I would keep dating Ty or not…and his response was to give Ty a black eye and ignore me for a month and a half."

"I never said this was your fault, Woods. But when did you

become the Angel of Drama?" Smiling, he stares at his crossword book. "What's a five-letter word for *polo participant*?"

"I dunno, man...a shirt? Like a polo shirt?"

• • •

After dropping JJ off at home, I drive. Drive, with no real destination. But then I realize where I want to go.

Soon I find myself standing beside the Cumberland River, the spot of my last real conversation with Henry. I open my journal and pull a pen from my pocket.

The dull ache still infests my body like cancer

Henry cancer

Only rather than killing me, this cancer lets me live, in a reduced sort of way

Without Henry, I'm living 75 percent of my life

And maybe some people accept that, settle for that, but I don't want to.

I find the log where Henry and I sat over a month ago. I root around beneath the rotting wood, groping for flat stones. I pull out several, stand, and take aim at the river. First I manage two skips. Then three. Will I ever get up to four? I search for more stones, discovering some brick-like rocks, which I launch into the river, creating big splashes.

I skip stones and throw rocks until the sun starts to set. Just as I'm getting ready to leave, I see a large splash in the river, so I jerk around to find the thrower of the rock. And there he is. Henry. Standing there with a handful of rocks, launching them into the river. No one knew I was coming here, so he must've just shown up, just like me.

He stares at the journal in my hand, and then looks away as he picks up more rocks and starts throwing them in the river.

I drop my journal onto the ground, reach down, and grab a huge stone, almost as big as a cinder block, and hurl it at the water. Then I pick a few flat stones and skip them each three times.

He picks up a tiny rock, probably no bigger than a golf ball, and flicks it into the river, creating the measliest splash ever. I glance at him, scared to say or do anything. I watch as he reaches down and picks some wildflowers. Sunflowers. Goldenrod. Queen Anne's lace. He slowly shuffles over and hands me the bouquet.

My tears are everywhere. I sop them up using my sweatshirt, and when I look at his face, he reaches around his neck and pulls off the silver chain that holds the plastic football charm, fingering it. He stares down at the charm, then finds my eyes and puts the chain around my neck.

"I'm sorry I fucked everything up, Jordan," he says, and then he's gone.

• • •

Later that evening, I'm huddled in the potting shed with my flashlight, writing in my journal.

> My fears have come true:
>
> I'm that girl who's lost all control and perspective because of a guy
>
> What do I say to Henry?
>
> Is there anything I could say to make things better?
>
> I finally have the charm I've wanted forever
>
> But it's just a shitty piece of plastic if it's not attached to Henry

All of a sudden the door to the potting shed creaks open and Mom crawls inside with me.

"How did you know where I was?"

"Sweetie, you've been coming here for years. Ever since that first time you and Henry played house."

"Oh." Mom really does know all.

"Your friends are here."

I furiously wipe my wet eyes on my sleeve. "Carter? JJ?"

Light from the porch illuminates the inside of the shed, so I can see Mom smiling. "Carrie and Marie."

What the hell? "Why are they here?"

"Carrie wants to talk to you."

"Oh."

Mom hesitates. "Look, sweetie, I wish you'd talk to someone. I hate watching you keep everything bottled up."

"I'm not! I've been writing in the stupid journal you gave me."

Mom puts an arm around my waist and drops her forehead onto my shoulder. "And I'm so glad you've found another outlet besides football. But talking to Carrie might be more helpful than writing in your journal."

I think back to when I told Carrie I slept with Ty, and I felt so scared, because she could've told everyone. But no one found out. And Marie didn't make a big deal of being my partner in music appreciation class. I like that she's kinda low-key, at least compared to the other cheerleaders. Hell, she knows what a flea flicker is.

"That's not a bad idea, Mom."

"Good. Want to go inside?"

I stand up, and together, we go out of the potting shed. Mom holds my hand as we walk through the garden and up to the porch.

Back in the house, after glancing at my red face in the bathroom mirror, I go to the foyer, where Carrie and Marie are waiting for me. "What's up?" I say.

When the girls see me, they glance at one another. Carrie clears her throat. "You okay, Jordan?"

I wipe my eyes again and force a smile. "Oh yeah—I'm fine. What are y'all up to?"

"Carrie needs your advice," Marie says, patting Carrie's back.

My advice? "Is this some kind of a joke? Did JJ put you up to this?"

Marie laughs. "No—for real. Is there someplace we can talk?"

"Sure—let's go to the basement." Carrie and Marie follow me down the stairs and we plop down on the couches. So now what? Should I offer them a drink? What would Henry want?

"You guys want to order pizza?" I say.

"Awesome," Carrie says.

"Can we get wings too?" Marie asks.

"Hell yeah," I say.

Marie likes wings?

I grab a menu from the desk, pull out my cell phone, and order the pizza and wings, then sit back down on the couch. "So what kind of advice do you need? Need my opinion on buying a new pair of cleats?"

"No," Marie says. "Guy advice."

I laugh loudly. "You must be joking."

"Nope," Marie says. "The issue is that Carrie totally likes Carter, but he doesn't want to date her."

"Really?" I exclaim, focusing on Carrie, whose face is all red. "I thought he liked you a lot."

"That's what I've been saying," Marie replies.

"Look, guys," Carrie says, "I *know* he likes me. But he doesn't want to get involved because he thinks Henry is still hung up on me."

I laugh. "Carter is so dense."

Carrie pauses for a beat. "I know, right?"

"Have you told Carter why you dumped Henry?" I ask.

"No..."

"So tell him."

"You don't care if I tell him about Henry?" Carrie says, raising an eyebrow.

"Of course not. Or if you'd rather, I can send Carter a text telling him to stop being a bonehead."

Carrie smiles. "Nah, I can do it. Thanks, Jordan."

"Now that that's settled, can we play some foosball?" Marie asks, eyeing the table in the corner.

"Let's do it," I say. The three of us head over to the table and start a tournament. Since they're guests, I let Marie and Carrie play the first game while I go upstairs and raid the kitchen for sodas.

When I get downstairs, only three minutes later, Marie says, "Your turn to play me, Jordan. I just slaughtered Carrie."

"Cool," I say, popping a Diet Coke open and setting it on the table. I grab the knobs and start moving my wooden men to hit the ball. One of Marie's wooden men steals the ball from me and slams it into the goal.

"Damn," I say. "Carrie, you could've warned me that Marie's a foosball prodigy."

"Champion of Cedar Creek Camp, three years running," Marie replies.

"So how are things going with Ty?" Carrie asks, taking a seat on a bar stool and opening her Diet Coke. When I look up from the foosball table, she's staring into my eyes.

"Fine." Lie.

"Just fine?" Marie exclaims. She swallows before asking, "Are you guys, you know, fooling around?"

I nod.

"What's he like in bed?"

I freeze—I can't believe she asked that, but he is hot, so I can understand why she's curious. "Unfrickinbelievable."

Not a lie.

"But?" Marie asks.

"Hooking up isn't everything," I say, trying not to think about how much I love Henry. Henry, who's probably gone forever. Friend or otherwise.

"You don't love Ty?" Carrie asks quietly.

I shrug and focus on the foosball game. "With Ty, it's like I have this amazing guy, and he's sweet and nice, and yeah, unbelievable in bed, but it's not all there, you know?"

"There are plenty of other guys out there," Marie says as she twirls the knob, knocking the ball into my goal again. "So if you want to dump Ty, everything will be fine."

"It won't be fine," I blurt out before realizing I'm speaking.

"'Cause Henry's not around?" Carrie asks, a frown spreading across her face.

"Yeah, and if he's not around, I might as well be with someone like Ty, right?"

Marie and Carrie exchange a look again and then Marie says, "If Henry doesn't know what an ass he's being and what he's missing, then screw him."

"That doesn't help," Carrie says, coming over and resting a hand on my back. "We're here if you want to talk about it."

"I just miss him, that's all." I feel tears welling again. "I hate that we don't play cards anymore. I hate waking up alone."

"That sucks," Marie replies. She digs the ball out of the goal and drops it back down in the middle of the table, and we start playing again.

I don't know what comes over me, but I feel like ranting. Ranting like wildfire.

"I don't get it. I mean, he told me he loved me and then just disappeared. How could he? We've been best friends forever and now he can't even talk to me? What the hell?"

"I bet he's just scared," Carrie says.

"I'm sure he'll be back to normal soon," Marie adds. "He stares at you all the time in class. He misses you too."

"JJ says Henry just needs to work through this himself." I hesitate before adding, "It's so much easier to talk to you guys about this stuff."

"You talk to JJ about your love life?" Carrie exclaims.

"JJ, the guy who ate a six-foot-long meatball hoagie in half an hour on a dare from Carter?" Marie says before scoring another goal. "Are you crazy?"

I laugh. I love writing in my journal, but I have to admit, talking with these girls is pretty cool.

Football player or cheerleader—doesn't matter.

We play foosball until the pizza comes, and then the three of us sit in front of the television and watch some crappy show where B-list Hollywood stars race around the world. Surprisingly, Marie and Carrie trash the show more than I do. How did I never realize that girls can have just as much fun, and have the same kind of fun, as guys do?

only father, redux

Pregame ritual:

Lounge on couch

Lower my pulse

Love love love the game

Play hard in my mind

Picture myself winning

Pray for fumbles

(by the other team, of course).

Not part of the pregame ritual:

Dad.

No way no how

Never has been

Never will be—

Until today.

He showed up in the basement

Wielding a DVD

A DVD of me, my film.

I sucked back tears

Football heroes shouldn't cry

Not even today.

the state championship

The night is cold; cigarette smoke and the scent of coffee waft through the crisp air. I'm bouncing up and down on my toes, trying to get warmed up. I wring my hands and, one at a time, I shake my feet, loosening up my ankles.

A quadzillion reporters are taking pictures of me. Tons of college coaches are here, but none are from Alabama. Mark Tucker isn't here either. Asshole.

The great Donovan Woods is here, sitting in the front row of the stands with Mom, Mike, and Jake Reynolds. The Tennessee head coach is with them, undoubtedly here to take a look at Ty, if he gets to play.

When I glance at Dad, he smiles and waves. Um, okay? I smile back at him, loving him for spending a whole hour with me this afternoon, watching film. Film!

Jake Reynolds yells, "Looking hot, Jor!" and whistles.

I shout, "You'd better not mess up my concentration or I'll bust your kneecaps, perv!"

Jake laughs.

Carrie and Marie come jogging up to me, their short red and black skirts whipping around in the wind. "Jordan!" Marie says,

"Who's the hot guy sitting with your family?" She peers over at Jake, who winks at her, nudges Mike, and points at Marie's butt. My bro shakes his head and goes back to eating his popcorn.

"Trust me," I reply, making a gagging noise. "Don't waste your time."

"I'm not interested," Marie says, putting her pompoms under an arm so she can examine her fingernails, which look freshly painted. "Kristen was asking me who he is."

I pause, then burst out laughing. "Oh. Well, they're perfect for each other! I'll introduce them after the game. Maybe he'll stop bothering me if he gets someone new to harass."

"And then maybe Kristen would stop being obsessed with Ty," Carrie says, rolling her eyes.

"Sounds like a win-win for all of us. So, did you talk to Carter?" I ask Carrie.

She smiles so hard I think she might faint. "He asked me out for next Friday night."

"Details!" Marie says.

"He's cooking dinner for me and his parents, and then he's taking me to a jazz concert thing at the Opryland Hotel in Nashville."

I feel this strange urge to jump up and down and giggle but decide to say, "That's cool. Very romantic," and pat Carrie's shoulder instead.

"Listen, Jordan," Marie says. "You should try the Statue of Liberty play you did at practice the other day."

I gaze up at the announcer's booth at the top of the bleachers and rub my hands together, trying to keep them warm. "You know, I bet they're thinking I'll bomb it to Henry first thing."

"Right," Marie replies, nodding.

"What are you guys even talking about?" Carrie says, sighing, then laughing.

"You'll see," I say, grinning.

"Captains!" the referee shouts.

"Gotta jet," I tell the girls before turning to run out onto the field.

"Good luck, Jordan!" they call out, jumping up and down and waving their pompoms.

JJ and I run out to the fifty-yard line, and when I turn to find Carter, I see him walking over to Carrie. She reaches up and gives him a hug, probably for luck, but then he picks her up and kisses her in front of the entire crowd. Everyone starts clapping and cheering for them, including me and JJ. Henry's grinning at them too.

Coach throws his clipboard on the ground and yells, "Carter, get your ass on the field!"

Pulling his helmet on, Carter jogs out to us, and both JJ and I shove him around a bit. "Thanks for joining us, hot lips," JJ says.

We're playing the game at Vanderbilt University, and since we have the better record, Woodbridge High calls the toss. They say heads. It lands on tails. I choose to receive the kick.

I run back to the sidelines, meeting Henry as he goes out to return the kickoff. We knock fists, then he knocks fists with Carter and JJ. I shove thoughts of Henry from my mind—I need to get in the zone, so I turn and look at the Woodbridge bench. A team from Western Tennessee, we've never played them before, and neither did my bro. I've never seen them play either. But I've done my homework.

The quarterback doesn't have a great arm, but he's quick and he's smart. He knows how to direct the field, but he carries the ball more than anything. I told Carter to focus on containing the QB, or he'll run it. Carter loves to sack the quarterback, but we can't afford to have him miss, because if the QB escapes, I don't think anyone on our team has the speed to stop him except Henry. And Henry can't play both wide receiver and defensive back. Besides, he's too thin to play defense.

Speaking of Henry, I also know the Woodbridge kicker has a much more powerful leg than most high school players. "Henry!" I yell when he's almost into position at the Woodbridge end zone. He sprints back over to the sidelines.

"Yeah?" he says, springing up and down, trying to keep his muscles warm.

"You know about this dude, right? This kicker?"

He lifts his helmet a little, and I see him smiling, his green eyes twinkling. Fog spills out of his mouth.

"Obviously, Woods. Why the hell do you think I was playing so far back?"

"Just checking."

He nods toward the stands. "So where are the Alabama coaches?"

I fiddle with my chinstrap and shrug. "Not here, I guess."

"Not here?" he exclaims. "But this is the last time they'll get to see you play this year."

I bite into my upper lip as it dawns on me that unless I do what Dad says and look at some other options, this may be the last time I ever really get to play. The last time I ever huddle under hundreds of lights and smell the freshly painted yard lines and hear fans cheering. The last time I ever throw my perfect spiral in a game.

"Henry?"

"Yeah?"

I take a deep breath. "Remember that time I was searching for crickets at your game, and the ball went out of bounds and I threw it back to you?"

"Yup," he says with a grin.

I return the smile. "Were you mad that I took your position?"

"Course not. I could see how much you loved playing ball…and that made me love the game even more. I've always loved catching your passes."

"If Michigan asked you to join their team, but then, like, made it clear you weren't going to get to play, would you still wanna go there?"

He pulls his helmet all the way off and stares at me. "No way. I want to play ball. And if that's why Alabama isn't here tonight, then it's their loss." He pats my elbow. "You can do better, and you know it."

"Henry!" Coach yells. "Could I trouble you to receive the kickoff, or should I send JJ out to do it?"

Henry runs backward onto the field, staring at me as he puts his helmet back on.

I jog to the benches, where I stand between JJ and Carter as Woodbridge gets ready to kick off.

Ty comes up behind me and whispers, "Henry knows about the kicker, right?"

"Yes," I say through gritted teeth. It's my job to captain this team, not Ty's. He still doesn't get that?

"Good," Ty replies.

Woodbridge kicks off and Henry catches the ball. Sprinting, he makes it to the thirty-yard line before he's tackled. We all scream and celebrate, yelling Henry's name.

"Woods," Coach says, "Take it up the gut."

"Got it, Coach." To see how good the Woodbridge defense is, Coach wants to test them by running the ball up the middle.

I jog out to the thirty and huddle with the guys. "Statue of Liberty to Bates." We all clap our hands once and break. JJ hikes the ball to me, I take three steps back and with my right hand, I pretend to throw the ball to Henry, who's running up the right side of the field. This causes most of the defense to change direction, and when they do, I hand the ball off with my left hand to Bates, who grabs it and darts up the middle of the field. The Statue of Liberty trick only works occasionally, but with this experiment, I can see that the defense is expecting me to pass every chance I get. Bates makes it eleven yards before getting tackled.

We run up to the line and I yell, "Blue fifty, red twenty, blue fifty, red thirty!" Red thirty is the cue. JJ hikes the ball and I throw it down the field to Higgins. A cornerback is all over him, and Higgins misses the ball and crashes to the ground. Incomplete. Damn it. The Woodbridge defense might be better than I thought. If we want to score, Henry's our best chance, but the defense is doubling up on him.

We huddle. "Post route to Henry. Take a hard left at the twenty-yard line," I say. Henry claps his hands. JJ hikes the ball, and Henry takes off down the field so fast he confuses the Woodbridge defensive line. At the twenty, a cornerback catches up to Henry, but Henry takes a quick left and catches my perfect pass and darts off. Taking huge strides, he barely beats the cornerback to the end zone.

Touchdown! I jump and yell and rip off my helmet. I pump my fist as we jog back to the sidelines, where I grab Henry by the jersey. "Nice!" I say.

I drink some Gatorade as I watch our kicker make the extra point, after which our defense runs out onto the field, led by Carter. Not allowing Woodbridge to get a first down is tougher than usual for us, but Carter manages to sack their QB once. But they still make it into field goal range. On fourth down, they go for a field goal from the twenty-five-yard line and score. We're up 7–3 when I run back onto the field.

Huddling with the guys, I say, "This time, Woodbridge is gonna be all over Henry. We've gotta throw them off a bit."

"What do you want to do?" Henry asks. He puts his hands on his hips.

I'm so nervous, I'm sweating, so I wipe my hands on my towel. "Red Rabbit to Bates?"

"Let's do it," Henry says with a clap.

JJ hikes the ball, I make a short ten-yard pass to Henry, he catches it and as the defense moves in to clobber him, he pitches it to Bates, who runs it up the left side of the field. He goes another ten yards before getting tackled.

"Hot!" I yell as we move up to the line. I give Henry a high five, then squeeze Bates' forearm. Our victory doesn't last long, because the defense steps up their game. I'm not able to get another first down.

When's the last time that happened? Last year's state championship.

On the sidelines, I sip my Gatorade and try to relax. I turn and look at my family, and Mike and Jake raise their fists at me. When I look at Dad, he gives me a thumbs up. Whoa.

By halftime, the score is still 7–3 Hundred Oaks, but the guys are pumped and we haven't lost our spirit. As we're running for the locker room, I see Dad and Mike waving Ty over to the bleachers. Ty jogs over and shakes hands with the Tennessee head coach.

I feel jealous because I know the Tennessee coach is taking Ty seriously. He's treating Ty like a real player, not some meal ticket, some beauty queen, some poster girl. But I'm the one who's holding her own against Woodbridge; still, none of these college coaches think of me as a real player. No one has made an offer except for Alabama. Every time a recruiter comes to a game, it's Henry and Carter and Ty they're looking at. Not me. Which I don't get, because girl or not, I'm an amazing football player. That's what it should come down to, right? That I can throw an awesome perfect spiral.

I don't even know what Dad was talking about when he said I should consider all options. Are there other options?

The third quarter starts, and I hear Coach through the speaker in my helmet. "Woods, run the ball for the first play. See how far Bates can get. As soon as we're within thirty yards of the end zone, bomb it to Henry. He can run faster than any of these Woodbridge players."

I do as Coach says. We run the ball until we're almost at the thirty-yard line. There, I yell, "Blue forty-two! Blue forty-two! Red seventeen!"

JJ hikes the ball to me and I take five steps back as Henry darts down the field. The defense is blitzing. Oh hell. The entire defense is coming at me. My offensive line is being pummeled. JJ can't hold off both the safety and the linebacker who are trying to get at me. JJ chooses to block the safety. Henry's nearing the end zone, and I only have about a second before the linebacker will crash into me. I've gotta get rid of the ball. Now. Just as I hurl it, the linebacker hits me low and hard, and I'm crushed to the ground. Then I hear our stands erupt.

"Touchdown!"

JJ yells, "Suck it, fools!"

And for a second, I'm celebrating, but then the pain hits me. Something is very, very wrong with my knee. I scream.

he stopped to get flowers?

Grasping at my left knee, I'm crying, but not because of the pain, but because I am terrified. What the hell did I do to my knee? Did I hear a crack? Did something rip? A tendon? My ACL? Oh God…my future…

Both Henry and Ty fall down next to me, Ty on my right, Henry on my left. Everyone's yelling.

"Just stay still, okay?" Henry says, carefully pulling off my helmet. He runs a hand over my hair.

"Jordan, are you okay? Talk to me, Jordan," Ty begs. "Oh God, please be okay…"

"Man, stop crying," JJ says, pulling Ty off me and dragging him away. Thank God.

Henry takes my hand. "Where does it hurt?"

"Knee," I say, panting.

"Okay, I'm not going to let anyone touch you," Henry says as all the guys huddle around me. "Carter!" he calls out, "Get these fools away from us!" Tears are pooling in my eyes, but I'm trying to show a brave face for my team, for Henry, who's caressing my hand.

I'm still staring up at Henry's face when Coach kneels down next to me, but I don't hear what he's saying because all I can concentrate on is the pain and Henry's fingers. But one voice knocks me out of this Henry trance: Donovan Woods's.

"Nobody touch her!" Dad says, kneeling down next to us. "Talk to me, Henry."

"It's her left knee."

"Oh hell—that's the leg she plants to throw." Wait, Dad cares about if my knee will be in good enough shape to throw passes in the future? "Has she tried to move it?"

"No. And I didn't let anyone else touch her."

"Good man," Dad replies, pulling a cell phone from his pocket. I listen as he calls the Titans' team doctor and tells him to meet us at Vanderbilt Hospital. Then he calls for an ambulance. "I don't want to risk further hurting your knee, so we're going to do this right."

A referee says, "Coach Miller, let's get her off the field so we can keep playing."

"Like hell you will," Dad says, glaring at the ref, who puts his hands up and moves away.

When the ambulance finally comes, Dad and Henry get into it with me. The pain is nowhere near as intense as before, so I'm able to speak. "Henry…the game? You should play."

"Who cares?" Henry says. In the past twenty minutes, he's barely let go of my hand. And I'm loving it. Maybe I should've hurt myself a month ago, I chuckle to myself.

"Dad?"

He cradles my neck with his hand. "Yeah?"

"I'm so sorry," I reply, biting my lips together.

He gives me a slight smile and says, "Everything's okay," and then gets back on the phone.

Dad calls his doctor again, telling him what's up, what my knee looks like, saying that from one to ten, I'm at a six on the pain scale. I don't even know what the hell that scale is supposed to mean. What does ten represent? Getting your head chopped off? Is one a paper cut?

At the hospital, the EMTs push me down the hall as Dad storms around making demands, private rooms and portable X-ray machines and shit, but Henry keeps holding my hand. Having driven separately, Mom comes rushing in behind us, taking my other hand.

"Mike?" I say to Mom.

"He stayed with the Tennessee coach to watch Ty. We couldn't leave your boyfriend there alone."

The EMTs bypass the emergency room and wheel me right into my own room, which reeks of sterilizer and hospital food, but I'm glad I don't have to share. Having the great Donovan Woods for a father does have its perks. The EMTs carefully move me from the rolling stretcher to the bed and wish me luck. A technician comes in with a portable X-ray machine.

"Do you know what you're doing?" Dad asks the technician. "If you make the damage worse and ruin her dreams of playing football in college I'll—"

The technician drops the lead blanket he was about to drape over my abdomen onto the floor. He looks like he's going to shit his pants. So does Henry, who's gaping at Dad. I'm gawking too. Dad cares about my dreams?

"Donovan, please," Mom says, grabbing Dad's hand and pulling him away to sit in a chair. The technician carefully cuts my football pants away from my left knee and slides a cool, metal plate beneath it.

"Any chance you're pregnant?" the technician says as he pulls the X-ray lamp over my swollen knee.

"No," Henry and Dad say at the same time.

Laughing, the technician says to me, "That true?"

I nod. He takes X-rays from a bazillion angles and then leaves. Standing up, Henry runs a hand over my hair. "Can I get you a soda, Woods? Anything you need, I'm your guy."

Using my finger, I beckon him closer and closer until his ear is right in front of my mouth. "Stay with me. Please. Sit here. I'm so scared."

He whispers back, "I won't leave until you tell me to. Promise." Henry takes a seat and grabs my hand again. "Woods, what do you call a ghost with a broken leg?"

I smile. "What?"

"A hobblin' goblin!"

"Oh God, you're so embarrassing, Henry," I say, giggling.

It turns out the only thing on TV Friday night is reruns of *Cops*, so Henry and I watch an episode while we wait on the team doctor and the X-rays. Our favorite story line involves a woman who called the cops because some men stole her jeans. When the cops ask her why she needs the jeans back so badly, she replies, "Because my heroin is in them!" Together, we laugh so hard at the woman's stupidity, it's almost like before.

The team doctor finally shows up to examine my leg. Dad wouldn't let any of the other staff look at it before Dr. Freeman got here. First, the two of them study the X-ray images of my knee more intently than they'd study the *Sports Illustrated* swimsuit issue. Whispering, Dr. Freeman points at my ligaments and Dad moves in close to examine whatever he's talking about. Then the doctor comes over and flexes my knee a few times. It hurts like hell, but I don't feel anything popping and I don't hear any strange noises coming from it. If I had to, I bet I could walk.

Dr. Freeman squeezes my knee. "Does this hurt?"

"No," I reply.

He squeezes it in a different place. "Here?"

"A little."

"I think you just sprained it. Nothing's torn, nothing's broken. You'll be up and walking around by tomorrow. Tonight, I just want to wrap it, but for the next couple months, you and I are gonna do some physical therapy, okay?"

"Of course!" I say.

Smiling, I laugh, suddenly feeling relieved. About my knee, about my future. Mom and Dad hug me, then Henry does. I'm the luckiest girl alive today, so I take a risk and give Henry a quick peck on the cheek before he pulls away from me. Staring in my eyes, he purses his lips and sits down with me again, holding my hand.

As Dr. Freeman wraps my knee, Mike and Jake finally arrive.

"Where's Ty?" I ask as Mike gives me a hug.

"Getting you flowers or something," Mike replies.

"He stopped to get flowers?" Henry mumbles, his mouth falling open.

"Why are you still wearing that uniform?" Jake asks. "You'd look great in a hospital gown, Jor. Especially if it opens in the back."

Mike and Dad roll their eyes at Jake, and Henry throws a bedpan at him.

Then Ty comes running into the room, carrying roses, his cleats nearly slipping on the slick floor. "Woods! Are you okay?" He hands me the flowers and drags a hand across my hair.

"Thank you." I smell the flowers and whisper, "I'm fine—just a sprain."

"Thank God," Ty says, leaning toward my lips. As he kisses me in front of everyone, I open my eyes for a quick peek at Henry. His face is blank as he stares out the window. He drops my hand as Ty continues to kiss me and stroke my cheek.

"Get a room," Jake says loudly.

I pull away from Ty. "The game?"

"We won!"

Henry and I shout, "Hell yeah!" and "Awesome!" and "State champions!" and knock fists. "The score?" Henry asks.

"14–3," Ty says, looking only at me. "We never scored again after you left. I was a wreck. I threw an interception."

I smile. "You? When's the last time you did that?"

"Don't remember."

Henry guffaws. Ty scowls at Henry, then whispers to me, "How are you?"

"I'm gonna be fine. Couple weeks of physical therapy and I'll be a brand new quarterback."

Ty closes his eyes, nodding. "Jordan, tonight was horrifying for me."

"For you?" I exclaim.

"Yeah…I couldn't handle it if anything serious happened to you," Ty whispers. "And it's only going to be worse at the college level."

"Ty, I'm not going to quit because I sprained my knee."

"I'm so scared something will happen to you. You're, like, one of the only things I have left."

Poor Vanessa. She'll have to live with Ty's paranoia forever, but at least I have a choice. I won't do something just because my boyfriend thinks I should. Not anymore. I never should've let Ty tell me Henry couldn't sleep over.

Maybe my life needs some physical therapy too.

I'm Jordan Woods. I lead a sixty-person football team, and I've been letting everyone else shape me. I want to be a rock again.

"Ty—I'm not going to quit. You'll just have to get over it."

"Tonight was just a sprain. But you could get permanently hurt in college."

"You don't think she knows that, man?" Henry says, taking my hand again.

When Ty sees our hands together, I think he's going to get mad, but he gazes over at my dad, who's standing by the window.

"Mr. Woods? You agree with me, right?" Ty says.

Dad rocks to his left side, shifts his weight, and coughs. "I might try to discourage my daughter from playing football, but I'd never stop her from doing anything she loves. That's her decision. If I had any say, I never would've let her join that Pop Warner team when she was seven."

Mom smiles at Dad and rubs his neck. I can't believe Dad feels this way. It's true—he never has told me I can't play football. Though I'm scared about my knee, I feel happier than I have in a long time. I mean, it's not like I have Dad's total support, but even having his blessing to do what I love is huge.

Ty's face goes red. "Fine…whatever you want to do, Woods. I've gotta get home to check on Vanessa. I'll call you later." He kisses my forehead and leaves.

I shut my eyes, and then I feel Henry moving closer to me. He whispers in my ear, "Let me know if you need anything, okay?"

Dad's doctor just told me my knee should be fine in a few weeks. Still, this injury terrifies me. What terrifies me even more?

What happens next with Henry.

• • •

Knowing that my knee isn't royally messed up, I feel like I've been given a free play.

A chance to make some choices.

Henry was right—I let everyone else's feelings affect my decisions.

Screw that.

I'm taking the ball and running with it.

Maybe they're not my top choices, but they're choices that are good for me, choices I can live with.

Some things I can't control; but some things I can. And I'm going to.

• • •

First I go to Dad's study, the girl-free zone, and use one of my crutches to push the door open.

"Dad? You know how you said I should consider all options?"

"Yep," he says, peering up from the sports' section of the *Tennessean*.

"I was wondering…if maybe you can…maybe you could…help me come up with some other options?"

Dad sets the newspaper down on his desk, leans back in his chair, and stares up at the ceiling. A smile blooms.

"Let me see what I can come up with."

• • •

"But I don't get it," Ty says, laughing and running a hand across his jaw.

"I think you're great, and I really love hanging out with you—"

"You're breaking up with me?"

"Yes." I reach out and touch his arm, and he shakes his head.

"That doesn't make any sense. Every girl at Hundred Oaks wants to go out with me…and you're breaking up with me?"

"I'm sorry—"

"Is this because of Henry?" he asks, confusion creeping across his face.

"No, it's really not. You're great—I just know you're not the right guy for me. And it's not fair to either of us."

"Look, I'm sorry I asked you to give up football. It was stupid of me."

"No, I get that you're scared of what might happen to me…to anyone you care about. I understand everything you've been through."

"Is this because I'm a better football player?"

"Jesus, Ty," I say with a laugh. "Sometimes you just aren't supposed to be with someone. You can't control everything, no matter how much you want to."

And even if Henry doesn't want to talk to me, I can still talk to him.

• • •

After school on Monday, I hobble over to Henry's rusty maroon truck, being careful to mind my knee, and tuck a note under his windshield wiper.

Dear Sam—I'm here. Whenever you're ready. Love, Jordan

one week since

On this lame Friday afternoon, I'm lying on my bed, alternating between fiddling with the plastic football charm and writing in my journal. I write:

No best friend + no boyfriend = no plans and no life

Neither of my parents has mentioned my breakup with Ty except to say they're still going to help him get through college, and Mom will keep taking Vanessa on shopping trips because she doesn't trust Ty or his grandfather with such an important responsibility.

Henry? Well, after I left him the note, several strange gifts started showing up. Like a giant stuffed panda holding a bag of chocolate-chip cookies. I devoured the cookies in about two minutes, but why the hell would he get me a panda?

In retaliation for the stupid panda, I called Marie and Carrie, and together, we dressed the thing up in girly clothes and smeared makeup on it. Then we wrote Henry's name on its white fur in lipstick and put it out in front of the school. Pretty lame, I know, but it actually made Henry laugh when he saw it. I spied on him from a window.

Then, the other night, Chinese food was delivered with a special fortune cookie. A handwritten fortune taped to the plastic read, "I'm sorry, Woods." So I tried to call and thank him, but he didn't pick his phone up. Of course.

In response, I had a pizza delivered to him with a message that read, "I forgive you. Stop being a bonehead" in olives. Apparently, my message barely fit on an extra large pizza! Man, Henry *hates* olives.

Then yesterday, a deck of cards, a pair of salt and pepper shakers, and a blank journal showed up outside the door to my room. I love the new journal—it's leather bound and the paper smells wonderful. And it makes me feel good, that maybe my interest in writing isn't totally lame, that I can be publicly proud of myself for something other than football.

But why can't the boy just freaking talk to me? Why all the covert shit?

My dad pokes his head in my room. "Can I come in?"

I hide my journal under the pillow and pick up my football. "Sure," I reply, sitting up.

"How's the knee feel?"

"Not bad."

"Let me see you extend it," Dad says, picking up my right foot and pushing and pulling my leg in and out several times. "Good. You're healing up nicely."

"Thanks." I drop my foot back on the bed and start tossing my ball.

"What are you doing this weekend?" Dad asks.

"No plans."

"How about taking a little trip with me? I don't have a game on Sunday."

"Where are we going? The beach? God, I could so use some heat and some fresh air."

Dad sits on my bed with me. "I was thinking Michigan."

"Michigan?" I say, sticking out my tongue. "It's colder there than it is here! Why the hell would we go there?"

"You wanted other options, right?"

"Yeah…"

"Look, I know I can't stop you from playing ball in college, but if you're going to play, I want you to go someplace where you'll be taken care of."

"Like where?"

Dad takes a deep breath. "Want to take a trip up to Michigan State with me? Their head coach is interested in you. He's an honest guy—I played against him in college."

I laugh loudly. When I said options, I meant Florida or Ole Miss or Tennessee, even. "Give up Alabama for Michigan State? Are you freaking kidding me?"

"Jordan—if you go to Alabama, I know you'll be doing great things like the charity program with foster kids. There's no guarantee you'll ever actually hit the field, but there's a 100 percent chance they're going to make you do stuff like model for their calendar."

I nod, clutching my pillow. "Michigan State would actually let me play?"

"As long as you keep playing like you are now, yes." Dad smiles. "They've seen some of your tapes."

"Do you think the guys on the team will be sexist?"

Dad laughs. "Probably. But there, at least you'll get to play. And the coach promised me you won't be paraded around like a piece of meat."

"That's good to hear."

Dad musses my hair. "So, what do you say? Can we at least go talk to the Michigan State coach? Maybe throw a ball around with some of his wide receivers?"

"Let's do it. When do we leave?"

"We can leave now. Get your bags packed. Bring some cleats." Dad stands up and walks out the door, but then pokes his head back in. "By the way, we're taking Henry with us. He doesn't know it yet, but we're going to stop by the University of Michigan too. I told his mom to keep him home until we get there." Dad grins.

I drop the suitcase I just pulled out of the closet. "Henry?" I say, gasping. "I'm not going anywhere with Henry."

"Yes—you are. Henry has worked too hard and too long on getting into Michigan to blow it now. He deserves this. And you and I are going to support him."

I nod and avert my eyes, which are starting to tear up again.

Dad sighs. "Why can't you and Henry work through whatever has been going on since September?"

"You should talk to him about this, Dad. Not me. I've been ready to work through it for weeks and weeks."

Dad shuts the door, comes back in, and picks up the football, twirling it in his hands. "What happened exactly?"

"What? You don't know?"

"Nope."

"Honest to God?"

"Honest to God."

I touch the plastic football charm. "Did you know that Henry liked me? As, um, more than a friend?"

"Sure. Who didn't?"

"Me."

"Well, we all thought you weren't interested."

This conversation with Dad is going far better than I ever could've imagined. Who is this strange Donovan Woods impersonator? "When I found out that Henry likes me, well liked me, as more than a friend, I went to him. I told him I was up for it. For trying…you know…to have a relationship?"

Dad nods.

"He said we couldn't date, but that we would still be friends. But he got weird anyway. He got mad about Ty and said some mean things. He never stopped to think about how much he was hurting me."

"What did he say about Ty?"

I can't tell Dad about how Ty didn't want me and Henry sharing a bed, so I say, "I told Henry that I couldn't do something with him because I was going to hang out with Ty. Then he said all this crap about Ty trying to control everything, and that I let everyone control me, which is probably true, but Henry just went nuts, Dad."

"Sounds like Henry was jealous. His pride was hurt. So he acted like an ass. Every guy does that from time to time."

"I get that. But I've been trying to make up, but he doesn't even return my calls."

Dad twirls the ball again. "So do you still like him?"

"I loved the old Henry. I barely know this new Henry."

"So it sounds like even if you went to him and told him how much you love him, it wouldn't matter, right?"

"Right. 'Cause I already tried. Doesn't that suck?"

Dad smiles. "A wise man once said, 'Nothing takes the taste out of peanut butter quite like unrequited love.'"

"Who the hell said that? Gandhi?"

Dad laughs. "Charlie Brown."

"I thought comics were supposed to be funny."

Dad tosses the ball to me. "One thing I learned a long time ago is that even if you think you're meant to be with someone, that doesn't necessarily mean you *get* to be with them."

Sighing, I laugh. "You're depressing too, Dad." Thinking of Mom, I say, "Does that mean you, uh, didn't marry the person you wanted to be with?"

"Of course I married the right girl. It just took a while to get her attention. Why the hell would a woman like your mom be interested in a jerk like me?"

I smirk. "There is that."

Dad picks up a picture of me and Henry from the shelf, a picture taken at Lake Jordan when we were thirteen. In the photo, I'm grinning at a trout I've just caught. And Henry's smiling at me.

"For what it's worth," Dad says, running his fingers over the picture, "I've never seen anyone run faster than Henry after you hurt your knee last week."

trips

We pull up in front of Henry's trailer, and Dad goes inside. A few minutes later, he comes out pulling a struggling Henry by an elbow and stuffs him in the back of the Audi.

"Yo, Woods." With dark circles under his eyes, Henry seems miserable.

"Hi, Henry."

"How's the knee?"

"Better, thanks."

And that's all we say the entire way to the airport. Dad has chartered a private jet to Ann Arbor so he doesn't have to "deal with the masses" on a commercial flight. On the plane, Dad makes us play a game of Monopoly with him and I kick ass, buying up Park Place, Boardwalk, and all those green properties that are worth a shitload. After Henry lands on Boardwalk, where I've just built a hotel, he has to mortgage his lame purple and orange properties. I giggle maniacally. Henry shakes his head at me and pouts. But now that we're actually playing a game together, I've seen smiles trickle across his face a few times.

After checking into the hotel, where Dad has reserved three rooms for us, he tells us we're going out to dinner with the University of Michigan head coach.

I throw my suitcase on the bed, unzip the bag, and pull out this new dress Carrie and Marie helped me buy, this black sweater skirt thing with short sleeves, and pair it with black boots. I want to look pretty for Henry because tonight is important for him, so I also put on some mascara and lip gloss.

I'm brushing my hair as my phone rings. I check the caller ID. Ty. I pull a deep breath and answer.

"Hey, Woods," he says.

I clear my throat. "Hey. Is everything okay?"

"Yeah." His voice sounds fine. Upbeat. "What are you doing?" he asks, so I tell him about the impromptu trip to Michigan, which surprises him.

"What about Alabama?"

I tell him it's probably not the right school for me, which surprises him more. "Dad thinks Michigan State might be a good fit for me."

"That's great," Ty says. "Text me after you meet the coach—I want to know how it goes. Michigan State's a great program."

I smile at my reflection in the mirror. "So what's up?"

"Your brother called and asked if I want to come to a party tomorrow night in Knoxville. You know, after his game against LSU?"

"Yeah."

"And I just wanted to see if that's okay with you. I mean, that I'm hanging out with your bro—"

"Definitely," I say, still smiling.

"We're friends, right?"

"I hope so."

"There might be girls at the party. I, um—" Ty pauses to cough.

I had wondered, if I found out Ty was dating someone else, if my heart would lurch, but it's still. "Have a great time. We're cool."

I'm glad he's willing to have fun, to let go, even if it's only one night. Maybe he'll relax a bit.

I chat with Ty for a few more minutes, arguing over who'll win in Sunday's Colts-Texans matchup, and I tell him to hang close to my brother at the party and to steer clear of Jake Reynolds and all his possibly STD-ridden minions.

Someone knocks on the door, so I grab my coat and wallet, and step out into the hall, finding Henry standing there in a suit and blue tie, which brings out the aqua flecks in his green eyes. I've never seen him so dressed up before.

Smiling, I say, "Damn, Henry, you clean up well."

He smiles back at me. "I know, right?"

I roll my eyes. "Ready to go?"

"Yup." Henry ushers me toward the elevator. From the corner of my eye, I see him looking me up and down. "You look really pretty."

Outside the hotel, we hop into Dad's town car and head to some fancy French restaurant where I won't know what anything on the menu is. Too bad Carter's not here.

The restaurant is dark and romantic and full of flowers, and I find myself wishing it was just me and Henry here, huddled over wine and champagne and crêpes or some shit like that. As we walk beneath beautiful chandeliers, alongside a wall made up of mirrors, my hand moves without permission, linking with Henry's.

"Thanks, Woods," he says, taking a deep breath.

He keeps holding my hand as we approach our table, where two men are waiting for us. They introduce themselves as the head and offensive coaches for the University of Michigan. After introductions, we sit down and I have a fit trying to decide what to order because it's all in French.

Following a bunch of small talk about the university and the Titans and how Mom and Mike are doing, the head coach takes a sip of wine and says, "So, Henry…my recruiter liked what he saw in Tennessee, and I love your speed, but you'll have to work extra hard on finishing your routes." What the coach means is some wide receivers get lazy if they know the ball isn't coming to them, so they won't run hard or try to fake out a cornerback. This is a dead giveaway to the defensive back that this will be a running play or the ball will be thrown to a different wide receiver.

Crazy. I'd never even noticed that about Henry. This coach must've watched the tapes closely. And I have a lot to learn.

"Yes, sir," Henry says. "Is there anything else I should do to improve my game?"

"Just keep working on your speed and your explosiveness, and I think you'll fit right in here."

I squeeze Henry's hand under the table as a smile edges on the sides of his lips.

• • •

The next day, a car takes me, Dad, and Henry out to East Lansing—home of the Michigan State Spartans. Dad told me not to wear a dress, but my sweats and knee brace and cleats, which makes me excited. I might get to throw a ball around with some college guys today!

Again, I did my homework last night—Googling on my laptop—so when we arrive, I recognize the head coach and the athletic director, who are waiting to greet us when we pull up outside the stadium. I expect it's because the great Donovan Woods is with us, so it surprises me when Coach Bryson shakes my hand first.

"We're so happy you agreed to come take a look at our program," the coach says, staring in my eyes. "I've enjoyed watching your tapes. You've got a lot of style on the field, Woods." Judging by his smile and firm handshake, he seems genuine. I think he actually wants me here, unlike crazy Coach Thompson at Alabama.

Coach Bryson and the athletic director shake hands with Dad and Henry too, and then we're off to see the inside of Spartan Stadium. Another good sign? I don't have to see all sorts of lame things like where to buy shampoo and where to see a piano recital; we go straight to the field, where a bunch of guys are standing around. I count at least thirty players.

They have a game versus Notre Dame today, their biggest game of the year, so I'm glad half of the team has time for me. I'm sure it's all because of Dad, but regardless, it makes me feel pretty damned good.

The stadium is just as beautiful as Alabama's. Maybe even more so. I take a knee and run my hand over the natural grass, digging my fingers into the blades, then gaze up at the bleachers. The place is so huge, I bet you could see it from space. I love the cool weather; it would be fun to play a bunch of games in snow.

"What do you think?" Coach Bryson asks, kneeling down next to me.

"It's a hell of a lot better than Astroturf."

"Agreed," he says, laughing. Another plus? Coach Bryson clearly doesn't care if I use language unbecoming of a lady.

"I love the stadium," I say. "It has a lot of character."

"Yeah—I've always felt like it's alive, you know? Kind of like New York City."

I nod, smiling.

"Want to meet some of the guys?" he asks.

"Definitely! I mean, if they want to meet me."

I can't help but wonder where the other thirty team members are. Could they be anti-girl, like the guys at Alabama?

"You know, I didn't tell them they had to come out early today. They were beside themselves when I told them you were coming to visit."

"Really?" I say. Henry snorts. Being on this field is giving me confidence, so I turn and say, "Shut up, Henry! Would you stop being so freaking jealous all the time?"

Dad and Coach Bryson laugh, and so does Henry. I'm glad he's smiling.

"Let's go, Woods," Coach Bryson says, beckoning me to walk across the field to the benches. Dad and Henry stay behind. None of the guys are dressed to play yet, as the game isn't going to start for hours, but they're wearing green and white sweats and they look ready to work out.

Another plus? These guys are just as hot as the Alabama boys. Sa-woon! Their starting quarterback, Todd Phillips, this buff guy with olive skin, black hair, hazel eyes, and a rugged scar on his jaw, steps up and shakes my hand. He's gorgeous and he knows it. "God, you're beautiful. I love your accent," he says, putting an arm around me, but I shove him away. Dad was right—sexist guys are everywhere. Phillips laughs at me, turning to Coach Bryson. "Coach—do I get to be her sponsor?"

"Oh, hell no," Coach Bryson responds, pulling Phillips away by the hood of his sweatshirt. "I wouldn't let a pig like you within a hundred feet of my own daughter. Go run a lap, will you?" All the other guys laugh, so I smile too. Phillips jogs off toward the track, blowing me a kiss. This time, I actually do catch the kiss, crumble it in my hand, and throw it to the ground, where I pretend to stomp on it.

"Ouch!" the guys exclaim, chuckling.

"Sponsor?" I say, focusing on Coach Bryson again.

"All new recruits get assigned a sponsor on the team—like a big brother, someone to show you the ropes. If you decide you want to be part of our team, I'll assign our freshman center, Seth Brennan, to you."

The guys say, "Damn" and "Figures" as they shove a younger, pudgy guy around. The pudgy guy, who I can only assume is Brennan, looks like a pinball being bounced between all these linebackers and wide receivers.

When he finally gets dislodged from the group, he comes over and, after smoothing his hair, says, "Nice to meet you, Jordan." He beams at me. "If we've got time before our game tonight, I'd love to show you around campus."

"What do you mean by campus?" I ask, thinking of Mr. Tucker's boring tour of the Alabama newspaper stands and bike racks.

"You know, where the best pizza place is, and where our gym is, and where the twenty-four-hour mini-mart is, important stuff like that. I'll even spring for a slice of pizza. And you've gotta try the smoothies at the mini-mart."

"Sounds great." I slap Brennan's shoulder.

"Wooo! Brennan's got himself a date!" one of the guys says, smacking Brennan's ass.

"How'd you manage that, Brennan?" says another guy.

A couple guys stare me down, narrowing their eyes. Checking me out, like they're trying to decide if I'm a circus show or the real thing.

"I'm grateful for the opportunity to meet y'all," I tell the team. "You've got a great program."

"Want to show us what you've got, Woods?" asks one of the

players, who I recognize as a wide receiver. According to the Michigan State website, this dude is pulling numbers almost as good as Jake Reynolds's, so I bet I'll be seeing him at the NFL draft soon. He drops a football into my hands.

"Hell yeah," I reply, bending my knee a couple times. "Check this." Henry and Dad are standing about forty-five yards away down near the goal posts. Tossing the ball up in the air to myself, I call out, "Henry!"

I hop back a few steps and hurl the ball down to my best friend, a perfect spiral. Seconds later, it lands right in his hands.

"Very nice," Coach Bryson says, and some of the guys whistle and pat my back, jostling me around. Henry tosses the ball up in the air and Dad catches it. When he winds up to throw it back, several of the players jog out because they obviously want to catch Dad's pass. They're shoving each other, acting like a bunch of boneheads, but they're boneheads I think I could grow to love, much like the guys I've grown up with over the past ten years.

Dad launches the ball down the field, but he didn't aim at any of the guys vying for the pass, but to me. As I catch the ball, I feel my eyes burning. This pass was a sign of respect.

Everything about this stadium, this coach, this team, this moment, feels right. I hope I can win the respect of the rest of the team, if it needs to be won.

For the next hour, Phillips shows me some moves, and I can already tell I could learn a ton from him. We run some plays with the wide receivers and we even do a drill where some linebackers rush at me and I have to get the ball off within three seconds. Then Henry and I show off our flawless hook and lateral play, Red Rabbit, which totally impresses Phillips. With his hand cupping his chin, he watches as I do a few handoffs to some running backs and gives me pointers. Unlike when I first showed up at the stadium, he behaves seriously, treating me as an equal, which I love in a leader.

Finally, Coach Bryson claps a hand on my back. "So what do you think?"

It's like what I told Carter. Sometimes you have to give something up to get something better. I'm willing to give up my fantasies of Alabama if it means I actually get to play for a coach and with guys who all respect me. Grinning and tossing the ball to myself, I turn to Coach Bryson. "I should explore all my options, but I think you're my number one choice."

He smiles and a bunch of the players start whooping and shoving me around.

Phillips slaps Brennan's back and says, "Brennan might finally get himself a girlfriend!"

I throw my arm around Brennan, which is difficult, as he's well over six-foot-four and must weigh 300 pounds. "You don't have to be so jealous, Phillips. Maybe if you weren't such a pig, you wouldn't still be a virgin."

"Ouch!" the guys say again, and I'm loving this place.

• • •

"And this is the pizza place I was telling you about," Brennan says, gesturing to a grungy hole-in-the-wall restaurant that looks greasier than my hair after football practice.

"Awesome," I say as we walk in. Brennan goes to the counter and buys us six slices of cheese. My kind of guy. We carry the pizza to an empty booth, and after taking a bite, I pull the salt and pepper shakers over in front of me. I stack salt on top of pepper, yank pepper out and salt falls straight down.

"Nice," Brennan says. "I suck at that game."

I grin. "Duh. You're a center."

"So what are you gonna major in, Woods?"

"Not sure yet," I lie, thinking of poetry. "Maybe physical therapy. What's your major?" I ask as I take another bite of cheese.

"Theater. Like stage management."

What? Brennan's a theater major? Crazy. "That's cool," I say, smiling big time.

"Yeah—I love acting. But obviously, I don't have the looks or the body for it," he says with a laugh. "So I'm doing behind the scenes stuff. Directing."

"So you think you're the next Spielberg?"

He grins. "Something like that."

Taking a deep breath, I say, "I lied...I actually want to major in creative writing."

"You can write plays for me to direct," he says, and we smile at each other.

• • •

The day is only getting better. After my tour and pizza with Brennan, I'm sitting with Dad and Henry at the fifty-yard line. Coach Bryson gave us tickets for the big game versus Notre Dame, and Henry and I are pigging out on hot dogs and cotton candy and nachos.

Each time some kid comes and asks Dad for an autograph, Henry pretends like they're asking for his autograph, and when they say they actually want Donovan Woods's autograph, Henry says, "Oh. Well, I guess I've gotta let old Don Woods get some of the attention."

Dad and I smack Henry's head several times.

Dad asks over the crowd, "So do you like this school?"

I lean near his ear. "I do." I hesitate before adding, "But can we check out some other schools too? Just so I'll know I'm making the right decision?"

He pats my good knee. "I'll set up some more visits. Maybe Purdue and Missouri?"

"Cool." I smile and cup my mouth, blowing warm air onto my hands.

The marching band is playing a fight song when Henry cups my ear with his hand. He whispers, "So, if you come to school here, and I go to UM, we'll only be an hour away from each other."

When he takes his hand away, I whisper back, "I know. But we can still be close, no matter what schools we go to. You know that right?"

"Yeah, it doesn't matter," he says, his breath hot against my face.

Then I give him a quick kiss on the cheek. He responds by running a fingertip across the back of my hand. God, I hope Dad isn't watching us.

Speaking of Dad, did he purposely set up the whole Michigan State thing so Henry and I could live close to each other? I grin at the great Donovan Woods as he autographs a Notre Dame foam finger for a little boy, despite that 1) Dad went to Ole Miss, and 2) Dad hates Notre Dame.

At one point, Phillips runs for a touchdown from the five-yard line, hopping over a cornerback. When he runs back to the benches, I yell, "You rock, Phillips!" and pump my fist at him, and he rips his helmet off and grins at me. He gives me a little wave and I feel myself blushing. Michigan State wouldn't be bad at all…

"Woods," Henry whispers as cheerleaders do a pyramid in front of us.

"Yeah?"

"What was that all about?"

"What?" I say, acting oblivious.

"You know...him," Henry says, gesturing at Phillips, who, while sipping his Gatorade, keeps glancing at me.

"Henry, stop being jealous! I wish you'd stop being such a pansy."

Henry laughs, then runs his hand along my thigh.

"Oh, hell no," I say, picking his hand up and putting it back on his own knee, and he chuckles.

He doesn't touch me again until we're getting ready to go. I'm pulling my jacket on when Henry rests his hand on the small of my back. Leaning near my ear, he whispers, "Can we hang out later?"

a lifetime supply of cookies and lemonade

Back at the hotel, I'm changing into my sweats when Henry texts me: Come to my room? #2205

I'm so happy I squeal, but I don't immediately respond. I'm gonna make him wait. But after about five minutes of doing everything from brushing my teeth to playing with the in-room coffee maker, I lose patience and text him back: On my way.

I knock on the door to his room. A few seconds later, Henry, wearing a T-shirt and mesh shorts, opens the door.

"What's good, Woods?" I walk in to find a window providing a view of the university, and a pitcher of lemonade and a bunch of chocolate-chip cookies sit waiting on the table.

His hair is as unruly as ever, hanging down to his shoulders. He wipes a few curls off his face. "So, it's really good to spend time with you," he says.

"Yeah…totally." We just stare at each other for a long moment, a moment that seems to last longer than an overtime. Then I rush forward and hug him.

He releases me a few seconds later, rubs my back, then takes a seat on the couch. He leans back and crosses his legs. After that hug,

I don't want to push it, so instead of joining him, I sit down on the bed and pull a pillow to my chest. I prop my chin on the pillow and rake a hand through my hair and peer up at Henry.

He coughs. "So, I, uh, know I should've called to apologize after Ty and I got into the fight," he says. Leaning over onto his knees, he focuses on the carpet. "I shouldn't have hit him. I'm sorry I was so stupid."

Tears rush to my eyes. "We were best friends for ten years—it's pretty unforgivable that you didn't call. That you haven't called."

The tears fall freely, and I dig the heels of my hands into my eyes, trying to stanch the flow, but it won't stop.

Suddenly I feel him sitting down on the bed. When I can open my eyes without a flood gushing out of them, I turn and see that he's got both hands out as if he wants to play the hand-slap game. A grin starts to spread across my face as first, I slap him upside the head, then I shove his chest so hard he flies back onto the bed. Getting up onto my one good knee, I stretch my other leg out to the side and punch him in the gut.

"Fuck, Woods!" Before I can slap his face, Henry rolls over and falls off the bed. When he pokes his head up above the mattress, I see he's cracking up.

"Man, you deserved every bit of that, and more!" I say.

"Are we even?" He crawls up next to me.

"Not yet." I punch him in the jaw and I hear a crack.

"Ow!"

I cringe. Shit, what's his jaw made of? Titanium? I shake out my hand. "I'm so sorry, Henry! I didn't mean to hit you so hard."

Eyes watering, he rubs his chin. "Finished?" He smiles.

I laugh softly. "For now," I reply, popping my knuckles.

He goes over to the table, where he pours two glasses of lemonade, hands one to me, and uses the other to ice his jaw. I hold my glass of lemonade up to my knuckles. He sees me icing my hand and we laugh so hard—just like before.

Still holding the glass to his jaw, he shuffles his socked feet across the room and digs around in his bag, finally pulling out a deck of cards. He sits back down on the bed, puts the glass on the nightstand, and starts dealing the cards into two stacks. "Let's play some war."

I grab the plate of cookies from the table and set it on top of a pillow. He picks a cookie, puts it in his mouth, and uses both hands to keep dealing. When all the cards are dealt, he takes a bite of the cookie and wipes his mouth, then looks down at the plate.

"Woods, where did all the cookies go?"

I've already eaten four. "You snooze, you lose, man. Call room service and order some more." He throws down a queen, I throw down an eight. He sweeps the cards away and up into his pile.

"No way—I'm not made of money."

"Oh, I didn't realize you were paying for all this," I say, gesturing to the lavish room. "Charge it to my dad." I throw down a five, he throws down a three. I sweep the cards away.

He grins. "Fine." Grabbing up the phone, he orders more cookies and lemonade, and even asks for some champagne too. He opens his wallet and pulls out a fake ID, showing it off for me.

"What's the occasion?" I ask.

He glances up at me and takes a deep breath. "You're the occasion, Woods. I've missed you so, so much."

Lowering my chin, I bite my lip. A tear drops down my cheek. I throw down an ace, he throws down an ace. I deal three cards facedown, and he mimics me. At the same time, we each drop a fourth card. He has a queen; I, a king.

He looks up at me again and grabs my hands, pulling me up against his chest in one motion. He leans back against the pillow.

"Am I hurting your knee?" he whispers as I drop my chin onto his chest and gaze up at him.

"No."

He closes his eyes. "You know what I regret more than anything?"

"No."

"Not kissing you in my room that day." He drags a hand across my head and rests it on my back.

I smile and try not to cry again. "Yeah, you were pretty stupid, man."

"I know I could never deserve you, but can I try to make it up to you?"

I smirk. "How?"

"A lifetime supply of cookies and lemonade."

"That's pretty tempting…" I clutch his side as he continues rubbing my back. His hand drifts up, and he sweeps my hair away, letting his fingers trickle along the nape of my neck.

"But?" he says.

"I want something else more than that."

"Oh? You gonna tell me what it is so I can get it for you?"

"Guess…"

He guesses right, because he takes me by the elbows and pulls my body up so our noses touch. His breath smells like chocolate-chip cookies. My favorite.

We kiss.

Finally.

"Will you stay with me tonight?" he asks.

"I'll stay as long as you'll let me." Somehow, even with my sore knee, I manage to straddle his hips and weave my fingers through his curls. "But we have to sleep head-to-toe."

"We can't tonight. I heard you haven't been washing your socks. In homage to me."

I giggle as he kisses my neck. "Don't test me!"

"So how do you feel about living in Michigan?" he says. "You can be my trophy girlfriend." Before I can smack him, he pins my arms to my sides and rolls me over, holding me down. We laugh and kiss again and again. He's a lot stronger than me now. He must be working out hard. I squeeze his biceps to get a taste. Rocks.

"What made you change your mind about us?" I whisper.

"When I stopped being such a wimpy idiot and stopped being afraid of losing you, I realized I'd already lost you because of how stupid I'd been, but didn't know if you'd give me another chance. I didn't want to talk…'cause I was so scared you'd get mad or reject me for Ty. I didn't know what to do. I'm so sorry." His eyes are clenched shut.

I kiss his forehead. "You are a wimpy idiot. But…I still love you."

"I love you too, Woods."

I grab a handful of his curls, yanking his face to mine. "If you ever leave me again, I'll fucking kill you."

Opening his eyes, Henry laughs and rubs his jaw where I just punched him. "Understood."

We kiss some more, and his soft lips are making it hot in here, so I pull off my sweatshirt, revealing a tank top underneath, and Henry focuses on the plastic football charm, taking it in his fingers. I hesitate, then pull the chain off and drop it around Henry's neck.

"Oh, thank God," he says, kissing the charm. "I've missed this."

"More than you've missed me?"

"Oh hell yeah."

I knock him off the bed again, and laughing, he climbs back up and kisses me. We make out for what seems like hours, pausing only for cookies and champagne.

"I'm not one of your cheerleaders du jour," I tell him when his fingers edge under my tank top. I bat his hand away.

He smiles, lies back on the pillow, and clasps his hands behind his head. "Admit it, you're my number one fan."

"Yup. I'm having T-shirts made."

Then we crawl under the covers with me at the base of the bed and he at the head. He shoves his feet in my face.

Dad told me that even if you're meant to be with someone, that doesn't mean you necessarily get to be with them. But sometimes? Maybe you do.

I guess we'll find out.

acknowledgments

Warning! This acknowledgments page is super-long because I practically had to field an entire football team to help me as I wrote this book. Also, please excuse the cheesiness.

Many, many thanks to my coach, ahem, agent Sara Megibow, and everyone at Nelson Literary Agency, for taking a chance on me and always being there. Leah Hultenschmidt, my editor and quarterback, thank you so much for loving *Catching Jordan* and for wanting to share it with everybody. A huge thanks to Aubrey Poole, aka real life cheerleader, for picking up my story and not wanting to put it down, even though it was a weekend and you had the day off.

I owe a ton of gratitude to Allison Bridgewater, who reads everything I write and gives the best critiques ever! You're awesome and I know you'll do great things in college and beyond. Becca Fitzpatrick—I'm in your debt. Thanks for giving me great advice when I needed it most. Thank you to Jessica Wallace, for falling in love with Henry first; Sarah Cloots, for teaching me how to write; Madeleine Rex, who, at fifteen, should be an editor already; and Ben Rusckowski, for always telling me the truth about my writing (and for being terrified of whales). Many thanks to Rebecca Sutton,

Jackie Kenneally, Karen Mlyniec, Sarah Gibson, Kate McHugh, Jo Morningstar, Ruthie Morningstar Lynes, Alisha Niehaus, Cassandra Marshall, Krista Ashe, Regan Means, Tiffany Reisz, Sarah Skilton, Alyssa Palmer, Jennifer Shaw Wolf, Natalie Bahm, Trish Doller, E. Kristin Anderson, Michele Truitt, Lynwood and Carol Dent, Marguerite Coffey, Leslie Moeller, Mike Jacobs, Christy Maier, Susan Curley, Bob Bryson, and Eric Stein for being great, supportive friends, reading my stuff and keeping me sane.

Thanks to my parents and brother and sister—for letting me make my own plays. Dad—thanks for reading all my writing and helping me make it better.

Finally, the biggest thanks go to my husband, Don, for never giving up on me and never letting me give up.

about the author

Miranda Kenneally grew up in Manchester, Tennessee, a quaint little town where nothing cool ever happened until after she left. Now Manchester is the home of Bonnaroo. Growing up, Miranda wanted to become an author, a Major League Baseball player, a country music singer, or an interpreter for the United Nations. Instead she became an author who works for the U.S. Department of State in Washington, D.C., planning major events and doing special projects, and once acted as George W. Bush's armrest during a meeting. She enjoys reading and writing young adult literature and loves *Star Trek*, music, sports, Mexican food, Twitter, coffee, and her husband. Visit www.mirandakenneally.com.